Books by the Author

The Danie Jaye Collection:

The Chase

The Taming of Lions, Vol. 1

The Pride of Lions, Vol. 2 (coming soon)

The Danielle Dexter Collection:

Stupid Love, A Salt City Diaries Novel

Stupid Love
A Salt City Diaries Novel

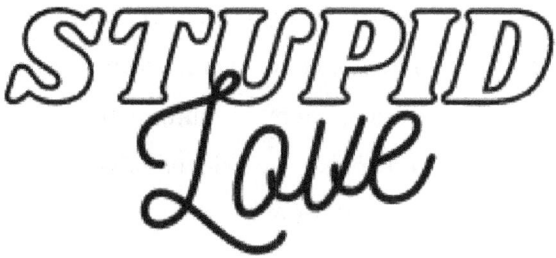

A Salt City Diaries Novel

Danielle Dexter

Danielle Dexter Books
New York

Copyright © 2022 by Danielle Dexter

Cupid's Arrow Publishing
All rights reserved.
No part of this book may be reproduced or transmitted in any form or by any means, electronic or mechanical, including photocopying, recording, or by any information storage and retrieval system, or otherwise—without permission in writing by the publisher.

Cover Design by Cupid's Arrow Publishing
Cover photo licensed by Cupid's Arrow Publishing
Names: Dexter, Danielle, author.
Title: Stupid Love: a novel/ Danielle Dexter
Description: First Edition | Cupid's Arrow Publishing 2022

This book is a work of fiction. Names, characters, businesses, organizations, events, and incidents either are a product of the author's imagination or are used fictitiously. Any resemblance to actual persons, living or dead, events, or locales is entirely coincidental.

International Standard Book Number:
979-8-9856286-0-9

Printed in the United States of America

To anyone brave enough to start over.

And to Ashleigh: No matter what lifetime, I would always search for your friendship.

"Love is stupid."

-Me

Introduction

Let me preface this introduction by saying that I have worked on this book on and off for roughly the better part of seven years. Do I need to repeat that for the people in the back? Yes, it took me seven years, multiple drafts, and various sets of characters to finally feel as though I've told this story in the best way possible. And when I finally put pen to paper, I knew what I wanted to accomplish, and that was to write a book I wish I had during some of my most challenging dating years. And let me tell you, there were a lot of them—spoiler alert!

As you probably already know, no one ever promised that love would be easy. And that very truth became somewhat of the theme for this series, which subsequently stuck to it like glue and hardened without any form of release. If love were easy, I wholeheartedly believe that our fascination and desire for it would be faltered. It wouldn't mean as much to obtain it if obtaining it was easy. It's the journey, the highs and lows, the heartbreaks, and the happiness that makes it all worthwhile. And I truly believe without a shadow of a doubt that love is made better only through the experience of encountering love that's not, well, *better*.

When I first sat down and decided that now was the time to work on this book (and finish it!), a friend of mine was going through a very tough breakup. I recalled a similar situation to hers that happened to me years ago when the guy I was dating no longer wanted to be together. *Ouch!* I was beyond heartbroken—so I could relate. And what was even more devastating was knowing just how much of myself was to blame for that heartache. *Double ouch!* But like her, when you are in the thick of things, you can't pick up on the obvious signs that the relationship isn't good for you—even when they are staring you right in the face. You are blind to the red flags. You want to believe that things are not what they seem, and you so badly want everything that you *do* see through those rose-colored glasses to be real. And it was those same stupid glasses that led me to believe that becoming "the exception" was possible as well.

Ahh, the exception. We have all heard that story where the guy chooses the girl against all odds because no obstacle—timing or otherwise—can keep them apart. Or the story where the "bad boy" turns good all because one girl's love has the power to change his heart forever. PLEASE. Let me tell you, love is not some romance novel or Hallmark movie. Relationships like that are not realistic. And if by chance they *do* ever happen, they never seem to happen to someone you know firsthand. You always hear about a friend of a friend who knows of someone that experienced the narrative you desperately want your relationship to fit into. *Am I right?* But how many of us have banked on being that exception anyway? *Are you raising your hand with me? Come on, don't leave me hanging!* I can't tell you how many times I have rolled my eyes at these clichés yet have secretly wished to be *that* girl. Then again, what do you expect after being force-fed fairy tale after fairy tale before we were even able to speak our first words? It only messes with our expectations when it comes to love. Trust me; love is far more complex than waiting for some prince to ride up on his white horse to save the day. Because with my luck, he'd get lost in the damn woods.

    Nevertheless, several years ago, when I was dating this guy (who I was head-over-freaking heels for) told me upfront that he wanted nothing serious. I thought: *Maybe, I didn't want anything serious either?* However, I never stopped to question what that *actually* meant. But when you spend night after night, and day after day with someone, at some point, you begin to intertwine lives whether you planned to or not. And the whole idea of wanting "nothing serious" gets completely tossed out of the window or, in our case, chucked out. That's when I began to believe in the idea of being "the exception." It didn't matter how many of my friends tried bringing me down to reality because I still came back with the same lame response: "But *it's* different. *He's* different. *We* are different." But here's the thing: We *weren't* different. It was the same damn song attached to a different-sounding melody, and I was just singing along like a tone-deaf idiot. There wasn't anything unique about our situation; it was just my feelings attached to it that were unique. Yet, there I was, believing that we were "one of a kind" just because with him, I felt something I had never felt with anyone else before. And what was even worse was realizing that feeling something different didn't always mean it was better.

Wanting to be "the exception" was like forgoing the saving princess metaphor and replacing it with becoming the actual knight in shining armor. I figured that if I initiated all the saving, someone would want to save me in return. But this guy and I were just two broken people (something we couldn't admit to ourselves or each other), and when two broken people try coming together, it never creates anything whole. **Remember that.** Not to mention, discovering that you played the part of the romantic bandage to someone's scorned heart (i.e., rebound) is not something I would ever wish on anyone. But for the sake of being transparent here, I both willingly and unwillingly played that part for several years until it eventually blew up in my face. It was like trying to plant a seed in cement and expecting something to grow from it.

Don't get me wrong, I have had my heart broken more times than I care to admit, but I know I've done some breaking myself. I'm not an innocent party here, yet, I can't even count how many times I have cried into my pillow at the unfairness of it all. The pitiful "why me" sob-fest was an activity I engaged in for years before I had chosen to rid myself of that self-deprecating behavior. *How?* you ask. Well, I channeled a lot of my thoughts and feelings into journals. And when I finally decided to take them out of hiding (when I was safe from repeating past behaviors or re-opening old wounds), I couldn't believe I had almost left them in boxes, collecting dust. There was so much honesty, love, and hard lessons that needed to be shared, which was why I committed to writing this series. So, I stepped out of my typical writing box—and comfort zone—and put that freakin' pen to paper.

    I initially thought this was a standalone novel but quickly realized that cramming everything into one book would be impossible. It just wouldn't give the story the justice it deserved. In the end, I created a great cast of characters to help deliver a story, although inspired by real situations, is still considered a complete work of fiction. So, if I've dated you (I'm laughing as I write this), please don't be that guy who thinks every guy I mention is you. Writing this was never about airing out dirty laundry. It was and always will be about creating something special where you find yourself flipping through the pages, yelling, "Yes! I know exactly how that feels!" It's a book to remind you that you are not alone. We have all been there. We have all done it. We have all settled for the wrong guy or loved someone we shouldn't have. And whether we are meeting people out in the real world or through a swipe on our phones, dating is the same. I'm just giving you a whole new way of looking at it.

Love,
Danielle

Disclaimer

As I mentioned in the proceeding pages, writing this book took longer than any other book I have ever worked on. My goal, if I succeeded, was to create a story that pays homage to life's many rollercoasters when it comes to matters of the heart. I hope that you feel connected to the emotions and insight I poured into every page. It's also important to note that although actual situations inspired this book, it is not a memoir. The characters have either been stripped of their true identities or entirely made up for the nature of storytelling. I have also changed as many details as possible while still delivering the emotions as raw and unfiltered as the day I felt them.

    For those of you who are on the cusp of turning thirty or beyond, we can easily say we have been through it all. However, what took me a long time to grasp, is that our past is our past. It happened for a reason—even when we're not aware of what that reason is. There is no need to run or hide it from the world. Why? Because it's a part of our story. It's what makes us who we are. It's what brings us to the next chapter in our lives. So, be easy on yourself; we have all made mistakes. We have all fallen in love with the "wrong" people (and I say this loosely because each person we have loved is technically *right* for us. Those "wrong" people help mold us into the people we are destined to become and help us love the person we are meant to be with, better). But we made those mistakes with the best of intentions. Maybe we ignored the red flags because we wanted to believe in the possibility that people or circumstances could change. Or that if we can see the good in someone, they could perhaps, see it, too. Trust me; love doesn't work that way—no matter how hard you wish upon that shooting star or cross your pretty, little fingers.

Next, I want you to recognize how truly blessed you are to have the friends and family that you do. I believe that it's important to thank them for lending their ears and shoulders to cry on during some of your life's most challenging moments. You would lack a tremendous support system if you didn't have them. And the people in my life are saints. I couldn't imagine my life without them.

While writing this book, I will admit that a lot of past emotions resurfaced. It was hard to let things I thought once dead and buried be brought back to life again. But for this to work, I had to become the most vulnerable writer and person to you. And I knew that I wouldn't be doing anyone a favor—including this book or any subsequent book after—if I decided to tiptoe around all the hard stuff. Therefore, I stomped all over it.

I'm fully aware that books such as these may come off as a little preachy at times. I get it. But who cares, right? Sometimes, the lessons we learn in life don't always come to us in the forms of songs, poetry, or pictures of rainbows and puppies. That's why I needed my past emotions and perspective on situations to be as authentic as possible. I needed my readers to see my main character at her lowest points so that they could appreciate her at her highest—much like me. This book would have never worked if I wasn't willing to be that vulnerable. And I would be doing a complete disservice to everyone by not being as transparent as possible. I'm just blessed to be able to look back on some of these memories and smile. And I can't express to you enough that I am equally as blessed to have gone through every bit of it—even the rough times because it's what brought me to where I am today. And it's what made me into the person I am as well.

Lastly, I want this message to sink in before you dive into reading: DO NOT compare your life to others. Do you know how they say that comparison is the thief of joy? Well, they weren't wrong. But sadly, I still struggle with this sometimes. It's something that I have to consciously work on every day so that I'm not too hard on myself when I'm comparing my authentic self to those who broadcast theirs in filters. We cannot measure our successes based on the supposed successes of others. We are not privileged to know what goes on behind closed doors in other people's lives. So, that picture you are comparing yourself to on social media may just be for show. One of the most eye-opening things a friend has ever told me was that no one ever posts a lousy picture. People want to portray happiness—perfection. They want the world to think they have it all—that everything in their life is perfect sans filter. But no one ever said that life was a race or that perfectionism was the finish line. It's not realistic or obtainable. Life doesn't care about perfection. In fact, isn't all the imperfections of life what ends up making it *perfect*?

Before you begin reading, I want you to know how grateful I am that you are holding this book in your hands. It means that I finally put on my big girl's pants (more on that later) and found the courage to publish it! I hope that you find the characters and situations relatable and that you highlight, dog-ear, and mark the hell out of the pages when you read something that speaks to you. I hope you laugh. I hope you gain perspective. Most importantly, I hope that this book touches your heart as it did mine while writing it.

So, a big THANK YOU to the ones I've loved, the ones I've lost, and the ones I settled for, no matter the cost. Each of you took part in giving me the greatest gift of all: Finding love within myself.

Here goes nothing…

Year One

What Ifs and Other Bullshit

November 2013

"I don't know why it has to be this fucking hard?" I sighed as I plopped down on my couch beside Leigha. The cushions enveloped me like a hug as I watched her reach over and grab the bottle of red blend to top us both off. Our purple-stained teeth and tear-stained cheeks said it all: Love sucked.

But was I wrong? I mean, why does love have to be this fucking hard? I can't tell you how much time I have wasted mulling over that very question, only to come up empty-handed each time. I'm fully aware that no one ever promised love to be easy. There is no proverbial arrow that strikes you in the heart, and love just magically finds you. Love is far more complex than that. It takes work. It takes time. And sometimes, it's downright confusing and messy at its core. So, as far as I'm concerned, Cupid could kiss my ass.

Still, we ask these questions, do we not? We want to know why things happen the way they do. We want to know if we said or did things differently, then maybe things would have turned out in our favor. Did our actions or inactions hold the magic sauce? As in, if I hadn't seemed too eager or if I had played "the game" differently, then things might have worked out the way that I wanted them to? Maybe then he'd still be interested? Or, perhaps, we'd still be together? But seriously, why do we do this to ourselves? Why do we agonize over the details—no matter how minuscule—in hopes of uncovering the deeper meaning of things? We could make things so much easier on ourselves if we didn't feel so compelled to dissect everything and just accepted things for what they are. And what they are is pretty simple: Things didn't work out—not because you responded too quickly to his texts or because you always seemed too available—but because it wasn't meant to be—end of story.

But who are we kidding? That's never the ending we are willing to accept, which means we will never stop dissecting every little detail until we mold it into the ending we'd much rather have. We are all too convinced that we must follow a specific formula or a particular set of rules for the object of our affection to reciprocate feelings—like it's some mathematical equation that leads to romantical bliss. We never stopped to factor in that even if we did everything by the book or played those "games" to a T, there would still be a good possibility that the reason he didn't reciprocate those feelings was because he didn't feel the same way you did. No, that would hurt too much to consider.

Instead, we analyze and decode texts, words, body language, length of response times, etc., as though it's a sport that provides value to every relationship situation or that we are aiding Robert Langdon in solving the Da Vinci Code. Asking: "Why didn't he call?" Or "What do you think he meant when he said what he said?" As though men are naturally cryptic beings. How about he meant precisely what he said? And that reason you are desperately digging for as to why he never called back? Well, it certainly wasn't because of some far-fetched reason you and your girlfriends came up with to soften the blow. And I know this is hard to hear, but the reason that guy didn't call was because he didn't *want* to call—it's that simple. But the truth is, we will never be satisfied with accepting things at face value. We want to believe in that teensy, weensy possibility that he didn't call because he was off saving the world where there was no cell phone coverage for miles or that his phone went missing when he helped his grandmother move. We want to believe that things are more complex than that, like a game that requires you to solve the puzzle before advancing you to the next level. And at the end of the day, we want to believe that the deeper meaning exists (especially when it benefits our narrative). Maybe it's because it makes things much more exciting or gives us the hope that things are not always what they seem. Either way, I know we will stop at nothing until we feel we have finally cracked the code.

So, armed with a bottle of wine, takeout containers, and our past experiences with love, Leigha and I tried extremely hard to crack that very code. We spent the past hour in my apartment begging for answers, hoping that one of us would have an epiphany that would solve at least my current relationship dilemma. But like always, it was the blind leading the blind. Because what do twenty-eight-year-olds know about love? They know nothing. Absolutely nothing. But the code for me was more of a Rubik's Cube where I had to twist and turn all the many possibilities as to why this guy led me on the way he did; why he was an asshole who wanted his cake and eat it, too; and why the hell I had to be the cake.

At our age, you would have thought Leigha and I would have had these answers already—or at least had our shit together to some degree—but we didn't. I would have thought I would have been in a solid relationship by then, too, but sadly, I wasn't even close to being in one. I wasn't even progressing towards those relationship milestones that I was sick and tired of seeing other people parade around on social media like Macy's freakin' Thanksgiving Day parade. And the only aisle I was close to walking down was the one at the grocery store. At least with Leigha, she was closer to a solid relationship than I was—even if it was far from picture-perfect. Still, when was enough, enough? When would we finally find someone decent enough to share our lives with? When would the games end? Because, at the rate we were going, we were both ready to wave our little white flags and call it quits.

I don't know about you, but I was exhausted. I was tired of having to deal with yet another failed relationship. Were my expectations so unrealistic that trust in a relationship was too much to ask for? Or that I allowed myself to get so caught up in the honeymoon phase that I completely avoided the reality of what the relationship was? Or maybe I just didn't want to admit to myself that I had no idea what I actually wanted, which was why I kept picking the wrong guys? It was something to ponder.

Had my situation been different, I might have just rolled my eyes at the whole thing and moved on, but it wasn't that easy given everything I had been through dating-wise. You see, it all began just over a year ago when I ended things with my ex, Mike. I had spent the better part of my twenties with him, and he, for lack of better words, treated me like garbage—hot garbage. And it wasn't until I got so fed up with trying to fix that mess that I decided to walk away from that dumpster fire of a relationship with the hopes of giving myself a second chance at finding love. And this time around, I thought the guy I had been seeing, with his intoxicating personality and wild abandon, could have been "the one." Not even freakin' close.

For most of us, our twenties are the years we devote to finding ourselves, whereas I spent the better part of mine doing the complete opposite. I lost so much of myself into another person that I eventually became so unrecognizable to myself. Even my reflection in the mirror looked like it belonged to that of a stranger. After a while, I had no idea who I was anymore. And on some days, sadly, I still don't. But I haven't stopped trying to figure it out. *That has to mean something, right?*

"I just don't understand why he strung me along like he did," I said after finishing my second glass of wine. "I honestly feel like he took complete advantage of me." I set my empty glass on the end table beside me.

"Girl, that boy needed a filler, and you were all-too-willing to play the part." Leigha peered over at me.

I should have been pissed at her for being so blunt, but she wasn't wrong. And the last thing I needed was a friend to sugarcoat how they felt to me. I had already been spoon-fed enough sugary lies to rot my teeth and heart that it was refreshing to taste the bitterness of truth for once.

"But you should have seen us when we were together. He would say and do some of the sweetest things. It just makes no sense how we got here—how he could flip the switch like that. What was the point of it all?" I leaned back into the couch with an audible sigh.

"Rachel, why does anyone say one thing and do another? Think about it: If he truly meant all those pretty little things he filled your head with," she pointed to her own, "then wouldn't he have made good on his word?" she asked, cocking her head towards me. "Wouldn't you two still be together right now?"

"Who knows. He didn't have to lie to me, though," I protested. "But it had to be done. I had to do something." I looked to her for reassurance. "I couldn't have very well left things as they were, right?"

"No, you didn't. And he didn't have to lie, but you also didn't need to lie to yourself either. Don't tell me that that little voice in your head wasn't trying to stop you well before all of this happened? You knew it was never going to work from the start."

"Which is why I ended things," I said as though my actions deserved some kind of trophy or recognition.

To be honest, I knew he and I being together was a shot in the dark, but I still felt like we *had* a shot. And I stupidly thought that was all that mattered. It's like when Mary Swanson tells Lloyd Christmas in *Dumb & Dumber* that he had a one out of a million chance of them being together, and he stupidly replied, "So, you're telling me there's a chance?" That was me. I was freakin' Lloyd Christmas.

But I had been down a similar road with him in the not-so-distant past, so it was easy to spot the same road signs telling me that we were heading in the same direction as before. However, I chose to ignore every last one, convincing myself that this time would be different. But I was just in pure denial.

Tell me, have you ever wanted to believe in a lie so badly that you begin to forget that it was even a lie in the first place? I have. Time and time again, I have done this. And as Maya Angelou once said: "The first time someone shows you who they are, believe them." But do we? I certainly didn't then, nor had I ever practiced that advice in the past either.

So often, I find myself making excuses for other people's behavior—I am notorious for it! I have made excuses for pretty much everything because making excuses was much easier for me to do than having to face the truth. But here's the thing: You can only hide from the truth for so long until all those excuses you made eventually reach the end of their fuse, and then, BOOM goes the dynamite.

Back when I was with my ex, Mike, that particular habit of mine exacerbated. Whenever he said something cruel, I excused it for him having a bad day or for me having said or done something to instigate that response. When he lied to me about something, I believed whatever excuse he gave me because I didn't want to open myself up to face the truth behind his lies. When he played mind games and manipulated me into getting whatever he wanted, I made up whatever excuse I could to justify it. After separating myself from that situation, I realized that my reasons for making excuses were just my way of surviving through the continual heartbreak he put me through. It was my defense mechanism so that I didn't have to feel too much. I knew that if I allowed myself to really feel the extent of those feelings, my heart couldn't take it. Excuses were my armor; however, they didn't protect me in the least.

I know all-too-well what it's like to give your heart to the wrong person. And even after having faced that realization many times over, it has never gotten better with time. It certainly doesn't age like a fine wine—that's for sure. When I finally came to terms with the fate of my relationship with Mike, it took me almost the same amount of time to sever that relationship entirely. I just wasn't ready to accept the fact that he wasn't the right guy—that I had devoted so much work into something that would never, well, *work*. And I also wasn't prepared to face the hard truth that his behavior towards me was not circumstantial but rather a result of who he was as a person. I was pretty much the mouse who couldn't smell the cheese. It was such a slow-moving process to break away from him that I found myself beginning to reject him like he was cancer or a foreign object that didn't belong. If you're familiar with it, the ache is a suffocating, heart-wrenching feeling that only dissipates with the break. And it was that very break that gave me my life back.

For years, I fantasized about the moment where I would finally call it quits, where I would tell Mike that I had enough and end the relationship for good. But what saddened me most about that fantasy was that I had spent a large portion of our relationship dreaming about it. Sometimes, I would see the door appear, but for whatever reason, at that time, I wasn't strong or brave enough to walk through it. Or maybe it was because he made me believe that things would be different that time around. Other times, when the door wasn't there, it seemed hopeless, as though the universe was punishing me for the life I had repeatedly chosen by wasting all prior chances I had of walking away. So, the last thing I wanted with this latest guy (more on him later) was to settle for the wrong person again. And that maybe what was currently happening in my love life was just a blessing in disguise? If that were the case, then tell me, how can something that feels so right be fifty shades of complete wrong for you? Go ahead; I'll wait.

All of the biggest hesitations in my life had always been plagued by the dreaded "what ifs." *What if he changes? What if he means what he said this time? What if this was the wake-up call he desperately needed? What if? What if? WHAT IF?*

For years, I held onto those "what ifs" like they were gospel. I wanted to believe in their possibilities so much that I rejected the emptiness they possessed. With Mike, they were all cyclical excuses he used to his advantage, leaving me constantly second-guessing myself and the fate of our relationship. They were tools he kept in his back pocket, which he only pulled out during the times he knew I had one foot out the door. He wanted me to believe in the "what ifs" as well because it helped delay what we both knew was inevitable. It was never so much about me or the relationship than what benefits he could reap from them—and that was bullshit. It was always about him. It was a narcissistic kind of love that swallowed me up whole for years. And there I was, almost a year later, surrounded by a shiny, new set of "what ifs," hoping that this new guy would have made at least one of them worth believing in.

Looking back on the moment I had decided to move clear across the country to be with Mike after he accepted a new job opportunity, I knew I was making a terrible decision the moment I made it. How I knew it was a terrible decision came down to its weight. Good decisions feel releasing. They are light and freeing—sans pressure. Bad decisions feel constricting, heavy, and somewhat paralyzing. It's similar to that feeling you have when you think you forgot to lock your door or turn your hair straightener off as soon as you pull out of your driveway. It's that nagging feeling that lingers no matter how many times you check the lock on the door or the outlet to make sure that damn straightener is unplugged.

Everything I had ever known or wanted up until that point in my life was quickly cast aside with one quick, impulsive decision. A decision that, quite frankly, I made because I was too stubborn to admit that it wasn't right or what I really wanted for myself. I wasn't brave enough to acknowledge that it was never about having "cold feet;" it was more about recognizing the signs that it wasn't the right thing to do. But, perhaps, I'm being a bit too hard on myself. It wasn't like I knew any of this at that time. After all, the past is the past, and I can't keep punishing myself for making mistakes that I wasn't sure I was making in the first place. It was easy for me to be impulsive with my decision-making back then because I was too immature at life to know what it was that I was sacrificing. Being young, we believe that we have all the time in the world, so that if we waste a little, it's OK. Well, my friend, time flies. And you can never truly make up for lost time no matter how hard you try. I wish I knew that then, too.

But if it weren't for my past, I definitely wouldn't be where I am today. Now, I'm not saying I was exactly where I wanted to be, but I can assure you I was happy that I wasn't where I used to be. With this current relationship dilemma living rent-free in my mind, I couldn't deny how much of a letdown it all was. I was so sick and tired of dealing with the unnecessary drama that I was just about to say, *Screw it!* And call it quits on love for good. One after another, I was continuously picking bad apple after bad apple off the dating tree, expecting something different with each bite. And when it came to this particular bad apple, like all others before, it had a worm in it.

I wish people wore warning labels so you knew what you were getting yourself into well before you got into things. There are no "guy facts" to read up on to know whether a relationship is worth pursuing. First impressions are tricky because everyone presents their best versions (you know you do). We want to be liked. We want to be desired. But when all that honeymoon dust settles, we are left with only our true selves. It only sucks when you discover you're left with someone that's not even close to the person you initially fell for—like they catfished their personalities.

So, is it fair to say that the decision I had made to be with Mike, or any previous guy for that matter, really that bad? Sure, there are a lot of uncertainties any time you enter into a new relationship—but such is life, right? If I had never decided to move across the country to be with him, I may have always wondered what could have been. So, did it actually matter what I chose? Not to mention, the girl who made that decision is far from the girl who would have made that decision today. We both have different wants and needs. We are two different people now. However, if we are as different as I am claiming us to be, why am I still making similar bad decisions? Why was I still falling for the wrong guys? If the universe was trying to teach me a lesson by continuously throwing the same types of relationships in my path, then obviously, there was a lesson I wasn't getting. I cringed at the thought. If that were true, I knew I still had a lot of learning ahead of me.

Like all relationships, there are the good times, and there are the bad. But what do you do when the bad outweighs the good? Well, for starters, you don't hold out for the good times like I did by suffering through the bad as though it were some consolation prize. It's never worth it. The cost is too great. Now, I'm not saying that every relationship needs to be perfect to survive, but the bad times shouldn't always be in the spotlight. They shouldn't be allowed to take center stage, defining the relationship in its entirety. Nor should we put so much of ourselves up for sacrifice just to make things work. And if I were being honest with myself, the relationship I had with this new guy was nothing more than another lesson I still hadn't quite learned yet.

I know that our hearts gravitate towards specific people at specific times for specific reasons (*Am I being specific enough?*) And sometimes, we may never know what those reasons are. So, again, I wouldn't be where I am today had I not made certain decisions in my life, and neither would you. Life is all about living and learning. Whether I cared to admit it at that time or not, I've experienced both sides of the coin with all the men I've dated.

From an early age, I always believed that love made anything possible. I believed it had the power to heal, the power to change, and the power to inspire love in return. But through my many attempts at loving Mike—or, again, any guy for that matter—I learned that no matter how much you love or do for a person, it doesn't mean they will reciprocate those feelings in return or that they would change because of it. When it came to Mike, it didn't matter how great I was or how great I was to him. It didn't matter how much of myself I sacrificed to make up for his shortcomings because, in the end, it only ended up depleting me more. I kept draining myself to keep him whole while in the same breath, calling it fulfillment. And had I been the best version of myself to this new guy, it still wouldn't have mattered. What he did wasn't about me. It bared no reflection on me at all.

So, just to put it out there again: Why does it have to be this fucking hard?

But it was. And there wasn't anything I could do about it. *It was what it was*, as they say. Whether I was still navigating my way through yet another disappointing relationship or not, the universe was begging for me to learn something here. But that was easier said than done, especially when emotion blinded my every move. I was letting my emotions reign supreme over logic as if my heart knew better than my gut. However, it all came down to what I *wanted* to hear, and my gut just wasn't getting the memo.

Still, I couldn't understand why he (this new guy) did what he did. I spent way too much time overanalyzing the situation until I backed myself so far up into a corner that I could no longer decipher what was real and what was pure speculation. Not including the hundreds of times I combed through our last exchange in my head, which I felt compelled to drag Leigha in on as well. I wanted to understand what couldn't be understood. I wanted to know *why*, as though his actions were personal rather than consequential. I couldn't understand why he could do what he did to *me* as if I was somehow exempt from this type of behavior—as though I could be the exception to the hurt. But I wasn't. And if it hadn't been me that he treated this way, then he would have positively done the same thing to someone else. However, I couldn't accept that. It wasn't enough. I needed the deeper meaning. I needed the bigger *why*.

What I can say is that love is, well, stupid sometimes. It makes us do and feel crazy things. And no one is immune from its effects—no matter how hard we try convincing ourselves otherwise.

"I just don't know why he had to string me along like that—or why I even let him." My face hit the palm of my hand in defeat. I looked over at the now empty bottle of wine, realizing that our problems outlasted the contents.

"We've all been there. You're not the first person who thought the ending was going to play out differently."

"I get that. But I just don't know how I got here again. You would think after everything I've been through that I would have known better—that things would get easier," I sighed.

Leigha laughed. "Things don't get easier, babe. We're just supposed to learn how to deal with this shit better."

"Well, that's just plain stupid." I rolled my eyes.

Let's go back in time, shall we?

Welcome Back, Parker

August 2012
(One year and four months earlier)

I moved back to New York at the end of that summer, and I was excited at the prospect of starting over. It was my chance at a new beginning. It was my chance at redemption. It was also my chance at creating a better life—one I could never have had with Mike. I knew that if I had any shot of pulling myself out of that heartbroken hole, then this would be the rope to help pull me out. And I couldn't have been more ready to grab hold of it.

New beginnings can often come off as cliché. We have all heard the story where the girl returns to her hometown to find herself after a break-up, dedicates her time to self-discovery, only to meet a guy who shows her why it never worked out with anyone else before. It's all a damn Hallmark movie, if you ask me. So, spoiler alert: This is not that story. But we all know that you don't find "the one" after only one attempt at dating. I knew I had many hits and misses ahead of me, but it wasn't like I was ready to start swinging.

My decision to come back home didn't mean that home was guaranteed to be the same place as I had left it. So much had changed in the few short years I was gone, including myself, that trying to search for some level of familiarity got lost. I began to see things through a new set of eyes, and the nostalgia for home quickly wore off after only a few weeks. Do you know that expression saying how you can always go home again? Well, no one ever promised that it would be the same place that you had left it.

However, something about Syracuse, aka "The Salt City," felt promising. Or maybe I was so drunk off its residual summer vibes that any city would have made me feel the same way. The smell of bakeries, pizza shops, as well as the mishmash of eclectic bars and restaurants that lined the streets, called to me. Downtown played host to many ethnic festivals from Italian to Irish, and the food was downright amazing. Nothing screamed Syracuse more to me than walking the streets downtown with food in hand, waiting for something magical to happen between each bite. Nevertheless, once I found a decent job, I found an even better apartment. It was then I was ready to begin again.

And now that I was back, two of my closest friends, Leigha and Jessie, were all-too-eager to get me actively back into our social circle. The minute my car passed the first exit into New York, they had already planned our first night out. To be honest, anything they planned I knew would end up being fun, but I just preferred some alone time to decompress instead. I needed time to deal with the quietness of my new life. I needed to face it head-on with no distractions. But I could only ignore so many pleas from them before I eventually gave in and met them out for dinner and drinks at our old stomping ground known for its small plates but large flavors.

"Let's toast!" Leigha exclaimed as she raised her glass. "To the ones we've loved. To the ones we lost. And to the ones we settled for no matter the cost. Cheers to new beginnings!" We all reached across the table, clinking our glasses together, creating a melody that sounded nothing more than a theme of survival. A beat that would have made Destiny's Child proud. (*Am I aging myself here?*)

But what was surviving exactly? For me, it meant spending the next phase of my life picking up the pieces and making sense of what was left and what was still needed to make me feel whole again. It also meant a much-needed recovery period that would, most likely, leave my head and heart spinning off their axels. But I was ready for it. I didn't come this far to give up so easily.

Truthfully, I had been ready for a while. I acted out this very life every chance I could, whether dreaming about it at night or thinking about it during the day. Every rendition left me more excited, and I couldn't wait to test drive the new woman I was becoming. I no longer wanted to settle for anything less than what I knew I deserved. I finally gave myself the room to be my complete authentic self, and I couldn't have been more blessed to have been welcomed back home with such unconditional love and support. It only validated my decision to leave Mike even more.

As I sat at the table, the world felt alive all around me. People were laughing and going about their lives just as I was in the process of restarting mine. I wondered what establishment and a solid foundation underfoot felt like. I even wondered if the strangers that filled the room wondered those same things, too. Or if they, like me, were starting their lives anew. It was hard to say. At times, because I was starting over, it left an aftertaste of loneliness and dread. And I was perfectly aware that when the night was over, I would be returning to my apartment alone. And, to some degree, it sucked. But it was far better than ever having to go home to Mike again.

Taking a bite of food, I thought back to earlier that morning, when Leigha called, begging me to come out for drinks. She mentioned the horrible date she had the night before.

"It was terrible. Are you home? I'm coming over," she said all in one breath. Twenty minutes later, she was at my door with coffee and donuts in hand.

"Come in." I smiled as she brushed past me in the doorway and headed towards the kitchen. Soon, she emerged with a half-eaten donut and powdered sugar decorating her face.

Leigha Michaels, a blonde bombshell, possessed more confidence than a group of a hundred women, whom I envied for always being so resilient and strong, somehow deflated like a balloon in front of my eyes.

"It was my third date in a row, and like all the rest, it was downright terrible," she huffed as she scanned my apartment for someplace to sit. "Can you clear a spot for me on the couch? You would have thought you'd be unpacked by now." Her nose curled in either disgust or disappointment—I couldn't tell.

"Well, one box at a time," I said. "So, your date—that bad, huh?" I changed the subject. "Should I go get the rest of the donuts from the kitchen?" I smirked while running my fingers through my freshly darkened hair. I was originally a blonde like Leigha but felt like I needed a change. I couldn't believe I talked myself into changing my hair so drastically, though. A fresh start didn't mean a new identity—at least, not in this case. There weren't witness protection programs for the brokenhearted.

"I just want to know what I'm doing to attract these guys. You're lucky you haven't started dating yet. You will not be impressed with what's out there." She took an aggressive bite of her donut.

"So, what happened? Let's hear all the shitty details."

"What *didn't* happen? It was a complete nightmare," she sighed. "He spent the majority of the date talking about himself—couldn't care less about me. I just don't get it. I'm almost thirty years old, and I'm still dating around like I was in my early twenties. Where are all the decent guys? Are there any left?" she groaned.

"I'm convinced they're hiding," I laughed.

"Are you keeping them in these boxes?" she teased, lifting one of the flaps as if to check.

"Saving the good ones for a rainy day." I smiled. "But you have dated some decent ones, Leigha. What about J—"

"I know who you are going to name, and no." She put her hands up in protest.

I rolled my eyes. "I don't know why you act like that. James was so into you, and you were—"

"So, *not?*" she cut me off. "Regardless, have you, Rachel Parker, ever stopped and asked yourself why dating has to be this hard?" She turned her body towards me, setting her coffee down onto her lap.

"All the damn time." I frowned, not realizing that it would end up being the same question she and I would religiously ponder over without ever coming close to an actual answer.

"How many bad dates do I have to suffer through before I have a good one?"

"Beats me." I shook my head. "I keep telling myself that there has to be a light at the end of this heartbreaking tunnel."

"Wishful thinking," she sighed again. "That tunnel is pitch black."

"Maybe, but I think us holding onto some kind of hope is the only way we're going to survive this."

As I was thinking back to that conversation, I wondered if I ever believed that there was a light. Looking across the table at Jessie, she had her share of romance woes like the rest of us, but it seemed like she was finally in a good relationship with a guy who had lasting potential. Who's to say that couldn't be Leigha or me one day? (I crossed my fingers under the table for extra luck). However, whoever said that finding love had to be a race? Or that the aforementioned light had to be a guy?

The light could very well mean finding acceptance and love for yourself and, of course, your life. (I silently cheered to that sentiment in my head). Moving on never meant that I had to find someone new.

When I got home later that night, I did a face-plant into my bed, feeling the coolness of my satin sheets against my bare skin. Without giving myself a second to come up for air, I muffled out a low-pitched scream into my pillow. I knew that if I yelled any louder, my neighbor, Agnes from across the hall, would come knocking on my door to check on me—again. Two weeks into moving in, she had somehow taken on a surrogate mother role by bringing me meals, houseplants, and unsolicited advice. During her little "check-ins," she often hinted that I should find a good man and settle down. *If it were only that easy, Agnes.*

The following day, I stared around at my messy bedroom at all the boxes still waiting to be unpacked. I knew I had a lot to do, but it felt extremely overwhelming at times, which was why I committed to only unpacking a few here and there, or whenever the mood struck. But there I was, at the brink of turning thirty, living a life I never envisioned for myself. Nor did I ever imagine having to start over during what I considered to be so late in life. But was it that late? Well, better late than never, I've always heard. But it was my fault for putting the breakup off for as long as I did. What a waste of valuable living time. Who knew where I could have been in my life had I grown some balls and done something about my situation sooner? That was all on me. There was no one else to blame. I had all the control, and I chose to be complacent instead—shame on me.

However, if you were to have asked me ten years ago where I thought I'd be at this exact moment, I would have probably said married with a family. Now, I found those projections to be oddly funny. No one, myself included, ever considers that life doesn't give two shits about what you planned for it. Mine certainly didn't. Yet, there I was, beating myself up for not living up to those expectations I had set for myself as though my life's dream board had caught fire. The mere thought of me not having reached certain milestones yet made me feel like it directly reflected on my successes in life. Therefore, I had to accept that this was my life—for now. It was nothing more than a resting place and not the final destination. And the only way it could have ever been the final destination was if I had chosen to settle there, and I refused to do that.

Truthfully, I half-expected that the universe would have smiled upon me by providing what my heart so desperately desired. I told myself, before leaving Mike, that if I were brave enough to fight for what I deserved, the reward would be instantaneous. Believe me, I understand how foolish that sounds now, but it was the only thing to push my ass out that door. I was no stranger to loss, heartache, or grief. In fact, I had sat with those tribulations for quite some time, but never once did I think they would become as consuming as they did. Along the way, I let them define me rather than allow them to inspire me to become a better version of myself. But what I failed to see was that the reward wasn't so much about finding love with another person but rather finding love within myself.

Of course, I would rather be alone than spend another day invested in a life I knew wasn't for me. However, it didn't take long to realize that my loneliness peaked when I wasn't surrounded by distractions. It reared its ugly head and made itself so unbearable to endure. The only thing that kept me going was knowing how easily I could have stayed with someone that wasn't right for me. How I could have easily settled and accepted my life for what it was rather than what it could be. So, I tucked away those negative thoughts in the back of my mind and laid them to rest. I didn't want them to stomp all over my progress thus far. I also didn't want the universe to think that I wasn't appreciative of this second chance. I was just having a hard time adjusting to it—that's all. But no matter how liberating it felt to walk away from a bad relationship, there were still times the side effects of loneliness ate away at me. Trust me; it scares me even to this day how easy it can be to settle. So, in the end, I would take loneliness over a lousy relationship any day.

Life is messy, and I was just splashing around in it like a kid in a rain puddle. During the first month of my breakup from Mike, I naively equated the chaos in my life as the proverbial side effect, or the transitional period blues, which directly resulted from my detoxification from the relationship itself. I desperately tried everything within my power to escape from it completely, which was just a fancier way of saying I wanted to pretend as though none of it happened in the first place—not a bright idea. Denial can sometimes be an even uglier place to reside than facing the pain head-on.

Still, I clung to the hope that my past would stay buried so that I could have a successful fresh start. It wasn't that I was making things out to be far worse than what they were, but I knew what I walked away from. And for so long, it had always been Mike and Rachel, Rachel and Mike. You couldn't say one name without saying the other. And I think that's why I wanted my name to start standing on its own and not be grouped or associated with any other. I wanted the world to know me without the "and" attached to it. But how was I to accomplish that? I moved back to my hometown—ground freakin' zero—which was the very place where our relationship started. It was almost as if everyone expected us to be together still—that we could withstand the test of time. I knew it wouldn't take long before I had to burst that bubble.

Although, the idea of starting over never meant that I had to jump into another relationship. You can't heal yourself with someone else (because we all know that never works). And you certainly can't find yourself within another person either. I'm perfectly aware that starting over can mean different things to different people, and I knew there were many people out there just like me who were trying to navigate the world being single after ending a relationship. And if that were the case, why did it feel so damn isolating?

Emotional Baggage

September 2012

I'm a very analytical person who ponders everything by nature—especially the "what ifs." I often find myself mulling over the same things, expecting different answers each time (*The definition of insanity, right?*). Why I torture myself this way is hard to explain, but I think it has something to do with my way of dealing with life's uncertainties (as if life's uncertainties needed to be dealt with, and I was the only person capable enough of dealing with them).

But I wasn't the least bit capable.

It was Sunday morning at the beginning of September when I decided to unpack a few more boxes. With coffee in hand, my phone vibrated with a text from my friend, Noah, who agreed to come over and help me tackle this chore.

Noah Crawford was a friend from college whom I lost contact with over the years but ended up reconnecting with when I moved back. Having rekindled that friendship, I had to admit that he had quickly become one of my most favorite people in the world. He was wise beyond his years, incredibly sarcastic, and never shied away from telling me what I needed to hear rather than what I wanted. I valued his friendship so much because he had always been there when I needed him the most—even when not asked. Aside from that, he had no problem calling me out on my bullshit, letting me know when I was being foolish, irrational, or if I was downright overacting about something. He was a friend I never knew I needed, and it felt as though he had resurfaced in my life at such a crucial time that I often wondered how the hell I survived without him for so long.

That's the thing with people. They come and go. And they come and go for reasons only the universe understands. I have heard that it's by no accident who we let into our lives or who leaves (but more on that later). Life is crazy. And I can say with the utmost certainty that if anyone were to ask me if I could have predicted where I'd be at this stage in the game or who I would be surrounding myself with, I would have probably laughed at the absurdity of it.

But friends are essential. And it's not how many you have; it's the quality of those friendships that mean much more. My mother always instilled in me that you can't view each friendship as the same because they are not all created equal. Each relationship we have is different, and you can't rely on the hope that your friendship will reciprocate someone's friendship in return. I have been friends with those who have betrayed me. I have opened myself up to those who didn't deserve my truth. And when you find yourself grieving the betrayal and loss of a friendship you never really had in the first place, you need to take a step back and look at the whole picture. Too often, we are quick to give ourselves over to people. We don't allow time to reveal who they are or what their placement in our lives should be. Instead, we just throw out VIP passes into our lives like candy. We assume that each person is good and then are shocked when they turn out to be the complete opposite. Knowing this helps establish boundaries. It does no one any service to have a relationship with blurred lines—love or otherwise.

There isn't one person I know that hasn't been guilty of forcing things to happen—and I am guilty as charged. We have gone above and beyond to make people like us and extend ourselves beyond our means because we are somehow convinced that it would give us the validation we so desperately sought. It's draining. Why we do this can never be fully answered or comprehended, even when we know full well what the potential consequences are. It's the curse of false validation. Luckily, the people I was surrounding myself with were not abusing their VIP passes or giving me false validation. They were true. They were special. They were amazing.

"It would be nice to clear off your couch finally." Noah pointed to the pile of boxes upon it before grabbing one and placing it onto the floor. He then grabbed the boxcutter from the end table and opened it up, revealing various kitchen items bubble-wrapped inside.

I didn't immediately respond because I was too busy picturing my apartment post clutter. It was slowly becoming (even though I wasn't 100% mindful of it at that time) the foundation for which I rebuilt my life. Rock bottom became the boxes and bags scattered about from a previous life I had fought so hard to leave behind. However, a part of me wished I could have just lit a match and set everything on fire, but I realized that no object is tied to a memory unless I invested the time to keep it there. These were my things, after all. They had nothing to do with Mike or anyone else—just me.

My life ultimately began the second I ended the one I shared with Mike. It was the first domino knocked down before the others quickly followed suit. Had I been braver a lot sooner, I would not have prolonged the inevitable for as long as I did, especially when I knew I wasn't living my best life with him. It was foolish. However, when you become so complacent and accepting of a relationship, no matter how bad it is (after spending so much time convincing yourself that things would eventually get better), you remain in the worst position of all: Settling.

I had one finger on that domino for years, wondering and waiting for a reason to pull it back. I always knew that leaving wasn't going to be easy, and the aftermath of it all left me feeling drained, defeated, and somewhat disconnected from reality. It was difficult to reveal to those who barely knew me, or my story, what I was going through—especially when most people at my age were saying their "I do's" and I was busy saying, "I don't." It was hard. But it wasn't like my story was any different from anyone else's because it wasn't exactly earth-shattering. So, then, why did it feel so unrelatable? In the end, leaving was the best thing I could have ever done for myself. And even on those days when I felt depressed and alone, I never regretted my decision for one second.

Through time, I have realized that breakups are hard no matter whose decision it is to end things. For me, I wanted the separation from Mike more than anything—actually, I *needed* it. But even with coming to terms with that decision, it still didn't make things any easier. Although to give credit where credit is due, I owe a lot of my strength to Jessie, who helped me get to that place of acceptance. She was the friend who took my hand and walked me to the door when I was too scared to make the journey on my own. Like Noah, she couldn't have played a better role in my life during that time. She made me face the truth I had spent years comfortably denying. She saw through every fake smile and empty word I had spoken, forcing me to acknowledge the kind of love I kept alive with excuses. *You want a better life*; she said to me one day. *Then you better fight for it, girl—before it's too late.* That's when I knew no matter how hard it was for me to leave, it would have been much harder should I have chosen to stay.

I wasn't trying to dwell too much on the past, but when you're unpacking items you haven't seen in a while, your mind has a way of inviting those memories back in. Until that point, I did my best to block out the past as best as I could. I wanted nothing from my past relationship with Mike to seep into my new life and pollute it. And yes, there were times I wished I could have gone back in time and changed a few things, but we all know that everything happens for a reason. So, why bother?

I am also a firm believer that life has the power to yank us backward to put us on the right path going forward. It's OK to take a few steps back sometimes. It doesn't translate into a setback or a delay but more of a chance to reassess where you are. It's about making sure you don't continue down the wrong path before you have no choice but to turn around and start the journey all over again. It's a complete waste of valuable time (and we all know how precious time is).

Now, we may not understand the need for the reassessment, but I believed that mine was due to the need to find my solid foundation in life—a new place to rebuild. And I will say, you certainly cannot begin to rebuild anything sustainable on a ground that is shaky beneath your feet. Taking those few steps back for me meant returning home. But returning home also meant that I'd have to face a lot of unsolicited questions, and the only way to limit all that noise was to remain in the shadows, so to speak.

Once I came back to New York, I decided to keep my social media presence very lowkey. My goal was not to make a big spectacle out of my situation or publicize Mike's wrongdoings (because you know how people love good drama). Therefore, I did my best to keep a certain level of privacy and not parade my business around. *Remember boundaries?*

Going public with any new relationship or even addressing one that has ended is a tricky status update to navigate, and shockingly, Mike managed to publicize everything he possibly could. So, after I moved out, he did whatever he could to get a rise out of me or find ways to make me jealous. But I didn't bite. I honestly felt none of those things. But I knew that was the only way he could try and hurt me because *hurt people hurt people.* I get it. But I wasn't hurting—at least not in the way he thought I was. He became so vocal about our breakup as though trying to get a jumpstart on being the crowd favorite, which made my intentions on staying in the shadows rather tricky. And I couldn't care less about any girl he tried replacing me with—they could have my place! As I said, I knew he was trying to hurt me or at least try to see if it would entice me to come crawling back, but again, I didn't bite. He truly believed at that time that leaving him was *my* loss (and not the other way around), but all his attempts failed miserably. Mike, hear me when I say this: Leaving you was my gain.

Unlike Mike, I remained single. I wanted to be single. I wanted this newfound time to be dedicated to myself. But my choice of staying single didn't mean that I was incapable of finding love. I just knew that I wasn't in the right heart or headspace to introduce a new relationship into my life until I was emotionally ready to do so. I needed to unpack the emotional baggage from one life before inadvertently packing it into the next. I didn't want or need that—and neither did anyone else. And I most certainly wasn't looking for a rebound. I was much stronger than that—better than that. **This was my recovery period.** Nor was I looking for a sequel. So, if fate was giving me a second chance to do things right, I was going to take that chance and run like hell with it.

Now, let's talk about being single, shall we?

Being single was once considered a "golden" status. It meant freedom. It meant discovery. It meant having the ability—and the time—for self-exploration and not feeling pressured to have your strings tied to anyone or anything. Not that those "strings" are synonymous with being put on a leash, but sometimes, it limits our abilities to live out our lives to the fullest when we are still trying to learn what our aspirations are or could be. (Unless, of course, you find someone who complements and supports those very things.) *Do I hear an exception?*

Now that I found myself single again, it wasn't reminiscent of what I remembered it once being like in years past. Every time I logged onto social media, announcements bombarded my feed regarding engagements, weddings, and babies, which completely overshadowed anything I was doing as a single girl. It seemed as though no one cared about my nights out with friends or that I considered adopting a puppy when half the girls I was "friends" with were pushing kids out of their who-has and playing house with their soon-to-be husbands. It made me feel like everything I shared paled in comparison. So, inherently, I felt this overwhelming pressure to essentially "catch up." *Tell me, am I alone here?* But being single at almost thirty years of age, I was suddenly being bombarded with all these looming milestones, earmarked with deadlines hanging over my head like dark clouds with impending rain. And it was those same deadlines that hung over my head, reminding me that I had to quickly check all the boxes before society began to question what the hell was wrong with me. But would that have happened? Would that so-called society really have judged me harshly on whatever I chose to do with the rest of my life? Or were those lies I told myself? I could have never imagined staying with Mike—or any guy for that matter—for the sake of being able to check a few of those milestones off the list. What then? The only thing I would have accomplished would have been hammering yet another nail in that relationship coffin.

"Do you find it hard being single?" I looked over at Noah as he was busy organizing a stack of books. His emerald, green eyes went from examining the titles to examining me.

"What do you mean?" he asked as he began placing a few books onto a nearby shelf.

"Do you find it difficult to be alone? Or do you constantly find yourself trying to fill that void with something—like another relationship?"

"I'm not sure. I just go with whatever feels right at the time, I guess. Why?" He cocked his head towards me.

"Well, since this is my first time being single in a while, I just don't know how to be single anymore. I've pretty much distracted myself since I moved back here, but I fear what will happen when all the dust settles. What then?"

"You need to just deal with it. As sucky as it may sound, you just have to. You need to be able to stand on your own because if you can't accomplish that, you will never be able to stand with someone else."

"Are you recommending this from experience? Or did you get this from some book?" I laughed.

"Perhaps both." He grinned. "But honestly, Rachel, it's true. You need to know that what may work for me may not work for you."

"I feel like you are slowly becoming my shrink," I smirked half-jokingly.

"Trust me, I plan on sending you my bill," he replied.

Timelines, Fairy Tales & George Clooney

September 2012

"Cut the crap," Noah said to me over the phone a few nights later. "You need to stop whining about being single like it's the end of the world. I thought you were going to take my advice and learn to just deal with it?" I heard him start the ignition to his car as his phone turned over to Bluetooth.

"Easier said than done," I sighed, pulling my bed covers over my face.

"Seriously, though, who cares if you're single? The only one making a big deal out of it is you. You're not the only one in the world to have gone through a breakup or who had to start over. There are far worse things to worry over, and this certainly isn't one of them."

"It's not about being single per se, Noah." I yanked the covers back down. "It's more about this sudden awareness of how my timeline feels completely off." I pulled myself into a sitting position on my bed. I had been down on myself that day because I had spent the better part of it scrolling through social media and committing the worst cardinal sin: Comparing my life to the lives of others.

Everywhere I looked—or didn't look—I was reminded of how alone I was. Even though a few guys had asked me out in recent weeks, I still wasn't ready to get myself back out there. I wasn't interested in jumping back on that horse, so to speak. None of them sparked any excitement in me to take that leap and consider saddling up. They all left an aftertaste of that familiar flavor of settlement.

I get it. I knew I didn't want to date—or felt ready to—but that didn't mean that I didn't feel alone. I wanted companionship just like the next person but knowing that what I wanted wasn't something I was ready to receive was a hard realization.

"What's a timeline anyway? It's not like we all have the same aspirations in life. So, why would everyone's milestones be the same?" Noah interrupted my thoughts. "And if you're telling me that I'm wrong, then sure, my timeline is off, too. But you don't hear me griping about it."

"Why not gripe, though? Aren't you at least a little pissed off at the universe that you still haven't found someone worth sharing your life with?" I asked. "Especially after all you've been through?"

"What's the point? It's not like I'm going to force a relationship to happen because we both know they never work out that way," he said. "Come on, lady, move!" he yelled at traffic.

"Makes sense," I breathed into the phone.

"What you need to realize is that we are all not on the same page. We will never be. And we also don't need to rush into a relationship just to say we have someone there. That's not something I want for either one of us. A warm body lying next to you at night doesn't equate to happiness, and it took me many bodies to figure that out," he laughed with recollection.

"But seriously, the only person in charge of my happiness is me. And it's about time you learned that too"—he paused for a moment as he parked his car—"OK? People start over at all ages all the time. You are not reinventing the wheel here. Your situation is not unique," he laughed again. "Everyone has been here, Rachel. It's just your turn now."

"Well, can I get a pass?"

"With Mike? You wouldn't have survived one."

I'm not exactly sure what happened later that day, but I knew that I needed to begin channeling my thoughts into a healthier outlet. As much as I loved talking to my friends and still planned on doing so, I just knew that I didn't need to beat a dead horse with them while I tried making sense of how I was feeling. So, journaling was the only way I felt like I could get out what was bottling up inside of me. Again, I wasn't reinventing the wheel here.

Guilt set in after I hung up with Noah. There was no way that he, or any of my friends for that matter, weren't tired of hearing about the same nonsense day after day. Just because I needed to process my emotions didn't mean that they needed to be my constant sounding board to do it on. It wasn't fair to monopolize our friendships with my problems. Don't get me wrong; it wasn't like I planned on never sharing anything with them again; I just knew I had to put a cap on it.

Deep into page two of my notebook, pen and paper suddenly weren't cutting it. Writing by hand wasn't fast enough since it couldn't keep up with all the thoughts rushing to get out of me. So that by the time I was three pages in, my hand began cramping until I could no longer write legibly. That's when I decided to take my thoughts over to my laptop instead. But none of what I started to write made any logical sense, but I knew it still needed to come out of me nonetheless. I didn't want to rely solely on my friends and family, especially when the tradeoff was listening to their unsolicited advice or judgment. And as much as I knew I needed it at times, there were other times I just needed a quiet ear. But even those ears, with the best intentions, grow tired of hearing the same things repeatedly. People can't help but start tuning out the racket. It's natural. I get it. Hell, I have even tuned myself out at times.

But it was then I began to throw myself into journaling more so than I had ever done in my life. In what I considered a safe place, I found expressing myself an essential tool in my recovery. It didn't take long before I began questioning if anything I was writing would be helpful to others. Would they find positivity out of it? That's when I humored the idea of starting a blog—an anonymous blog. But the minute I decided to create a website (thanks to a little liquid courage), I froze. I had no idea what to write about. And suddenly, my safe place didn't feel so safe anymore. I didn't want to feel judged—even if no one knew who was behind my words. I didn't need to feel any worse than how I was already feeling, and my attempts to start something—whether worthwhile or not—were sabotaged entirely by my insecurities. So, in a matter of minutes, all inspiration within me depleted much like the remaining wine in my glass.

It wasn't like I was dating. It wasn't like I was getting myself back out there. Nor was I having the slightest bit of fun navigating through my new life. Instead, I was spending an enumerate amount of time wallowing in self-pity, and when I stopped to face that awful truth, I recognized that I was in that predicament all because of fear. I was afraid of what moving on would show me. And I was afraid of the possibility that the next relationship I found myself in wasn't going to be any better than the relationship I had left. What if people judged my decisions? What if people were unkind when I was still so very fragile? Although some were already doing that at the hand of Mike's dirty work—so, what was the difference? And what if those same people came with their torches? What if? What if? What if?

Looking back, I couldn't believe that I gave two shits about what other people thought of me. No wonder I lost inspiration at that moment. I wasn't doing anything inspiring! I deserved to live the life I fought so hard for. So, it was about time I put forth the effort into trying to live it. I didn't need to explain myself to anyone. And I certainly didn't need to divulge details of my personal life to strangers to justify my reasons for moving on or my reasons for whatever other decisions I made for myself. It was no one's business but my own. And if Mike wanted to dedicate his time to fabricating the truth, then that was on him. I had to swallow the urge to be defensive. I didn't need to play that part to satisfy his ego. There was nothing for me to defend because the truth did that for me on its own. And regardless of what others believed or didn't believe, I knew the truth would eventually come out in the end. I just had to be patient. I had to stop caring so much.

I have read countless self-help books in hopes of getting that much-needed clarity that I hoped my blog would provide. Then again, who was I to give advice to anyone that I wasn't strong enough to even listen to myself? Yet, there I was, about to use my laptop as the new sounding board. Would the world listen? Better yet, would I?

I eventually shut my laptop down for the remainder of the night. I had to get out of my apartment. I needed fresh air. So, I called up my friends and suggested a night out.

Loud conversations from nearby tables sucked our small little table up and enveloped us in like a cocoon. Our waiter, Davis, who claimed us to be his favorite regulars, already brought out our usual choice of appetizers before we even had the chance to set down our menus. I loved that about this place. You always felt like family.

That particular night didn't make it into my memory bank because of how much fun we had or how great the food was, but more because of the great conversations we shared. Because of that, I couldn't help but wonder if times like these were just as important to my friends as they were to me, or were they simply a memory tossed away without a second thought?

"Everyone has had their heart broken at some point," Jessie said after a mouthful of food. "But it's not like we can't recover from it. We eventually get back on our feet and start over," she said. "For example, after things ended with my ex, Greg, I thought I would never love anyone as much as I loved him. Now look at me, I ended up meeting Jordan, and I couldn't be happier." She smiled, making the corners of her mouth touch her two dimples like the game, Connect the Dots.

"Yes, and you both plan on living happily ever after—blah, blah, blah! We get it!" Leigha rolled her eyes.

"I don't know if you two have heard, but Rachel over here had a meltdown earlier today," Noah teased.

"I did not have a meltdown." I punched him in the shoulder. "I had an emotional rant, that's all. There's a huge difference."

"Is there?" He peered over at me.

"A meltdown over what exactly?" Jessie interjected as her eyes narrowed towards me. I hadn't exactly kept her in the loop regarding my woes.

"Timelines," I said. "Mine just feels like it's off."

"Who cares about stupid timelines." Leigha took a quick swig of her beer. "Take it from me, I'm taking things slow and not rushing into anything—and neither should any of you. Just have fun."

"Coming from the girl, who, not too long ago, was bitching about her terrible dates," I mocked.

"Touché." She tipped her beer towards me.

"But when you move at your own pace, timelines don't seem to matter much anymore. I don't know what dumbass came up with the whole concept, but it's all a bunch of bullshit," Jessie stated.

"I blame the movies," I crooned. "Think about it, for years, we have watched these unrealistic fairy tales that have completely warped our ideas and expectations about the way love actually is. No wonder everything about relationships fall short. There aren't any princes in shining armor."

"Well, that's obvious. I could have told you that," Noah cut in. "But what other expectations don't match up for you?"

"We have been made to believe that one day some prince will ride up on his white horse to save the day and steal our hearts. As I said, we have watched so many happily ever after's that just thinking about it repulses me," I said, pushing away my food as though I had lost my appetite.

"Wow. No wonder I've always been hyper-focused on what kind of car a guy drives," Leigha snickered.

"Does it have to be a white car?" Noah joked. "You know, because it's a white horse?"

Jessie punched him in the opposite shoulder from where I had struck him earlier. "Real cheesy there, Noah."

"Ouch," he said while rubbing the spot where she had punched. "Just so you three ladies know, I'm probably the only guy in the universe willing to sit and talk about this nonsense with you. The least you can do is let me throw in a cheesy joke or two."

"Rachel does have a point now that I think about," Leigha responded, completely ignoring Noah. "I remember watching *The Notebook* thinking about how much I wanted a guy to do what Noah did for Allie. Tell me, where is the guy willing to write 365 letters professing his undying love for me? Men don't hang on or try that long—or do they?" She turned to Noah.

"Why are you looking at me? Wrong, Noah," he laughed. "You think I'm some spokesperson for all the single, straight men out there or something?"

"Then how long do you normally mourn a failed relationship?" she countered.

He shrugged. "Depends on the relationship. They're all different, Leigha. Some I have easily bounced back from because there wasn't much invested in them, while others, it took a bit longer."

"Yeah, but how much longer?" Jessie butted in. "Like, are we talking weeks or months?"

"I don't know. I'll go home and check my breakup diary and get back to you." He rolled his eyes.

"But no guy would ever write that many letters, right? I can't even get a guy to text me back half the time," Leigha continued. "There aren't any guys grabbing me in the rain telling me how our love isn't over, just before passionately kissing me under the soft glow of a streetlamp."

"My exes would sooner push me in a puddle rather than cradle me in the rain," Jessie laughed.

"It's no surprise why we are depressed," I said. "We create exceptional men in our heads and then get disappointed when the reality doesn't match up."

"We definitely don't hold boomboxes over our heads outside of bedroom windows either," Noah smirked. "Or, at least, that's what we decided in the last single men's meeting."

"Who would want that anyway?" Leigha scrunched her nose to meet the crease in her forehead. "The last time someone tried waking me up with music, I almost fought them. It wasn't pretty."

"I think in the movie you're referring to, it happened during the day, so you would be fine," Noah replied just as Davis brought us our second round of drinks.

"I got one!" I exclaimed, almost spilling my new drink. "What about *Pretty Woman*? Where is my Edward Lewis climbing up a balcony to prove his love for me despite his fear of heights?"

"You don't have a balcony," Noah pointed out. "Where the hell do you expect this guy to climb?"

"It's the thought that counts, Noah. We can't even get men to climb a set of stairs for us," I said.

"That's not true. Not all guys are like that. Some put in the effort." He looked at me pointedly. "Although, I wouldn't suggest you become a prostitute to test that theory either."

"Obviously," I said.

"The problem with you girls is that you think every relationship—every romance—is the same. There are millions of different love stories out there, which means millions of different types of men, yet you are expecting us all to be the same."

"We're not expecting you all to be the same, Noah. But is it so hard for men to be decent sometimes?" Leigha questioned.

"There *are* still good men out there." Jessie smiled while staring down at her phone. It was apparent she was texting her boyfriend, Jordan.

"Well, good for you and lover boy," Leigha scoffed. "I have dated enough men to know that I have probably dated every single type of guy out there. And for every hundred bad dates, I'm maybe blessed with a halfway decent one."

An hour later, we said our goodbyes. Noah offered to walk me to my car because I had no choice but to park around the corner from the bar due to the lack of parking spots.

"Seriously though, do all girls just sit around and talk about that garbage?" he laughed while saying how he thought we wasted too much time on the subject.

"I guess we do. And it's not garbage," I turned to him, "I think we are onto something."

He shrugged. "I think the only thing you girls are on is too many cocktails. But, you know, I've been thinking a lot about what you said regarding timelines, and I think I have the perfect solution for you. What you need is to take a page out of my hero, George Clooney's handbook for a while. Think of him as your mentor."

"What?" My brow furrowed itself right into a noticeable question mark.

"You know, George Clooney," he emphasized. "If I know him like I think I do…"

"You don't know George Clooney, Noah."

"Well, *if* I know him like I think I do, then I know for a fact that he never cared about some stupid timeline. I mean, look at him! He was considered the most eligible bachelor for years. I would bet my entire life's savings that he would have died with that title and not batted an eye about it. But lo and behold, he found someone—the *right* someone—that changed all of that."

"So, you're saying that I should be a serial bachelor? Or a bachelorette—George Clooney?"

"Yes, just like George Clooney."

"Well, I *am* adorable." I fluttered my eyelashes. "So, I guess channeling him wouldn't be too much of a stretch," I teased.

"Aww, look at you. You sound just like Georgie already." He winked.

Exorcising the Demons

October 2012

I knew I was a mess—whether I cared to admit it or not. But knowing what I know now, I can fully acknowledge my ignorance on the matter. I don't know how I ever expected to walk away from a warzone of a relationship and not acquire a few battle scars or two. Or why I thought that everything would be peachy keen as soon as I waved goodbye to that shitshow. **Those were terrible misconceptions of mine.**

For years, I knowingly fought a losing battle—one where I knew I would never come out as the winner. Yet, there I was, day after day, putting up the good fight just so that I could continue perpetuating a lie. My demands were quite simple: I wanted trust, respect, and most importantly, love. But the man I chose to spend the better part of my twenties with was incapable of giving those things (especially when it involved any effort on his part).

What I had learned with Mike was that he could be whatever person he *wanted* to be. He was masterfully skilled at portraying an image of himself to the world that others bought into without any reservations (no wonder he could get people to judge me so harshly after I left). He embodied the literal meaning of being a wolf in sheep's clothing. He was *that* convincing. Hell, he even had me convinced for years! But through time, as anyone not being true to themselves would, he became exhausted. In his defense, you can only pretend for so long before you are no longer able to keep up with the charade. It can be taxing on even the most strong-willed person.

I had spent most of our relationship trying so hard to unearth the good guy out of all the darkness that surrounded him. It was almost as if I felt obligated to be his keeper. I never signed up for the role that had me constantly begging for him to change and one where I was foolishly demanding things that were supposed to be naturally given. It was all just a complete and utter waste of precious time and love. Why am I telling you this? Well, for starters, you can't demand something from someone, ever. Even if you are successful at getting it, it's never genuine. I sacrificed so much of myself to make up for what Mike lacked, making it one of the most self-depleting relationships I had ever encountered. It's sad to think that I loved someone so much that while trying to fix them, I was breaking myself in return.

They say that people only show you the sides of themselves that they want to show you. And I can't express to you enough how much I believe that to be true. Unfortunately, Mike was very comfortable exposing all sides of himself to me—the good and the bad. I think he knew that I would be too afraid to call him out on his shit or that I would be too nervous for people to find out what our relationship was really like behind closed doors. He knew I never wanted the world to see that I was allowing him to treat me the way he was. So, he manipulated me into thinking it was best to sweep everything under the rug—letting him be the person he wanted to be no matter what I felt about it in return. He forced me into letting him live his life how he saw fit without any regard to how I wanted to live mine. But we all know what happens when things continuously keep getting swept under the rug: Eventually, someone trips.

But he was right. Sooner or later, I knew I had to make a decision. So, I rested my proverbial sword down and walked away without ever once looking back. I no longer wanted to fight for something—or someone—that wasn't worth fighting for.

Trust me, I'm perfectly aware that my situation here is not unique—but that's the point. We have all been with a "Mike." Not to mention, I'm not the only person who has ever felt this way or has ever been with someone—better or worse—and knew they weren't the one for them. By sharing my perspective, someone out there in the world may find my experience relatable. Maybe I would be the one to phrase things differently in a way they'd understand? I bet they, like me, never thought they'd end up having to start over this late in life. Well, OK, I guess it's not *that* late. But I had plans for myself! I had a future for myself—and this wasn't it.

As a result, my life appeared disjointed—like I was stuck at a crossroads with neither road leading anywhere. I was directionless because I had no clue what I wanted or where I wanted to go. All I knew was that I needed to go somewhere.

Still, my life just didn't seem to match up with the lives of others. Once I set myself on this new path, I became pretty hard on myself. I began blaming myself for all the wrong decisions I had made thus far. Like: How I let myself stay in a failing relationship for years, knowing that it would have never lasted, but was too afraid to do anything about it. I hated to look at myself in the mirror, believing that I had ruined my life for the sake of "love"—and it wasn't even anything remotely close to being love. But here's the kicker: I can't change the decisions I had made, nor could I ever right my supposed wrongs. The only thing I could do was accept what had happened and make a promise to myself that I wouldn't let history repeat itself. I had to learn. I had to grow. I had to move on.

When I first moved back to New York, Jessie was there when I signed the lease to my new apartment and the one on my new life. That was the beginning of what she called my "rebirth." Having been through a pretty hard breakup herself, she understood a lot about what I was going through. She could understand all the feelings I had a hard time articulating and knew how to occupy my mind when it began leading me astray.

"You realize," she declared, "that this is the first time you can decorate your place however you want, right?"

I looked around at my new apartment, taking in the barren walls and spaces, believing it to be this incredibly new and exciting blank canvas awaiting my personal touch. Jessie Duncan, one of my oldest and dearest friends, wanted to be present for every moment of my new beginning. She knew what it was like to start over and how lonely it felt while doing so.

"The best part of being single and living on your own again is that you can come home, take your bra off and drape it over the damn lampshade if you wanted. You can leave your makeup all over the bathroom counter without some guy telling you to pick it up. And"—she paused momentarily— "you don't have to share your closet space with anyone."

"Now that's a perk I never considered!" I smiled while imagining all the shoes I could own without encroaching on someone else's closet space.

"Why don't we go out and do a little shopping before the movers get here? We have a few hours or so, so we have time." She looked at me.

Jessie and I are alike in many ways, but we couldn't be more opposite style-wise. I have always preferred a muted, classic color palette, whereas she is all about colors and patterns. I often wished I could be as bold as she was, but I could never quite get myself there. And as we began pushing our shared cart down aisle after aisle, I started to get nervous when she suggested that we only focus on buying décor for my new place. Within a matter of minutes, she had the cart filled with various shades of pink.

"Jess, I don't think pink is the right color for me," I scowled while looking through the contents she had tossed into the cart. She had pink pillows, bedsheets, picture frames, and whatever else she could get her manicured hands on. Our cart was reminiscent of my teenage years. The only items missing were some blowup furniture and a few teen heartthrob posters.

"It's not exactly my favorite color either," she acknowledged while tying her long brown hair back into a ponytail. She would do that whenever she was about to tackle a project or get serious about something. "And it's not about being your favorite color either." I watched as she tossed a few more throw pillows into the cart. "It's about what it represents."

"And what exactly does it represent?" I humored her.

"Your life without a guy. You would never be able to buy this stuff if you were living with someone else, so you might as well go crazy while you still have time."

"So, what, I'm rebelling against all men with various shades of pink?" I grinned, holding up one of the throw pillows as an example. "Is it like their kryptonite or something?"

A few hours later, the movers arrived at my place, where they began unloading all the furniture and boxes until my once empty apartment started bursting at the seams. So, Jessie and I did what anyone would do to take the unpacking edge off: We opened a bottle of wine, turned on some 90's throwback music, and began unpacking as much as we deemed necessary.

"You have to believe in the pink." Jessie smiled at me. "It's all about you now—all you. No one else. Your life is changing, girl. Own it."

"Hasn't it changed enough already?" My body slumped over the box I was sorting.

She turned towards me. "I get it. Mike was a complete asshole. He was all kinds of wrong for you, and no matter how good you were to him, it didn't matter. It would have never mattered. He was always going to be an asshole. Trust me, been there, dated that," she huffed. "But you can't allow him to continue taking up headspace any longer. Work that shit out the best you can. Exorcise the demons," she said just as she grabbed the power drill to hang up the curtain rods. "You don't want them haunting you well into the future. Make peace and let it all go."

She couldn't have been more right.

Nothing much was coming out of me—or being exorcised—in terms of my blog. And I had the sneaking suspicion that it was all due to the inescapable amount of fear eating away at me. I feared that if I allowed myself to do this, I was exposing myself—my true self—to the entire world. I didn't want or need that. Not that I planned on signing my name to every post, or any post for that matter. I had already settled on remaining anonymous well before I even created my website, but that didn't mean the fear subsided with that decision. Anonymity doesn't truly exist in this internet age as much as we would like to believe that it does. So, I couldn't rid myself of the thought that someone, somewhere, could figure out that it was me. Not that I planned on discussing anything too personal or top secret. It wasn't a place I intended on airing out my dirty laundry either. *But you get what I'm saying, right?*

    I felt creatively constipated. And I began to worry that all the feelings I had circulating inside me would become lost as soon as I tried to release them—as if they, too, feared what would become of them. They would have no choice but to retreat to their subsequent hiding spaces, forcing me to continue to allow them to live rent-free inside of my head. My first instinct was to call Noah to discuss my dilemma, but he was away at some work conference, and I didn't want to be that friend who constantly needed help from constructing an excellent sandwich to constructing a good blog. But just as I was about to try and solve my own problem for once, Jessie called. *Maybe she sensed my distress signal?* But when I answered, she greeted me with the sound of her screaming for joy that she was offered a new job, and not just any job, but a job she had wanted for years. The only caveat was that this dream came with a catch. She would have to move, and she would have to move out of state.

"When would you have to leave?" I asked, trying my best to sound as supportive as I could when deep down inside, I couldn't bear the thought of her leaving. It was selfish of me, I know.

"In a month. I'm moving to Virginia."

"I'm really happy for you," I lied through my teeth. It wasn't that I wasn't proud or happy for Jessie; I just selfishly relied on her always being close by and being there whenever we needed each other. But who was I to hold her back just because my life was a mess? It wasn't her responsibility to put it back in order.

"I know you don't want me to leave," she pointedly addressed. "But it's an opportunity I would be foolish to pass up. You understand this, right?"

"Of course, I do," I said, feeling bad she felt my lack of enthusiasm. "Have you told Jordan the news yet? What did he say about it?"

She hesitated. "To be honest, he faked his happiness worse than you did—if you can believe that," she chuckled. "He wasn't exactly thrilled about the whole long-distance thing either. So," she paused, "I suggested that he come with me."

"Really?" I was shocked. I knew she was serious about Jordan, but not *that* serious.

"I don't know why he made such a fuss when I suggested it, though. The boy constantly complains about his job and how he wants to get out of Syracuse.

You would have thought he would have jumped for joy after I handed him that golden ticket."

"Well, maybe he will come around, Wonka," I teased.

"Maybe," she laughed. "You do think I'm making the right decision, right?" she beckoned my support.

No matter how much I wanted her to stay, I knew the best thing was for her to go. She needed this. It didn't matter what I wanted or needed or whether the uncertainty of her relationship with Jordan laid in the balance. Opportunities such as those don't come around that often, and she would have been foolish to turn it down on account of my selfishness or Jordan's.

"You have to take it," I said.

So, she did.

Later that night, with a box cutter in one hand and a glass of wine in the other, I slid the blade across the top, opening the flaps of another box I had failed to unpack. But I knew I had to start somewhere. I knew I couldn't delay this process any longer.

Inside was what I had predicted: pieces of my past—pieces of me. You would have thought I opened a memory box from a past relationship, but sometimes, it's just as painful to be reminded of the past relationship you had with yourself as though you were an entirely different person altogether.

The more I retrieved from the box, the more I realized how much of myself felt fragmented and lost. Packed away were lost pieces of the girl I once abandoned, waiting to be rediscovered. I cringed, thinking back on how I allowed myself to be so complacent with nipping and tucking parts of who I was to appease someone else. It was hard to accept. And it didn't take years of complacency to feel those effects—it was almost instantaneous. But like everything else, I ignored it. I thought those feelings would have diminished over time or gone away entirely, but they remained under the surface, waiting for the perfect opportunity to show their faces once more.

To avoid confrontation, I placed many restrictions on myself to deter as much conflict as possible with Mike. He didn't like my independence. He didn't like my desire to pursue any aspiration—no matter how big or small. He didn't enjoy my unpredictable and spontaneous nature. He didn't like surprises. He liked knowing where I was and what I was doing at all times. He liked control. And all those things he once said he loved about me suddenly became the source of all the things he hated.

Seeing bits and pieces of myself made me realize how much I was willing to let go of. However, while trying to make peace with my past, I inadvertently left behind parts of who I was. I didn't want that. It wasn't good for me. It made me forget what made me, *me*. It felt horrible to be in a position where not only was I looking for love (well, eventually), but also looking for a way to love myself again—and the right way this time. I knew it would be tough to piece together all that was broken, missing, or taken away to begin rebuilding—or healing. What I was sure of was that the glue I needed to put those pieces back together wasn't going to come from a new relationship or anyone else—it had to come from me. I couldn't look outward to fix inward. *Do I need to repeat that for the people in the back?* I had to hold myself accountable. I had to keep myself together on my own because that responsibility should never fall onto the shoulders of anyone else—no matter how much they tell you that they don't mind you leaning on them.

But Jessie was right: I had to exorcise these demons before it was too late.

Eventually, I emptied several more boxes until I buried myself in the center of my living room floor. Countless notebooks I unearthed that used to be my place of refuge—the place I went to when I couldn't handle reality. It was where I channeled all my thoughts and feelings when I wasn't comfortable admitting to anyone what was going on with my life. Those notebooks were my safe place to run to when I needed to escape. They were always there, ready to listen. And I often wondered what they would have said should they have been able to speak.

    I flipped through a few pages, recalling past emotions I once poured into my writing. But through time, the intensity of those emotions dissipated. They were not as intense or palpable as they once were. I tried recalling how I felt in those moments, but I knew I had grown too much to allow myself to backpedal. It was time to set those demons free. It was time to move on. That's when I knew I needed this blog. It was exorcise or die.

Big Girl's Pants

November 2012

I gripped the edge of my kitchen counter for support. From the corner of my eye, I looked out the window, watching as a few neighbors got into their cars. Everyone was going about their lives as though they had no idea that the world had just ended. Well, at least, mine felt like it did.

    I was having a meltdown. It was Sunday morning at the beginning of November, and there I was in my kitchen, bent over the sink, desperately trying to fight back the tears. Oh, how I wanted to let them loose—how I needed them to break free. But I thought it would have weakened me if I had allowed them. What then? And why was I viewing crying as a weakness anyhow? Maybe instead of judging the act, I should have just let it happen—let the tears fall where they may. But no matter how hard I tried to fight those damn tears, they eventually came. And they came with a vengeance.

This is what you call a meltdown, Noah, I thought. And it was all because I found out that Mike was publicly saying some hurtful things about me. And the crazy part was that people believed him. His words spread like poison until I found myself cornered with my back against the wall, trying hard to avoid the sting. I was vulnerable. I took everything at that time personally. I thought it was unfair for people to discredit all that I went through just because that was Mike's way of dealing with my continual rejection of him. Shouldn't they know that there are always two sides to every story? But, unfortunately, the only side being told was the lie.

Yeah, I get it. I shouldn't have cared. But something about that morning, mixed with the current emotions coursing through my body, pushed me inches away from a breaking point I had no idea I was even close to reaching. I wanted to scream out the truth just to shut off the noise from the peanut gallery. But no one deserved VIP treatment into the intimate parts of my life just because I wanted to give Mike a taste of his own medicine. I had to let it all go. I had to let them believe whatever they wanted to believe, no matter how painful it was to remain quiet. I had to ignore the rude messages cluttering up my social media. I had to turn it all off. I couldn't allow people to barge through my door and invade my privacy. So, I nailed that baby shut.

Even if I had decided to make a public statement of sorts, there wasn't one thing I could zero in on that contributed to the breakup. There wasn't a particular reason that was just too hard to overcome because there were many reasons. And I knew that by summarizing them all to a mere "obstacle," it would have been demeaning to my decision to leave. It was much more than that. I left because I deserved better. I left because I refused to be treated the way he chose to treat me. I left because I didn't want to accept the "love" he was willing to give me when I knew I could be loved better. And I left because I didn't want to continue sharing my life with someone who didn't value some of the most important aspects of what makes up a healthy relationship: Trust, honesty, and respect. It certainly wasn't because I cheated. And besides, he was the one who cheated me out of a good life.

"You know," Noah said to me later that day, "people only believe his lies because that's the only thing they are hearing. Mike isn't an idiot. He uses your silence to his advantage—always has. But you should never feel like you can't defend yourself if you want. Just don't think you owe anyone an explanation because you don't."

Noah was right. But after marinating in how I felt for most of the day, I somehow understood Mike's perspective on things. What an awful burden for him to bear, having to carry his past offenses into his future. The last thing he wanted was to have his past affect his future—no different than me. But instead of letting it go, he needed to do his version of damage control. He wanted to paint a better picture. If I were to have spoken out, it would have probably hindered his ability to rebuild his life as quickly as he wanted. Somehow, I understood that. Was he sorry? No. I never once received an apology during his countless attempts to win me back. Asking someone to come back isn't an apology. Nor was him telling me that he would change (for what would have been the hundredth time or so). I didn't understand why he used me as the scapegoat for all of his problems. That's another role I didn't sign up for. But somehow, through all the hurt and confusion still stirring within me, I understood. I finally understood.

 I found the physical reaction of me falling apart to be somewhat of a beautiful thing—my saving grace. It signaled that it was officially time for me to pull myself together. I wasn't going to allow him to hurt me any longer—that was and always had been in my control. It was about time I got it back.

 The sudden emotional chaos wreaking havoc on my soul became the foundation for which I had no choice but to redefine myself. I could have easily stayed in that slump and pitied myself, but I knew that investing any more emotion into those things would have been a waste. I needed to put on my big girl pants and be happy. The amount of effort was the same.

So, I turned that sadness into motivational fuel and that motivational fuel into bravery and finally started writing.

Blog Post #1

Well, Excuse Me

He was self-absorbed.

Initially, I blamed it on whatever was going on with him, whether it was a bad day at work or the fact he woke up on the wrong side of the bed. And no matter how badly he treated me, I was always armed and ready with the next excuse to justify it.

By making excuses for his behavior, I developed an unhealthy coping mechanism as a result. I made those excuses—not because I felt like people needed to hear them, but because I needed to hear them to feel better. Or perhaps to believe in the false reality of our relationship because I was too afraid to face the truth.

Through time, that uphill battle changed the dynamic of our relationship forever. Yet, I remained loyal to him like some pathetic, little puppy dog. Don't get me wrong: he did throw a few proverbial bones my way to make me think he still cared. But looking back, it wasn't enough. Nothing would have ever been enough.

We did break up a lot, though. Back and forth, we swayed like a pendulum, playing this game with each other where we would engage in cyclical conversations with me demanding that things change for the better and him promising me that they would. Perhaps, we both desperately wanted to believe that things would eventually change, but those beliefs were always short-lived like all his other promises.

During those brief breakup periods, I thought for sure that I could sustain a life without him. There wasn't a single person in my life who rooted for our relationship. They had difficulty offering support when they saw everything that I refused to see myself. He wasn't good for me, and the only one who didn't see that was *me.* I tried my best to convince everyone, including myself, that things would be different each time we got back together—that he would finally change. But the most important (and hardest) thing I ever had to learn was this: YOU CAN'T CHANGE ANYONE. And you can't expect someone to change when they don't want that change for themselves. People are who they are. So, if you don't like something about the person you are with, you need to ask yourself whether it's something you can live with and accept or something you simply can't.

And it's OK if you can't. You don't have to bend yourself to meet another person if the bend is borderline sacrificial rather than a healthy compromise. And yes, I understand that people *can* change. But when you think about it, is it an actual change or just the act of them making amends? As in, they made a mistake and are doing their best to learn from it. However, if they continue to make the same mistake over and over, then it's not a mistake. It's who they are. And that is not a behavior you have a prayer of changing. They would need to want that change for themselves—you can't want it for them.

The back-and-forth dance we danced set the tone for our relationship. It was like a game we played that had no ending (because how can you end a game when you can't declare a winner?). And ashamedly, I admit, that every time he crept back into my life to "win me back," I somehow let myself believe that his actions were out of love. But he didn't love me; he loved the idea of me. He wanted the best of both worlds and for me to repeatedly show up to play out any role he cast me into.

Who knows, maybe he did love me. But even so, that didn't mean I had to accept the love he was willing to give. I had to be the one who had control over my life to determine what was best for me and not set the bar too low. My expectations should be defined by me—not anyone else. There were many times I let myself settle and adopt that "it is what it is" mentality, but how could I have ever truly loved myself when I was so willing to settle the way that I did? I couldn't have.

You know, one of my friends said to me a few years back, *you end all these stories about him by saying that you think deep down inside that he is still the same guy you initially fell in love with—like everything that happened after was the lie. It's the biggest excuse you have made to yourself by denying the way he treats you. But have you ever stopped to consider that he is just an asshole and that you fell in love with the lie but settled for the truth despite it?*

She was right. He would never be the guy I thought he was when we first got together because that guy never truly existed. He only surfaced during those convenient times when he wanted to get back together or win me over after a fight. He would say and do all the right things, and I stupidly fell for it each and every time. I became one of those people who fell in love with the mask and not the face behind it. However, when (well, let's call my ex, "**M**") **M**'s mask started falling off, I was in complete denial of the person left behind. That wasn't the version of **M** I knew. He was a con artist of the heart. Yet, I can't tell you how determined I was to get that "real" guy back that I sacrificed so much of my truth to make up for his lies. And how strongly I held onto that faux mask in hopes that he would choose to wear it permanently—a lot of good that did.

I could go on forever. I could divulge much more, but what would be the point of that? It doesn't matter what he did or didn't do. It only matters what I felt and what I did about it. I wasted a lot of time trying to fix him when I could have easily put that time and effort into myself because I, too, wore a mask. I wore one that told the world that I was happy when deep down, I was miserable. I lied so much to myself that it began to hurt more than the lies **M** told me. But like any bandage, you just have to rip that sucker off and start the healing. Otherwise, you will forever give the illusion that you are injured, and I refused to play the role of the victim a second longer.

Love, Me.

I stared at my laptop screen with my mouse hovering over the publish button like a plane, unsure if it was safe to land. Seeing my feelings put to words was cathartic. What a sweet release it was to no longer have them lurking about and taking up prime real estate in my head. Re-reading my post made me wish that I could go back in time and knock some sense into my young, foolish head. But unfortunately, life doesn't offer do-overs. Nor does it offer a time travel option; otherwise, wouldn't we all be climbing into our respective time machines? There would be no accountability and sense of right or wrong or even regret. But I have seen enough movies to know that messing around with time never ends well. So, I guess it's best to leave it well alone.

I was sincerely pleased with my first post (and not that I had any idea of my blog's overall purpose). My goal was not to feel alone in this. Maybe to have someone reach across cyberspace to figuratively hold my hand and say, *You've got this, girl. We've all been there. We will get through this together.* Or, maybe, just to hear other people's stories (if they would be willing enough to share). So, I turned on the comments section, hoping that might be the case. Nothing good ever comes without taking a few risks, so I was willing to start taking some.

Later that night, Jessie, Leigha, Noah, and I went out for dinner. Glancing around the table, I wanted to tell them all about my blog but immediately cowered behind each bite. *What if they judged me? What if they thought it was a dumb or foolish idea?* I hadn't even had the conversation with myself on what would be considered off-limits regarding what I would write about, so I felt a twinge of guilt when I imagined any one of them making an appearance in a future post. It wasn't like I planned on using personal or identifiable information, but I'm sure they would want the option of giving their consent.

What became like the glue that bonded our group together was ironically the same thing that could potentially tear us apart. What if they disapproved of me being so open about my life, and by consequence, theirs?

The idea started out as small and innocent, created out of my desperate need to find perspective, but I was well aware that it could easily take on a life of its own if I didn't keep a careful eye on it. But what if people found what I had to say helpful? What if my blog was to become the beacon of healing for the brokenhearted like me? Would people be upset to know that it all derived from a clueless and inexperienced source? A source who portrayed the illusion of mastering the art of bicycle riding yet could hardly pedal without using training wheels. It wasn't like I had answers to all matters of the heart, so why was I putting so much pressure on myself? No, it was all too soon to think about all that. I was overreacting because I finally posted my first entry, which was why my anxiety felt the need to feed into every probable reason for me to go home and completely erase it from existence. But sometimes, when things feel a little scary, maybe that's when you know you are onto something good.

Besides, my friends were having a good time. Everyone seemed happy—even if none of us were precisely in the places in our lives we wanted to be. We were each beautiful, little disasters still searching for answers to calm the chaos to unlock our individual destinies. Jessie, out of everyone, seemed closer to unlocking hers than the rest of us—and that was OK. I had to remember that not everyone had to be in sync (this wasn't like our damn periods).

I wondered if Fate had a plan for me. And if it did, what did it need from me so that I could finally obtain it? What was it going to cost for everything to fall into place? And would I be willing to pay that cost? It was time to, once again, put on my big girl pants and find out.

Are You There, Fate? It's Me, Rachel

December 2012

"Are you there, Fate? It's me, Rachel. I was hoping you could answer a few things for me," I said aloud as if Fate personified into someone standing before me. But no one answered. There were no signs that my message was received. No answers were sent down from the heavens to give me the clarity I desperately sought. There was nothing but silence. Therefore, I decided to reach out to Fate another way. Hopefully, I would get an answer this time.

Blog Post #2

A Date with Fate

Do I believe in the almighty Fate? Would it be safe to assume that no one has any control over where they are headed in life? That everything, down to what we choose to eat for breakfast, is all predetermined by Fate's design? And should we suddenly decide to detour by going off Fate's path, like selecting a bagel over a donut, Fate would then steer us back into the right direction? Or would we have simply lost our way forever? I'd pick the donut just to find out.

So, often, I find myself making poor choices in life. I am impulsive at best, primarily because I rely heavily on emotion rather than logic in my decision-making process. Sometimes, without any hesitation, I let my emotions climb into the driver's seat and take the proverbial wheel, so to speak. For the longest time, I used to believe that my heart was the best navigator, providing me with the best guidance through some of life's most challenging obstacles, that it held my best interest close to it and would never steer me wrong. Unfortunately, even if it did hold my best interests, it never stopped to educate itself on the knowledge my gut was privy to all along. The gut is unbiased. It doesn't consider emotions, like love, when presented with information. When it comes to the heart, if it's presented with information that either hurts or disagrees with the dominant feeling, it guards itself against the truth. It wants to believe in the best-case scenario instead of facing the reality of the situation.

I finally realized that it was no longer about me choosing between following my heart or listening to my gut but instead finding the balance between the two. *Why couldn't they just work together, right? Just get along already!* It would have made some things in my life a hell of a lot easier and less complicated. I will admit, however, that as a creature of habit, I still allow my emotions to climb into the driver's seat from time to time with the hope that my gut would be brave enough to call shotgun.

So, the question remains: If I choose the wrong path, will Fate guide me back in the right direction?

I have never personally banked on this assumption as my safety net while navigating through life. But now, as a single, almost thirty-year-old woman, I wondered if Fate was *actually* trying to steer me back in the right direction? That, perhaps, **M** was the detour? I wondered even more if all my past heartaches were a part of the damage control from past detours? Then again, and only to complicate matters more, maybe Fate *needed* me to go off course. Perhaps all those detours we take in life help us appreciate the destination even more. If the saying is true that *everything happens for a reason*, then, perhaps, we are all supposed to lose our way now and again. Maybe losing our way is the only way to find ourselves?

Just a thought.

Love, Me.

An hour later, I pondered over my words with a pint-sized container of ice cream. I stared at my laptop screen, noticing that time was almost midnight. But, unlike Cinderella, who lost her shoe, the only thing I was losing was sleep. Sleep, however, evaded me more as I allowed the floodgates of my mind to remain open. I couldn't believe how much was bursting through, begging for me to find a home for them somewhere. *Tomorrow is another day*, I thought, as I placed the empty container of ice cream on my bedside table and climbed into bed.

Danielle Dexter 💜 *Stupid Love*

"How come in the movies, the single girls always look like they are having the time of their lives?" I asked Leigha. She came over a few nights later for movie and takeout night. "Then," I continued, "when the main character—the ultimate clichéd, single girl—least expects it, she meets the elusive 'perfect' guy and lives happily ever after." I rolled my eyes, reaching for the Chinese takeout carton.

"It's a bunch of commercialized bullshit probably written by a bunch of oblivious men." Leigha took a bite of her food. "It's as deceiving as those happy bitches in tampon commercials, which were probably also written by men. What the hell do they know about periods?" she laughed. "Let me tell you; it would be a cold day in hell before I run carefree on a beach in a white bikini. It's just not realistic."

"True." I raised my chopsticks in agreement. "But we buy into that garbage, don't we? We want to believe falling in love is a Point A to Point B scenario and that there is a strong enough tampon to withstand that much-needed run on the beach—white bikini and all."

"Well, I don't know why being single at the brink of our thirties feels like we've been kidnapped and tossed onto the Island of Misfit Toys, but rather than toys, it's boys." Leigha weighed her thoughts over her noodles.

"I think it's because, when we are single, we feel like the last single people on earth," I groaned.

"We probably are. And now look at us. We are stuck trying to date through men who have either been rejected or have too much baggage that Delta wouldn't even check it. It's like their homecoming, and we are Sadie Hawkins. They hold all the power."

"Luckily for me, I haven't ventured out yet."

"Stay home," she laughed. "Perfect example, do you remember, Steve?" Leigha's eyes widened as she grabbed her cell phone out of her bag. "He sent me a text message the other night, asking if I wanted to hang out."

"Steve? Isn't he the one who wanted to open a microbrewery in his parent's basement?" I laughed.

"That's the one!" She raised her hand. "Anyways, he texted me, and I just about fell out of my chair. I couldn't believe he had the nerve."

"Did you respond?" I reached for my drink.

"Hell, no. Any guy who messages you at 11:00 at night asking to 'hang out' doesn't want to hang out—you know what I'm saying?" Her head moved like a bobblehead.

After taking a sip, I asked Leigha the question I had pondered in my latest blog post. "Do you believe in Fate?" I asked.

Leigha shrugged. "Sometimes. Why?"

"I'm just curious, that's all. I mean, do you ever wonder if everything we have gone through in the past and will go through in the future is all part of some predetermined plan? Like there is a bigger picture for our lives that we can't see?"

"It's a beautiful theory, but to be honest, I think too many people romanticize the idea of Fate. Like, its Fate that I met this guy at a certain time, or that it was Fate that I went to the coffee shop at that exact moment I met the love of my life. When it's nothing more than a happy coincidence."

"So, you think life is all about coincidence and chance?" I countered.

"Pretty much." She nodded.

Putting all my cards on the table for Fate was a gamble. Was I willing to take it---especially since I had nothing else to place my bets on? I had to believe once again that everything does happen for a reason without a shadow of a doubt. And that maybe I shouldn't blame myself so much for my past decisions. Even if life was full of coincidences and chances, it still wasn't enough to perpetuate the blame cycle.

"Do you believe in Fate?" I asked Noah later that night when he called.

"Why are you asking?"

"Well," I yawned into the phone, "I ask myself all the time: What if *this* or what if *that*. And I wonder, does it really matter? If Fate is the one in the driver's seat, then would it even matter what I end up choosing? Wouldn't the choice be Fate's and not mine?"

"I don't believe in focusing on the 'what ifs' in life, Rachel. If things were supposed to work out a certain way, then they would have. I don't have the time or energy to question every little thing in my life had I not missed that bus, train, or whatever. I've learned that we miss that shit for no other reason than we missed it. If Fate wanted my ass on that bus so bad, it would have made my alarm clock go off on time. You feel me?"

"Or maybe Fate *wanted* you to miss it?"

"No, it was my choice. I chose to stay in bed longer."

How could I have argued with that?

Mistletoes & a Lawnmower

December 2012

'Tis the season for singles awareness! There is nothing like the good ol' holiday season to remind you of just how alone you are. My only advice to all the single people out there is to proceed through all social media platforms with caution. The last thing you need is to be bombarded with nauseating pictures of couples, or worse, announcements of engagements and those annoying pictures that couples post showing off what they bought each other. (Side note: It's lame. Don't do it.)

    The Christmas Creep came just as I finished the last few pieces of Halloween candy that I had stashed in my office desk drawer. My hand was still inside the bag when Christmas music began flooding the airwaves well before Thanksgiving even wrapped up. I don't think anyone, including myself, is ever fully prepared to face the holiday season alone. There are too many chances of running into people you hardly ever see (like having to face those relatives that only come around the holidays who just can't wait to catch up on what you're doing with your life. Like, *No, Aunt Debbie, I'm not married. But I did spend last night elbows deep in a tub of ice cream watching re-runs on Netflix—so, thanks for asking!*) Then, just when you thought you were in the clear, you're stuck having to perform the same song and dance describing that: *Yes, Aunt Carol, you overheard me talking to Aunt Debbie? No, I never once considered the fact that my eggs will be drying up soon. Thank you for reminding me! Would you be so kind as to pass the cranberry sauce?*

I decided to spend my morning at work, avoiding doing work at all costs. And no better distraction was having the chance to work on my blog while I ate the breakfast of champions: the rest of my Halloween candy.

As I was about to dive into my third blog post, I was shocked to discover that some unknown reader had read my first two posts. *Who in the hell found my blog?* Either way, it was exciting to know that I had a reader out there. Maybe that person typed in their search bar: Lonely, single girl creates blog—and found me? Then again, it was just a reminder that I had yet to come up with an official name for it. I just settled for the computerized generic name the website pre-populated for me until I could create something better. So, the fact that this mysterious person found me was rather shocking.

But just as I was about to put my fingers to the keys, Tina, one of the office assistants, knocked on my office door, reminding me that the company holiday party was next weekend. Apparently. Because it was taking place much earlier than it had in prior years, she wanted to make her rounds to ensure that no one had forgotten. Tina wasn't one for email. She always believed in personal interactions and prided herself on never sending an all-staff email in her career.

"You know how everyone is so busy around the holidays"—she beamed from the doorway— "We just have too many people with conflicts in their schedules, so this was the best way to ensure that everyone could make it!" She clasped her hands together. Tina also lived for party planning and made any excuse—big or small—to make everything a celebration.

Since Christmas wasn't anywhere close to being on my radar, I altogether forgot that the holiday party was coming up. If I'm being honest here, I didn't care too much about it, only because I wasn't exactly in the holiday spirit. I dreaded going to the party alone since we were told we could bring a plus one. But since I had neither husband nor boyfriend, I would most likely be that one guest who lingered too long at the bar or food table, avoiding all social interaction. *Can't freaking wait.*

When I moved back to New York, I knew that I would be limited in finding the ideal job, especially in the creative sector. Had it been a bigger city like New York City, I may have had a better shot at finding the job I wanted. Instead, I ended up settling (story of my life) for what I could find here, which was a job at a local magazine specializing in—wait for it—all things local! They discussed anything from food, music, venues, events, and more. My job, however, was responsible for interviewing local people who were making names for themselves in the community, such as business owners, philanthropists, politicians, authors—the list went on. Having majored in Political Science with a minor in journalism, the magazine felt like I would be an excellent candidate to interview local politicians. Once, I hinted at wanting to write something different, my boss, in his ever-famous condescending tone, told me to "write what I know." *Write what I know? Well, I know you're an ass. Should I write about that?* Nonetheless, that pretty much discouraged me from ever wanting to bring up the subject again.

Knowing I had no intention of ever making this job my career, I took the offer in hopes of eventually finding something better. Although, the job did have its perks like flexible working hours and the ability to work from home or from anywhere I wanted, which made having an office rather pointless when you considered how many times I actually used it. But the position didn't give me the creative freedom I desperately wanted. Even with my last job, it felt like I was placed in a box and told not to color outside the lines. Thankfully, with my new blog, I had someplace to focus all of my creativity.

"So, I will see you there, right?" Tina asked, still lingering in the doorway. "I don't recall ever getting your RSVP." She referred down to her clipboard.

"Sure," I said, very noncommittal, which I knew wasn't lost on her. But instead of pressing me any further, she moved on to the next office in hopes of receiving a warmer welcome and a happier response.

As soon as she walked away, I texted Noah to see if he would be free to accompany me, but apparently, he had planned a trip to Michigan to visit his family. So, that sucked. After him, I texted Leigha the same thing, but instead of texting back, she called me.

"Sorry, girl. This new restaurant is taking a lot out of me. I'm exhausted," she yawned into the phone. Right before Jessie received her job offer, Leigha also got one for a head chef opportunity at an up-and-coming restaurant downtown owned by a celebrity chef famous for competing in various television competition shows. He was loud, eccentric, yet very, very talented. Lately, it seemed that Leigha lived and breathed the place without much respite.

"I bet. So, I guess I will be going alone." I frowned into the rest of my Halloween candy just before throwing the remaining pieces into the trash.

"Unfortunately, I just don't see a free Saturday in my future for a long time. We still have so much to do before we officially open our doors. And it certainly doesn't help matters when *he* keeps changing his damn mind on the menu every other minute," she said, referring to her new boss.

"That blows."

"You're telling me. All I do lately is work," she sighed. "Don't get me wrong, I am appreciative as shit for this opportunity, but if I'm giving up any free time, you bet your ass I will be spending it sleeping."

"Can't say that I blame you. If it makes you feel any better, I haven't done laundry in over two weeks, and I ate dinner the other night with a spatula because I was too lazy to wash any dishes. I'm the poster girl for people who have just given up," I laughed.

"You're preaching to the choir, girl. I'm a chef, for heaven's sake, and the other night, I had a bag of skittles and a glass of wine for dinner. I convinced myself it was fruit," she laughed. "But I have to go. Break time is over."

My parents already had their house fully decorated for the holiday season. No sooner did the Thanksgiving turkey come out of the oven, my dad was already on the roof hanging up Christmas lights. My mom even had a box of leftover decorations she no longer needed in case I wanted to decorate my apartment as well. Truth be told, I never gave decorating for the holidays any thought. I planned to get through the holiday season as quickly as possible, but no matter where I turned, Christmas peeked out of every crack and crevice like I was living inside of a made-for-TV Christmas special.

"So, you started a blog, huh?" my mom asked as she poured us coffee. "Is this something for work?"

"No, it's not for work." I smiled. "It's more of a personal pursuit."

"What's it about?" she asked as she walked to the refrigerator to grab the creamer.

I shrugged. "That's the million-dollar question. I thought it would be nice to create a space to write out my feelings to avoid dumping them onto everyone else. Other than that, I have no idea." I reached for the coffee mug she set down before me.

"Well, you used to love journaling. I'm sure if you looked back at old journals, you might find some interesting material to use," she offered.

"Maybe, but something inside of me tells me that it's not a good idea to dwell too much on the past, you know? I feel like I should be focusing more on the present." I slumped a little in my seat. "I'm just so back and forth about this whole idea that I continuously question if it's worth the risk," I said after taking a sip of my coffee. It burned the tip of my tongue, forcing it to snap back and hide behind my teeth in retreat.

"What do you mean? I thought you said that it would be anonymous?" She interrupted as I continued rambling on.

"I get that, but what if people figure out that it's me? That's not something I am ready to deal with, Mom. Who wants the world to know their business?"

"Then why put it out there?" She cocked her head towards me. "Why even create this blog in the first place if you are afraid of what everyone may or may not think. Stick to a journal then."

"But then I wouldn't be able to possibly help others…" My voice trailed off as I realized I had answered my own question.

She smiled. "I think you should just follow your heart on this one. I can't tell you what to do or not to do."

"I don't know, Mom. It's not as if my heart has been the best navigator."

"It always has, Rachel; you've just always chosen to take your own path."

"Maybe," I considered. "I suppose being anonymously vulnerable isn't that bad."

"You're a strong girl; you can do this. Think about what strength it took for you to walk away from a relationship you had for over seven years." She looked at me supportively. Since I announced I was leaving Mike, my parents were both equal parts shocked and relieved. They were shocked that I finally made the decision yet relieved that I finally decided to *actually* make it.

"You should be proud of yourself," she continued. "Just think about all you've accomplished in this past year." She reached across the table and touched my hand. "Consider this blog like your secret diary, but no one has to know the author."

And that's when the idea hit me. I knew exactly what I would name my blog: *The Salt City Diaries.* I would discuss what finding love is like in Syracuse, NY. It was perfect. It hit all the right notes. My excitement towards it reignited, and I suddenly couldn't wait to get started.

My visit to my parents, although short, gave me the necessary insight I needed. Following my heart was easier said than done, and the advice was borderline cliché at best, but it was still solid advice, nonetheless.

However, I doubt my mom knew how often my heart led me astray, or maybe, she was right that I had always been the one leading. It was hard to say. Perhaps I never truly listened to the directions my heart was giving me? I wanted to talk to Noah about it but quickly discovered that he was closer than a phone call away. Finding my apartment door unlocked, I opened it to discover Jessie and Noah seated at my dining room table, and I was sure it wasn't because they both somehow knew I needed advice.

"What are you both doing here?" I asked, sliding my shoes off by the door.

"I came over here to make dinner because my apartment lost heat, and I wasn't about to freeze my ass off waiting for them to fix it. Then, when I got here, I found this one sitting outside your door." Noah cocked his head towards a very upset-looking Jessie.

"Yeah, OK, but how did you get inside?" I asked.

"I had a spare key made in case of an emergency." Noah shrugged as though it were no big deal.

"And this qualifies as an emergency? Noah, you could have easily gone out to eat—" but just as the words slipped out of my mouth, Jessie burst out crying. Her head fell into her hands, where it remained for several minutes, collecting enough tears that I feared she could drown. Noah rubbed her back as he glanced in my direction, letting me know he had no idea what was happening.

"Jess?" I made my way over to her and sat down. "What's going on?"

"It's over!" she wailed. "It's so fucking over!"

"Jordan?" Noah mouthed across the table at me.

I rolled my eyes in response. I knew it had something to do with Jordan—that much was obvious.

"Why is it over? What happened?" I tried extending my hand towards her, but it wouldn't reach. Instead, it rested a few feet away as though ready to take action should it be recalled for consoling duty.

"What happened?" she repeated my question back to me. "He's a lying asshole—that's what happened!"

"You're going to have to elaborate here a little." Noah rested his hand on her shoulder.

She rubbed the wetness from her cheeks onto her sleeve before looking at him. "So, you know how I asked Jordan to move to Virginia with me, right? Well, I had to go and do a little apartment hunting this past weekend, which he said that he was too busy with work to come along." She paused for a second to ask for a glass of water. Then after a few sips, she realized that water wasn't going to cut it and immediately switched her order over to wine. "Well, I got back this morning and went straight to his place to show him what I found. I was super excited about this one apartment, but he was on his work phone when I got there. My phone was dead, so I saw his personal one sitting on the counter—" she paused again before taking a sip of the wine I fetched her. She stared off in the distance as though watching the scene replay in her head.

Noah's expression matched the confusion I was feeling inside. I shook my head with anticipation of hearing the rest.

"But as soon as his screen unlocked," she began, "ugh, all I wanted was to show him the apartment I found. The apartment, mind you, that we were supposed to move into together." Her head fell into her hands once more. I knew that feeling all-too-well and dreaded what was yet to come. "Then," she breathed through the gaps in her fingers, "I saw there were these messages on his phone from some app—" she stopped abruptly.

"What app?" I probed as gently as possible, but it didn't initiate much of a response.

"Is she breathing?" Noah mouthed to me.

"Jessie?" I touched her shoulder as she instantly sprang to life.

"And do you know what I saw? That jerk left some freaking dating app on his phone where he had a ton of unopened messages. So, naturally, I opened every last one. He had conversations going back several months ago. Months! They were even sharing pictures." She looked at both of us as though it was our job to fill in the blanks. "The idiot never deleted anything." She looked mortified, as though the words sounded worse aloud than what they did in her head.

"Tell me, you confronted him, right?" Noah asked.

"You're damn right I did. I grabbed his phone and threw it at him. And do you know what that asshole did next?" She looked to both of us again as though we should have already known what was coming next. "He denied it! He tried telling me that it was some mistake or, get this, spam! Like, dude, are you serious? I saw the pictures. I know what you look like naked."

"Then what happened?" I leaned in.

"He tried saying that it wasn't him—that again, it was all some huge mistake. He even went so far as trying to convince me that he went on some website where people sell stuff and that he must have gotten a virus that caused all those crazy messages. He said he was looking to buy a lawnmower." She took a large gulp of her wine, almost finishing it off entirely. "He acted like I had no clue how technology worked—as if an app could just magically appear on his phone loaded with fake messages that were all coming from his freakin' cell phone number."

"I don't want to point out the obvious here," Noah interjected, "but it's snowing outside." He pointed towards the window. "What the hell does he need a lawnmower for?"

"I realize that, Sherlock. I mean, come on, the asshole has tattoos, for crying out loud. What would be the chance that some computerized virus or spam account would release pictures of some naked guy with the same build and identical tattoos? He's an idiot."

"An even bigger idiot to think that you would even buy into that nonsense," I responded.

"Just to play Devil's advocate here, but maybe he wanted to beat the summer rush by trying to get a good deal on that lawnmower?" Noah looked at Jessie, almost regretting his words entirely.

For a moment, I thought she would choke him, but instead, she burst out laughing.

"Was it a push or a rider?" Noah continued. "We need these details! This would help determine how much skin he had to show." He smirked.

"Enough, Noah," I laughed.

And that was goodbye to Jordan.

It was Saturday—the day of my company's holiday party. I settled on a black cocktail dress and a pair of nude heels but still wasn't the least bit into the holiday spirit. *Bah*

Humbug. Still very much in my head, I had a hard time finding my way around the emotional maze I constructed for myself like I was the mouse all over again who couldn't quite smell the cheese. I was stuck. The maze felt never-ending, with no exit in sight.

It was only 9:00 a.m., and I somehow found the repetition of stirring my spoon into my coffee rather soothing. I watched as the cream slowly faded into the blackness, completely altering the color and taste. Where does the cream end and the coffee begin? The cream became absorbed and inevitably lost as a result of my stirring as it married into the blackness, becoming one with it. Had I not stirred, the cream would have sunk to the bottom with less effect. And I believed that was what happened to me once. For years, I prayed to be stirred equally into that of another, only to have sunk to the bottom with no spoon caring enough to find me.

Noah was seated across from me, watching as I stared off into space. I was rudely stewing on my thoughts as though he wasn't even there. I finally ended up turning my attention over to him just as he pulled his phone out of his pocket in an attempt to fill in the dull silence between us. Occasionally, he would look up from his phone as though waiting for the chance I'd begin paying attention to him so that he could put it back into his pocket for good. But still, neither one of us spoke. Mornings like these happened from time to time, and for some strange reason, I could never tell when it was considered a comfortable silence between us or the calm before some unknown impending storm.

"OK, out with it. What's going on inside of that head of yours?" His eyes met mine.

"I'm just thinking." I frowned.

"Well, duh, I could have told you that. What exactly are you thinking about?"

I hesitated for a moment because I was unsure whether I wanted to mention anything about my blog to him. I knew he was a good friend—patient, kind, and understanding, but he was also blunt and would have no problem shooting down the idea for one second if he thought it was stupid. And the last thing I needed was for him to tell me it was stupid when I suddenly began to feel like it wasn't. Still, he was the first person I wanted to tell. So, I did.

"Well, I started a blog—an anonymous blog," I blurted out. "It all came about when I wanted to find a place to work out how I was feeling—maybe even create a place to help other people who are in the same boat as me?" I said as though it were more of a question than a statement in need of validation.

"Really?" He leaned back into his chair. "Well, it may be a good thing for you. No sense in keeping everything bottled up."

"Are you serious?" My eyes widened. "I would have bet that you were going to tell me it was a bad idea."

"It's not a bad idea, Rach. Millions of people create blogs every day. Besides, it's healthy to have an outlet. It helps."

"So, you're supportive of this?" I asked, unwilling to believe what I was hearing.

"I'm supportive of you always. I think it's a great idea. What do you have to lose?" He leaned back into the table.

"Depends on what I choose to write about, and if people figure out that it's me," I answered.

"This isn't *Gossip Girl*," he laughed out loud. "Don't think I forgot how you forced me to watch that entire series with you." He smiled. "It's not like you are bashing people under some anonymous name. Tell me that you're not planning on doing that, right?" He looked at me pointedly.

"What kind of person do you think I am?"

"Then what do you have to worry about? My only advice is that if you choose to write about real life, just be as cryptic as you can. I take it you plan on discussing your past with Mike?"

"I would have to, wouldn't I? It's the reason I'm at this place in my life right now," I said. "But that doesn't mean my blog has to live there. People don't need to know the intimate details to understand my journey. I can talk about things without actually talking about them, you know?"

Noah nodded his head as though trying to understand. "Well, a lot of people may find what you have to say relatable. It's not like you're the only person in the world to experience a breakup."

"Or they may find what I have to say boring and uninformative."

"*Or* it may be exactly what they need. You won't know unless you try." He smiled reassuringly.

"Thank you for saying that." I smiled back.

"Who knows, you could very well become the Taylor Swift of literature," he teased.

"From George to Taylor?" I rolled my eyes.

"Well, I knew you were trouble when you first walked in." He winked.

Later that night, I pulled into an empty parking spot at one of the most prestigious hotels downtown. As much as I had always wanted to look around inside, I wished I could have done just that. But sadly, handing out a few holiday exchanges before quickly heading back home to my Netflix account just wasn't in the cards. It would have been an impossible mission to achieve. Even Tom Cruise wouldn't have been able to find his way out of this party early.

The banquet room had an explosion of red and green amidst those white Christmas lights strung around every doorway and window. In the center of each table were small tealights floating inside small glass bowls of water with holly scattered about the white linen tablecloths like glitter.

As soon as I walked in, I grabbed a glass of wine and a small plate of appetizers because I figured it would help with the awkwardness of having zero people to mingle with by keeping my mouth occupied. It wasn't that I didn't get along with my co-workers; I just didn't know them that well. Being somewhat new and not having anyone to pal around with made going to any work event a complete dread. And I knew I would have to suffer through countless introductions as people wanted to introduce me to their significant others while I would have to come up with some clever response as to why I came alone. I could very well create a fake boyfriend, who, unfortunately, had to work (*Damn him*), but I knew everyone would see through that bullshit.

"Is this seat taken?" I looked up from my place at the table to see a guy I had never met before, who I assumed to be someone's date, pointing to the seat beside me.

Clearly, I must have misheard him because the entire table was empty. He had his pick out of nine other empty seats.

"No, it's not." I smiled out of politeness.

"Not that into holiday parties, I take it?" he asked as he set his glass down on the linen-draped table, moving a few of the holly berries out of the way to make room for his drink.

"Is it that obvious?" I smirked. "I mean, they are OK. I'm just not feeling that jolly this year."

"So, no trees, stockings, or mistletoe in your future?" His finger ran along the side of his glass, drawing a line in the condensation.

"No tree. No stockings. And definitely no mistletoe," I confirmed.

"That's too bad," he chuckled. "I'm Dan, by the way. I just started here about a week or so ago. I don't think we've met?" He reached for my hand.

As I began introducing myself, I suddenly realized who he was. "You're Dan Wilson, right? Or should I say Dan the Food Man? You're that food-scene blogger we hired for the magazine? You have quite the impressive following." I recounted the information to him as if he wasn't aware of who he was or his credentials.

He laughed. "You flatter me. But yes, that's me." He put his hands up, letting me know he was guilty as charged.

"Wow." I sat back in my seat. I was very familiar with his work and always admired his passion for food well before I knew my boss wanted to acquire him. The acquisition was part of the magazine's plan to transition from strictly paper distribution to more of an online presence. I was excited when I heard the news. I had been a fan of his for a while and couldn't believe that I would have the chance to work with him.

"Looks like you could use another drink. What are you having?" He pointed to my empty glass.

"Some red blend they are offering." I took the final sip as though I refused to let any wine go to waste. "I'd be happy with anything, honestly." I watched as he got up from the table to refill our drinks. No longer did my Netflix night sound as good as it once did. Who knew that I would have been sitting next to Dan Wilson? It was equal parts exciting and intimidating all at the same time. I kind of hoped we didn't end up talking too much shop, because what writer, such as him, would be interested in my boring work? It held no comparison to food.

"You sure you don't care that I join you, right?" he asked as soon as he came back to the table. The question lingered in the air the same amount of time it took for him to get our drinks. "As I had said, I'm new here, and this table seemed less intimidating." He grinned.

I wasn't entirely sure what he meant by "less intimidating," but I just went with it.

I marveled at how Dan looked exactly like his pictures in his blog. Nowadays, you never know how close a person resembles their photos with all the filtering and editing we have at our fingertips. His ruffled chestnut brown hair was styled into the perfect "just got out of bed" look by the way it hung over his ears like a mop. He had hazel eyes like mine, but they hid behind black-framed glasses, giving him an effortless hipster-like vibe. He looked as though he belonged in a coffee shop penning his first novel.

Well beyond the plated dinner and dessert, we sat and talked while everyone around us mingled and danced. Surprisingly, there wasn't much lull in our conversation, considering how rusty I was with talking with the opposite sex (Noah excluded). And I was even more surprised to find him asking a lot of questions about my work and seeming interested in what I had to say. I knew he wasn't too familiar with my column—and I wasn't even near to having the impressive following that he had—but I had the sneaking suspicion that after the night was over, he might venture into reading some of my work.

On the other hand, when it came to his blog, he spoke very passionately about it (something I could hardly fake with my column). Whenever he was deep into explaining something or contemplating my many questions, he had a habit of removing his glasses from his face before putting them back on as though the action in and of itself helped him think.

"So, you obviously love eating other people's food, but do you make any of your own?" I asked, spoon-deep in my tiramisu.

"I'm not that bad." He smiled. "My grandma taught me a few things when I was younger, so that was helpful. We would spend Sunday mornings making homemade pasta and sauce." He leaned back in his chair with his drink in hand. "You should have seen her kitchen back then; we would have pasta drying in every corner of the room. It was magical."

"Sounds it." I beamed. "Do you still do that with her?"

His quiet momentary detachment from our conversation answered my question. He ran his hand through his hair before removing his glasses once more. "No. She passed away last year." His finger circled the rim of his glass.

I didn't know what to say other than to offer my condolences. Having lost a grandparent myself, I could understand where he was coming from. Mourning the loss of a loved one takes time, and there isn't anything anyone could say or do to lessen the pain or the time it takes to get through it (if you ever really do get through it). His face told me it was best to try and change the topic quickly and gently. His saddening expression was prominent. I quickly learned that he was the type of person who wore their emotions on their face, much like the shirt on their back.

Having spent another hour talking about whatever came to mind, I looked down at my phone, realizing how late it was getting. Not that my car would have turned into a pumpkin, but I just knew it was time for me to head home. Not to mention, it's always best to leave on a high note rather than staying longer and risking that dreaded lull.

"I probably should get going," I said before taking a sip of water which we had both switched to after dessert.

"Yeah, I should probably be heading out as well." He got up from the table to join me. "It was nice meeting you, Rachel." He smiled as he put on his coat. "Let me at least walk you out. Downtown can be a bit sketchy at night."

As we made our way through the banquet room towards the exit, Tina approached us. "Thank you both so much for coming!" She clasped her hands together in excitement. "Did you have fun?" She looked from me to Dan.

"Loads," I appeased her. "Thanks for putting on a great party," I added out of politeness.

"Really? Do you think so? I tried my hardest to top last year's party without going over budget, but you know me." She smiled. "I hate leaving out any detail—even the smallest." She pointed up at the doorframe to the small mistletoe hanging directly over Dan and me. Appearing quite pleased with herself, she offered up a quick smile and made her way towards another group of co-workers, making their way towards the exit to leave.

"Too much enthusiasm with that one." I rolled my eyes jokingly. "Sometimes, I wish she could bottle some of it up and sell it. I would totally be a buyer."

Dan smiled. "Well, as I said, it was really nice meeting you, Rachel Parker," he said as he reached in for an unexpected hug. There I was, embracing the lingering scent of his bourbon mixed in with the musky cedarwood cologne that permeated the small space between us. I caught myself inhaling deeply at his scent, causing a fluttering sensation within my stomach. I couldn't remember the last time I felt butterflies for someone. Maybe someone should bottle that up instead?

"It was nice meeting you, too," I finally responded, pulling away just as he planted a kiss on my unsuspecting cheek.

What the hell? I had no idea how to react. It was as if my mind decided the best course of action was to confiscate all rational thoughts and replace them with a clapping monkey instead. In my defense, that was the most action I had received in quite some time, and because of that, I had no idea how to react. Even if it were just a peck on the cheek, it was enough to send a crazy rush of emotion pulsing through my veins like it were a makeshift pinball machine. I couldn't remember the last time I felt this way. *However, was I really ready to feel this way? And for someone that I worked with?* Either way, I felt *something*, and it wasn't easy to simply snap my fingers and be done with it.

"Can I call you sometime?" His voice punctured through the heavy air of silence filled with my abated breath. "It would be nice to know someone around here."

After giving him my number and making that awkward trek back to my car (which was only a few feet away from where we were standing), I couldn't help but wonder if he asked for my number for work or pleasure. Then again, was it wise to get involved with someone I worked with? We all know what they say…

From a distance, he stood back, watching me climb into my car. But just as I was about to shut my door, I heard him call my name. I leaned my head out, meeting his gaze. He shouted: "Maybe you didn't want a tree or stocking this year, but you couldn't escape the mistletoe!" He smiled back at me.

And with that, he turned around, leaving me with this fiery pit of emotion churning in my stomach that was hot enough to melt the snow around me.

Matters of the Heart

December 2012

Noah was the first person I told about Dan. I didn't even make it back to my apartment that night after the holiday party before I was already calling him to dish out the details. I chose to call Noah because I wanted a guy's perspective on the evening. With my luck, he would be the one to tell me that I read too much into everything—that I made things out to be more than what they were. But as soon as I got him on the phone, he had similar news to share. Noah met someone, too.

"Go figure," he chuckled. "Look at us finally putting ourselves out there," he said as I placed him on speakerphone so that I could get out of my dress and wash the night off my face. I stared at my cheek in the bathroom mirror, admiring the invisible imprint left from Dan's kiss that I would no sooner be washing down the drain.

"Well, the jury is still out on my situation. I could very well be making a big deal out of nothing. For all I know, he was just trying to be a friendly co-worker," I sighed.

"The guy spent the entire evening pretty much only talking to you, and then he ended the night with a kiss—"

— "On the cheek," I interjected.

"Either way, it's something. I certainly don't go around kissing my co-workers," he pointed out.

"I suppose," I wavered. "I don't normally—or at all."

"Well, before you head off to bed, I want you to know that I invited Katie, the girl I met, to come visit here next weekend. I would like you to come out with us one night so you can tell me what you think of her. I'd really like your opinion."

"Isn't that moving awfully fast?" I asked while slathering my face with lotion.

"Who's to say what is considered fast and what isn't? It's not like I don't know her. We went to the same high school."

"Still, it may not exactly rise to the level of meeting the parents but having her come visit is a pretty big step, Noah."

"Either way, it's something," he replied.

"I suppose," I wavered again.

The weekend came much sooner than expected—or that I wanted it to, for that matter. It wasn't that I didn't want to meet Katie; it was more because the idea of having to give Noah my opinion after only just meeting her had my stomach in knots. The last thing I wanted was to get involved in matters of the heart because people tend to take those things personally. And the very last thing I wanted was for Noah to get upset if my opinion didn't match up to his.

"Noah has told me so much about you," Katie said after releasing my hand. By the tone in her voice, I was surprised she didn't go in for a hug. "He says you're like the sister he never had. That's so great."

"Noah tends to exaggerate," I teased while picking up on how she quickly defined our roles, with me being the proverbial sister and her the soon-to-be girlfriend. The girl was already marking her territory.

We spent the evening discussing random things, from what we did for fun down to the crack in the saltshaker—all of which we politely smiled and laughed about to keep the conversation going and the evening from turning into a boring disaster. I tried slipping in as many questions as I could to Katie, which made me feel like I was more on a date with her than Noah was. From what I could tell at surface level, she seemed nice, attractive, but way too settled and content with her life back in Michigan. The way she spoke about her job (which she loved), her apartment (which she also loved), down to her yoga classes, and the life she built for herself, which she also loved, loved, loved! It made me somewhat concerned with what that meant for her and Noah's relationship. The only way I saw things working out between them was if Noah decided to move back home—something he swore he'd never do.

"Have you talked to Jessie today?" Noah asked as soon as Katie excused herself to go to the restroom.

"Really? *That's* your first question as soon as she leaves?" I pointed towards the restroom, where Katie walked off.

"You obviously like her," he said confidently.

"Yeah, but Noah, I doubt she would ever move here. Have you given that any thought? Long-distance relationships rarely work out—no matter how optimistic you both are from the beginning."

"It's too early to even think about all that, Rach. We can cross that bridge when the time comes, but seriously, before Katie comes back, have you spoken to Jessie?" His eyes narrowed.

"She texted me earlier, but I was in a rush to get here, so I didn't answer. Why?" I reached for a French fry, wishing I could order more.

"Oh." His eyes widened as he took a sip of his drink. "Then, I'm not going to say anything until you speak to her." He leaned back into his seat as though distancing himself from the conversation.

"So, we're playing that game now?" I rolled my eyes at him. "Why don't you just tell me, and then I can act surprised when I call her later."

"Yeah, OK. You're a horrible liar. She will hear right through that crap," he laughed while stealing one of my remaining fries.

"Just tell me," I said as I tried snatching the fry back.

"Fine." He leaned into the table as he put the stolen French fry in his mouth. "Apparently, and you didn't hear this from me, but she and Jordan are back together."

I gasped loud enough for the woman seated behind me to jump in her seat. "But he cheated!" I exclaimed.

"Yep, our little cheater, cheater, pumpkin eater, begged her to take him back. According to her, he promised that he would never hurt her again—blah, blah, blah. Said that it was a 'momentary lapse in judgment' or something."

"That was no moment," I scoffed. "That was a handful of moments—a shit ton of moments."

"Yeah, well, she agreed to take him back." He put his hands up in defeat. "He told her that he would even quit his job and move down to Virginia to be with her."

I couldn't believe it. I didn't want to believe it. The only momentary lapse in judgment was on Jessie's part, having taken him back. But it's so easy to shout an opinion from the peanut gallery on what someone else should or shouldn't do with their life—because it's not *your* life. Had it been me, who knows how I would have felt? So, could I blame her? Love removes all logic.

I wondered if the feelings of loneliness and desperation to fix what was broken (two things that have the power to make us act in ways we never would with a clear head or heart) were what made her want to mend things? I understood that Jordan was someone she had strong feelings for—possibly, even loved—but what kind of love was he giving her in return when he was capable of doing what he did? And instead of acknowledging that the trust was gone, she invited that hurt right back in. I also understood that matters of the heart were never black and white, but this was too grey for my liking. My gut immediately sensed it was a bad idea.

"Noah, you know just as well as I do that when someone destroys the trust in the relationship, there is a slim chance of resurrecting it. It changes everything.

Sure, some people come out stronger for it, but that's not the majority," I sighed, crossing my arms against my chest. "Things will never be the same between them because no matter what Jessie says or does from here on out, she will constantly be reminded of his betrayal." I knew very well that those reminders would linger in the times they were apart or when he didn't call or text her back—even when his phone would go off in her presence. She would find herself in a constant state of wonder and worry—and I didn't want that for her.

"Rachel, you can't speak for Jessie. Just because we would react differently doesn't mean our reactions are right. It's her life. And I doubt that she is thinking about all those things right now," he said. "So, we are just going to ride this out and be as supportive as we can."

"And be there for her when it all goes to shit." I frowned.

"Yes, and we will be there when he plans on buying a weedwhacker next."

I wanted to laugh, but the sad part was, my gut knew it was bound to happen eventually.

Two days had passed, and Noah finally reached out to get my assessment on Katie. He didn't divulge too many details about the rest of their time together, but he did say that he would call me after he finished running a few errands. But just a few minutes after hanging up with him, my phone started to vibrate.

"Figures. You couldn't wait until later, huh?" I answered. "You're so predictable, Noah," I continued as I poured myself a cup of coffee and sat down on my couch.

"What? Who's Noah?" A male voice greeted my ear, causing me almost to spill my coffee. The voice didn't belong to Noah. For a split second, I thought that it might have belonged to Dan (wishful thinking), but when I looked down at my phone, I realized it was Mike. The one time I didn't check my phone before answering, it had to be him—just my luck.

"What do you want?" I asked.

"I'm good, and how are you?" He laid his sarcasm on thick as though he were spreading it on like peanut butter. He proceeded to tell me that he had just split from his most recent girlfriend. "Yeah, I just realized that things were not going to work out between us," he paused as if to gauge my reaction. "And you know," he continued, "it had me thinking about us, and about how much I missed when we were together,' he said, which just translated into him being the one who got dumped, and he was back trying to fill the ever-revolving void.

But I was no filler, which was another role I refused to play. Nor would I ever consider going back to him. But there he was, talking to me, spewing those same tired lines I've heard him use thousands of times over. I could have easily parroted them back to him, but I resisted the urge. I honestly didn't know whether he wanted me to pity him or say that I missed him. But neither one of those scenarios was going to happen. So, I did what any rational person would do in that circumstance: I hung up.

Leaning back into my couch, I tossed my phone onto the cushion beside me. I hated that Mike felt like he was entitled to be as intrusive as he was. Enough time had passed since our split that I would have thought he would have accepted things by now, but it seemed he was still deep-rooted in denial, trying to win me back—or whatever he wanted to call it. I was over it, and I wished he would have been, too.

As for Dan, it would have been nice if he had been the one who called. It had been over a week since I last saw him at the holiday party. I didn't even have the luxury of accidentally bumping into him at work since he was constantly working remotely—either at some restaurant or at home. So, a part of me hoped he would have at least texted, but all I heard were crickets—lonely, sad, single crickets.

I wondered, *Why? Why hadn't he reached out?* And because of his unexpected silence, I couldn't help but steal cursory glances at my phone, looking for either a missed call or text, only to be greeted with an empty screen instead. But what did I expect? It was only after I decided to just forget about Dan contacting me altogether did he finally reach out. *Go Figure.* It felt similar to that feeling of finding your missing car keys after you stopped looking for them. He texted, asking if I would like to grab dinner that Friday night. But before I had the chance to respond, Jessie called.

"Well, look who it is," I answered, getting up from the couch to begin cleaning. Cleaning has always been my preferred method of distraction. It keeps my mind off things and the dust out of my apartment—win, win! Not to mention, I was slowly cleansing my apartment of pink and replacing it with colors that didn't remind me of Pepto Bismol. *Sorry, Jessie.*

Jessie had been impossible to reach since my night out with Noah and Katie. After several failed attempts, I had the sneaking suspicion that she was purposely avoiding my calls. She probably knew that Noah had told me the news, and I wasn't too happy with her decision.

"Hey." Her breathy tone emitted through the phone. "How are you?"

"I'm fine. How are you?" I already hated how robotic and forced our conversation was sounding. It was unlike either of us to behave that way, and I couldn't help but assume that she was trying her hardest to tiptoe around the Jordan topic.

"Ugh, I don't know! One minute, I'm fine, and in the next, I'm not. It's like, I want to believe him, Rach. I really do. But I can't—not after what he did. It's too damn hard. Every time his phone goes off, I think it's one of those girls. I mean, do you blame me?" She paused for a second to gather herself. "And I read into everything he says or does as though it's some form of infidelity meter. I'm just pissed that he made me this way," she cried.

I called it. But I don't tell her that.

"It doesn't have to be this way, Jess. You can walk away. You don't have to put yourself through this heartache," I said. "You deserve better."

"I know it sounds crazy, but for some strange reason, I still love him. I want to believe that he's sorry for what he did and how he would never do it again, but taking him back doesn't erase what happened, you know? It makes things much worse. At least being apart," she said, "I didn't have to worry about whether he was being faithful or not. But no matter what I do, I know it's going to hurt. I just don't know which is worse."

"It's tough. I can't imagine how you must be feeling, but I also can't imagine putting up with what Jordan did either. You don't need to settle for someone else's shitty behavior when you did nothing to deserve it," I said. "I understand that people make mistakes, but there were plenty of opportunities he could have stopped, but he chose not to. He only stopped because he got caught—there's a difference. Who's to say how long it could have gone on if you didn't figure it out?"

"I know. You're right. The sad part is that I would be telling you the same thing. It's so much different when it's happening to you."

"But I don't want to be right, Jess." I sighed. "Listen, when I was going through some hard times with Mike, someone gave me a little piece of advice that I wished I had listened to sooner. Do you want to know what it was?"

"What?" she asked.

"It's that when someone hurts you, you believe that because they were the source of the pain, that they would also be the source of the healing. We invite these people to stay in our lives in hopes that they will remedy the wound they inflicted. But the sad part is, we never heal that way. Healing comes from within. It comes from that same place that tells us that we don't have to rely on anyone else for our happiness. Sound familiar?"

"Yes," she groaned. "I told you that."

"Exactly."

"Now, I understand why it's so much easier to give advice than take it," she laughed halfheartedly. "But do you honestly think Jordan would do it again?" She practically begged me for an answer. Unfortunately, there wasn't a crystal ball for me to look into to give her the answers she desperately sought. If I had one, I would have looked into it for myself—trust me. Lord knows I could have benefited greatly from it.

"You know what they say, 'once a cheater...'" she exhaled.

"I guess just give him the benefit of the doubt and see what happens"—was all I could say— "Time has a funny way of revealing the truth to us even when we are not ready to see it. I would just keep my guard up as much as possible."

We hung up shortly after, even though I wanted to tell her all about Dan and how he had asked me out to dinner, but Jessie wasn't in the right frame of mind to even share in on that excitement. Besides, that call needed to be about her, not me.

I threw myself back onto the couch, forgoing my mission to clean. I stared at Dan's unanswered text once more, wondering if I should accept his invitation or not.

But I knew that I needed to; even if it ended up being a terrible idea to its core, I needed to figure that out for myself. I needed to open myself up again. I needed to get back out there and not just talk—or write—about it. It was time to open myself up again.

I met Noah later that day after he asked that we meet up at a little diner around the corner from my apartment, Ella's. Ella's was known for its waffles, pancakes, and a line that would sometimes wrap around the restaurant full of hungry, anxious people waiting to get in.

Walking in, I found Noah already seated in one of the grey upholstered booths with a goofy smile painted across his face. It didn't take a genius to realize that his smile wasn't intended for me, but it made me happy to see, nonetheless. It had been a long time since he allowed himself the opportunity to try and move on from his ex, Courtney. Unlike Mike and me, he pined after Courtney for years. His heart was broken far beyond anything I could have ever imagined mine being. The difference was that I wanted my breakup from Mike; he did not want his from her.

Here's the backstory: Noah dated Courtney for almost five years and was days away from proposing before the surprising split. He knew he wanted to spend the rest of his life with her, but then one day (as all stories go), he discovered that she didn't want the same thing. She was cheating on him with some guy she had met at work. Coming home for lunch unexpectedly one day, he found her and the other guy together at their apartment. It crushed him. And from what he told me, he wasn't the same for a long time after that. Girls came and went because he had a hard time trusting someone again after what had happened. The relationship changed him and the way he viewed love, which was why I was so surprised at how unreactive he was to Jessie's situation. Maybe it went back to the same idea that it's far easier to give advice than take it.

As I made my way towards the booth, I remembered what Noah had said to me a few months back when we recounted past heartbreaks. He said that love doesn't hurt, betray, or devalue you. It is not something you tuck away in your back pocket or save for a rainy day—it's ever-present. And if the person you are with treats it as an option, then you are simply an option, too, which is not love by any definition.

Like Noah, I knew what it was like to exhaust so much of yourself into a relationship only to get nothing in return. As I had once done with Mike, he, too, had given Courtney everything. And where did that get him? Nowhere. He was left with all of his personal items boxed up and left outside of his apartment door—like he was the one who hurt her. How could she ever apologize for that? How could Jordan? It's so easy to say there is no going back. But I have to ask: How can you love what you can't trust?

Noah's face beamed from across the table while his crooked smile remained perfectly plastered between his blushing cheeks. I knew that whatever it was must be good because I had never seen him that happy before.

"OK. Spill." I looked at him.

"Before I do, I have to ask, are you nervous about your date with Dan tomorrow?" He set his menu down upon the table.

"Really?" I cocked my head towards him. "You're over there looking like you are two seconds away from bursting at the seams, ad you want to talk about my situation?"

"Just tell me. Are you excited? It's been a while…" His voice trailed off.

"I'm perfectly aware of how long it's been, Noah. And yes, I'm excited, but I'm also extremely nervous. Not to mention, I work with him. So, if this date doesn't go well, I don't think it would be a good thing for either one of us," I said.

"Don't go into it with that attitude. Just relax. It's not like this Dan guy is 'the one.'" Noah laughed.

"What's the point then?" I smiled.

"The point is to relax," he confirmed. "It's just a date."

"So, now that we've got that out of the way." I shrugged him off. "What's going on with you?"

Leaning across the table as though he was about to reveal a secret, he placed his hands upon mine. Noah and I had never touched hands before, so the action felt strangely intimate—even for us. He began gushing about his time with Katie and how their chemistry was nothing short of amazing. They had already made plans for her to come back and visit, and he couldn't wait to start planning.

"So, then you are going through with the long-distance thing, huh?" I asked, knowing full well he had planned on it well before I even addressed my concerns. "Aren't you afraid it will get old fast—all the sexting and no sex?" I laughed.

He shook his head. "I'm afraid that *I* will get too old too fast. Listen, she's a great girl. And who's to say what will or won't happen? I should at least give it a try and find out. Don't you agree?"

"Whatever makes you happy," I said just as he quickly released his hands off mine. He removed them so fast; you would have thought he had been stung.

Blog Post #3

Where's the Love?

I have always wanted (besides a promising career) to be loved—really loved. The kind of love that is unconditional, strong, healthy, adoring, trustworthy, and safe. As sucky as it is to admit, I wanted it bad. I wanted it so bad that I have unknowingly searched for it throughout my entire dating life thus far and never realized I was even doing it. I searched for it in every relationship I was in by settling for what was right in front of me and stupidly calling it "love." I searched for it with examples—no matter how farfetched—from movies, books, and the perceptions of other relationships I had encountered along the way. I searched for it at every stoplight, grocery store, bar, and restaurant, only to come up empty-handed or disappointed with what I had found.

But at the end of the day, the only love I should be focusing on is the love I have for myself. THAT is true love. I shouldn't be afraid to be alone. I shouldn't be scared to come home to an empty apartment, no matter how unwelcoming and desolate it may feel—because it doesn't have to feel that way! I'm in control of how I react to my surroundings. So, if I don't like them, I need to change them. I need to be the one to see things better—to appreciate the hard times as equally as I do the good. I need to allow myself the opportunity not to feel bad about being without a partner because having someone there doesn't mean they are worth having in my life. All of this is in my control. My life and heart are in my hands.

Part of the problem was that I was made to feel like being attached was expected—a requirement. Because of this, I had never given myself the time to feel true detachment. *I mean, who likes being alone?* I understood going into this that there would be moments of ups and downs, but no one fully understands anything until you are actually in the situation. We can speculate all damn day, but it doesn't mean anything until you are in the thick of it. I wonder if George Clooney ever felt this way? I wish I could call him and ask.

Love, Me.

Like Riding a Bike

January 2013

Date night had arrived. Dan planned on picking me up in a few hours for the dinner reservation he made at some downtown restaurant, making it a point to say he would also be simultaneously reviewing. The way he talked up our evening left me wondering whether he invited me on a work outing or an actual date. Either way, I spent the day like a sack of nervous beans until almost an hour before he was scheduled to pick me up, which at that point, I exploded into a full-blown panic attack. I sat in the middle of my bedroom amongst a massive pile of clothes, trying to determine what outfit to wear on this date or non-date.

But seriously, how was I supposed to know how to dress when I had no clue what I was dressing for? The pressure was all-too-much. It was all-too consuming.

Even trying to do my hair and makeup left me with a level of confidence that kept diminishing with each stroke of a brush.

That cold January evening, I ran to my bedroom window, opened it, and breathed in the fresh, winter air. I was freaking out. I lingered by the window longer than I should have and was surprised to find that I wasn't covered in icicles when I finally decided to pull my head back inside of the room.

Knowing that Leigha was at work and probably unable to answer my call, I called her anyway. I was desperate. I needed her advice, and I needed it badly.

"Calm down, girl," she said as she switched our call over to video. I positioned my phone on my dresser to be hands-free while trying several outfits to get her opinion. "You need to go into this with zero expectations—and I'm saying ZERO. Trust me; you will only stress yourself out for no reason."

"Have you been talking to Noah? I think he told me something similar," I responded after trying on another outfit.

"Now, what's wrong with that one? You look good." She pointed at me through the phone.

"You don't think it looks like I'm trying too hard?" I stared down at my cleavage, peeking through the top of my shirt. Even my jeans were almost a half-size away from being called leggings.

"Would you rather it look like you didn't try?" She cocked her head towards the phone.

"I just don't know if this is an actual date or him asking me to tag along on some work adventure of his. When we last spoke at the holiday party, I lingered too much on the topic of how cool I thought his job was and how much fun it would be to tag along sometime…"

"So?" she cut in. "If it's a work thing, who cares? Then the pressure is off. Problem solved." She wiped her hands together in conclusion.

Feeling a bit too exposed in the outfit I had tried on, I ended up trying on a few more until I settled on a pair of dark skinny jeans, a loose-fitting blouse, and a pair of booties I had yet to break in. I styled my hair in loose curls with just the right amount of volume while I kept my makeup simple. Leigha gave me her stamp of approval, making my level of confidence rise by the time Dan picked me up and all brushes were down.

"I'm proud of you, girl. You clean up well." She clapped.

"Thanks. It's just stressful, you know? I haven't been out with a guy since Mike, and he and I barely went anywhere together the last year we were together."

I watched as Leigha was trying to multi-task between managing the kitchen at the restaurant and managing me. Most people wouldn't have the patience to do both. Yet, there she was, mastering it like a pro.

"You will be fine," she said after letting me know she had to get back to work. "It's like riding a bike. These things have a way of coming back to us naturally—like muscle memory."

Muscle memory or not, I couldn't help but notice how much of my emotions felt scattered—much like the clothes across my bedroom floor. I reapplied another layer of lip gloss, wondering, riding a bike or not, was it all too soon? Was I moving on too quickly? Meaning, have I healed enough of myself to get back on that proverbial bike? Who was to say either way? Then again, what is considered the right amount of time? Most people would have probably found themselves in a new relationship by now—even Mike had a few. So, what the hell was my problem?

Why do we do this to ourselves? Why do we drive ourselves into total emotional frenzies all because of nerves? And why was I so concerned with whether I was moving on too quickly? What did that even matter? Shouldn't I be the only judge of that? Whether this was a date or not, I still made the evening out to be much more than it had to be. So, I decided to worry about other things, like: *Should I order dessert? Or do I have to wait until he decides to order one first? Ugh, the blouse I am wearing is white! What if I spill food or drink down it? I'm the world's biggest slob whenever I wear white clothes. I'm a total dirt and stain magnet. Should I change? Should I pack a bib? Or, maybe, I could just tuck a napkin into my collar before taking my first sip or bite…*

Total mind chaos.

But being that this was my first date (or non-date) in a while, Leigha wasn't too far out with comparing it to riding a bicycle. After settling into a good conversation with Dan at dinner, I realized even more that I put too much pressure on myself by unnecessarily complicating things. I needed to ease up on myself a little. I deserved a little grace.

"So, you said that you've been looking forward to reviewing this place," I said before taking another bite of my meal (which none of it made onto my shirt, thankfully). "What do you think so far? I see you've been taking notes."

"It's not bad. I'd definitely come here again," he said as he set his phone back down on the table.

"What would you rate it?" I asked, not knowing how to steer our conversation away from work and onto another topic. The more we lingered on the subject of work, the more I was sure that it was a non-date than a date after all.

"I'd probably give it 3.5 stars out of five."

"I've noticed you rarely give out five stars," I responded.

He laughed at that. "It's sort of on purpose. I mean, don't get me wrong, I have handed out a few five-star reviews, but I can't do it as much as I would like to. It would lessen the appeal, don't you think?' He winked as though he was letting me in on some secret of his, which in turn, made me smile as if I were the only one in the universe privileged to know it. I probably would have let that smile linger a few seconds longer had he not been so engrossed in taking notes and pictures of his food for his blog. Again, I mentally checked all those signs into the non-date column.

"I'm anxiously waiting for the 315 Eatery to open next month," he said with a mouthful of food.

"The 315 Eatery?" That was Leigha's restaurant. "My good friend Leigha is one of the head chefs there," I said. "She works under Connor Green, that celebrity chef."

"That's cool. I have already reserved my spot for the soft opening next month. I heard spots were going fast because you know how people are around celebrities." He rolled his eyes.

"Not a fan of his?" I asked.

"No, total fan. I just want the chance to taste his food besides just meeting him."

I nodded my head as if I understood or even cared for that matter. But just as I was about to take another bite, I saw someone I never expected to see. And I know what you're thinking: It's Mike. It has to be. Well, it wasn't. Nor was it Connor Green.

I couldn't believe it. I almost choked. I dropped my fork onto my plate just as my jaw practically hit the tile beneath my feet. It was Jordan—and he wasn't alone.

There, wrapped up in his arms like an extension of his body, wasn't Jessie. The mystery girl smiled from ear to ear as she petted his arm as though someone had just handed her a puppy. Nothing about their behavior seemed platonic or new. Their mannerisms suggested comfort, which only time could achieve. But wasn't he supposed to be working on things with Jessie? Did I miss something? No. Jessie would have told me if things between them had changed.

My stomach felt sick. Was this girl one of the many girls he had met through that dating app? I couldn't even look at my food anymore. I lost my appetite thinking about how I agreed with Jessie about giving Jordan a second chance when we both knew he couldn't be trusted. What kind of friend did that make me? Now, look what happened. I should have just told her to walk away before any of this had the chance of happening again. Because of that, I couldn't help blaming myself.

I mean, just look at him: He jumped right back on that cheating bicycle (*Muscle memory, right?*), riding around without a care in the world—especially Jessie's. It made me question if he had ever been faithful from the beginning. He looked all-too-comfortable and settled in his actions—like it was a part of his DNA. It was apparent none of what happened was circumstantial. It was purely character-driven. It was because of no other reason than him being one hell of a shitty person—and my friend definitely deserved so much better.

"Is everything OK?" Dan looked at me from across the table. I had almost forgotten he was sitting there after what I had just witnessed. Meeting his eyes for just a second, I quickly positioned them back onto Jordan. Curious, he turned in his seat to see what drew my attention away from him. "Someone you know?" he asked.

I nodded. "Unfortunately."

"Do you need to go talk to him?" He peered over at me as though to gauge my reaction. "But by the look on your face, you don't seem happy to see him. Ex, I presume?" His brown arched with curiosity.

"No. He's my friend's supposed boyfriend." I leaned back into my chair with an audible sigh. Already I was dreading the moment when I would have to tell her all of this, which made me pissed. I was pissed at having been placed into this position. I no longer cared about my date—or non-date. All I cared about was wanting to give Jordan a piece of my mind, which I knew I would never have the courage to do. I wasn't one for confrontation, so I felt paralyzed at the very idea of it. Either way, something had to be done. But what?

Dan took a long sip of his drink. "And I assume the girl with him is not your friend?"

"You are correct. Repeat offender that one is." I shook my head. "They were supposed to be working things out..." My words trailed off into a whisper before getting lost in the commotion that surrounded us. Again, I wished I had told Jessie to walk away. But with all matters of the heart, it's always damned if you do, damned if you don't. So, there I was, damned because I didn't.

"Got it." He took another sip of his drink. "What's this guy's name?" he asked as he emerged from our table.

"Jordan," I said with all eyes on him.

"And your friend?"

"Jessie."

"Excuse me," he said as I watched him make his way over to the bar where Jordan and his date were seated. I leaned further into my chair to get a better look as an uncomfortable conversation between Dan and Jordan continued to unfold right in front of the mystery girl, who sat wide-eyed, looking back and forth between them. And with each second that Dan stood beside him, Jordan's bodyweight shifted in his seat.

Suddenly, as Dan's lips stopped moving, Jordan's date jumped up, shoving Jordan in the chest just before grabbing her purse and storming out of the restaurant. I no longer felt safe in hiding because it only took a matter of a few breaths before Jordan's eyes found mine. All I could do was shake my head in disappointment. "How could you?" I mouthed in his direction. But, of course, he said nothing in return. All he could do was walk out of the restaurant and hopefully out of Jessie's life for good.

"I can't believe you just did that," I said just as Dan returned to our table.

"I doubt I left a lasting impression, but at least we defended your friend. I'm not one to condone cheating." He shook his head.

Suddenly, I wanted to move my chair closer to his and blast through that grey area that once served as a limbo between date and non-date. "You want dessert?" I asked, reaching for the menu without caring that he didn't ask if I wanted dessert first.

When I came home that night to my apartment, I slipped out of my shoes and into a pair of fluffy slippers when an idea came to me. But just as quickly as the idea struck like lightning, it dissipated just as fast. Either way,

I knew I needed to get this idea down before it was officially gone for good.

After logging into my blog, I decided to go back to the beginning and give it the introduction it deserved. Having one mystery reader who probably wouldn't notice that I chose to sneak one in was better than having many more who would. It was time to ignore all my insecurities and fears of how others might perceive my thoughts and feelings. It was time to get busy. Liquid courage holds no candle to the courage people find from hiding behind their screens. I knew some things needed to be said, and after what happened tonight to Jessie, I needed a strong voice, and I needed it to be mine (even if I didn't plan on admitting that it *was* mine).

The internet isn't safe like a journal would have been. We all know that. I know that. So, my identity meant nothing in the equation of making that decision. Who I was—or wasn't—held no weight in what I was trying to accomplish. Besides, I knew other people needed a sounding board to ask the questions we were tired of berating our friends and family with. We needed each other. I needed them. I just couldn't wait for *them* to show up.

"OK. All I have to do is be honest—not only with myself but also with my future readers. Should be easy, right?" I laughed unconvincingly because I knew that was easier said than done. My fingers hovered over my keyboard, unsure as to which one was brave enough to make the first move. However, grouped together, they were only brave enough to reach for the glass of wine I desperately needed to pour.

Hello, Single Ladies! I started to type just before deleting every single word. "What kind of crap is that? What, am I starting a dating service or something? And why the hell am I talking to myself?" I shook my head.

I couldn't believe how fucking hard it was. But if my spirit animal, Carrie Bradshaw, could do it, why couldn't I? For starters, she was braver—and didn't write anonymously. But at least she knew what to write about while I was sitting there clueless on where to begin. The blank page stared back at me as though mocking my ability to write anything worthwhile. Perhaps, this was a bad idea after all. And I should've just quit while I was ahead. Then again, was I ever even *ahead* in the first place? Hardly.

As Noah had said, it wasn't like I was reinventing the wheel here. I was a thousand percent certain that there were millions of other blogs out there that were just like the one I was struggling to create. It was nothing special when you compared it against the masses. But I wanted this, and I needed this, so I didn't care.

The past few years had been hard. Dealing with a breakup and having to start from pretty much scratch made it feel like my entire world was turned upside-down and inside-out. While it seemed like everyone else was on the right track with their lives, I was busy trying to find my way back to one with absolutely no roadmap to guide me.

One thing that ultimately changed since the last time I dated was how people were meeting. When I first met Mike, there weren't any dating apps to navigate through. I get it, it's not earthshattering, but I was part of the AIM generation, so, to me, it was. My generation downloaded mixtapes, wrote cryptic away messages, and watched as MySpace paved the way to the world of social media as we know it. No one downloaded anything onto their phones in hopes of finding someone worthy to date or hook up with in a matter of minutes. I remembered how excited I was when my phone had the snake game on it (*Am I showing my age here?*) And I definitely didn't have the experience of meeting someone with a quick swipe of my finger. Honestly, I have always been a firm believer that nothing worth having should be that easy to obtain. You know, easy come, easy go? But does anyone meet organically anymore? Yet, I found myself in an ocean full of fish that only the worm of instant gratification could hook.

Then again, I did meet Dan organically, right? Maybe meeting people the "old-fashioned" way was still a thing—not that Dan and I were anything more than co-workers at this point.

"What do you think of online dating?" I asked Leigha later that night when she called me to vent after work. It was just after midnight, and I was still up thinking about my blog. I knew it was a subject worth exploring and wanted her opinion.

"I think it's more about buying into the idea of someone—their highlights, so-to-speak—than who they really are. It's the first impression—and it's entirely controlled because no one would post a bad picture of themselves or write about their negative attributes or baggage. They will sell the shit out of themselves to get that swipe. What we see is just for show. It's designed to grab our attention," she answered. "Like a sales gimmick."

"True. But people do that on social media every day. It's not like anyone posts anything negative there either per se."

"Again, it's all a highlight reel. It's like when you see those couples who constantly post pictures of themselves and how happy and in love they are because they need outside validation. They need it because they are not getting it inside their own relationship, no matter how hard they try to convince themselves otherwise. But then, BAM, they end up breaking up. Why? Because no one wants the world to know about their problems or how unhappy they really are. They want to buy into the façade just as much as they want us to. It makes you wonder who we are creating our social media accounts for."

"Never has anyone spoken truer words," I laughed.

"It's all about perception, babe. No one wants you to find them undesirable. Why—" she yawned— "are you thinking of going on a dating app? Did your date tonight not go well?"

"No, it went fine—if it was even a date, to begin with…" I said, still trying to decide. "He ordered a ton of food, and we spent most of the night sampling it all while he took notes. So, who knows? I'm just asking about dating apps out of curiosity." I was honestly more curious to know why people in relationships, like Jordan, downloaded them in the first place? Why was he so wrapped up in the idea of remaining available to the world when, in reality, he wasn't? I felt terrible for telling Leigha about the night's events well before I told Jessie, but it wasn't exactly easy news to share. I was afraid of how Jessie would react, and I knew I needed to digest what happened before I tried feeding it to her.

"You have to be kidding me?!" Leigha sprung to life, forcing me to yank the phone away from my ear. "That asshole!"

"I know. I know. And I have to be the one to tell her because we both know Jordan won't do it. And if by chance he does, what kind of friend would that make me if I didn't try telling her first? Either way, I hate being involved in this," I groaned.

"People can be pigs sometimes. I don't get it. Actually, I do," she paused for a second, "it's because we keep inventing more ways for them *to* be pigs. They can easily download an app and have hundreds of people to browse through like they are window shopping for a car."

"Or a lawnmower," I interjected.

"Exactly," she agreed.

"Yeah, well, we also put ourselves on them—so, what do you expect?" I countered.

"I expect that people be honest. If you're in a relationship, you are a piece of shit for broadcasting that you're not."

I laughed. "It's sad that we have to air on the side of caution with that one. It's like we have to assume that there's a good chance that the men we are swiping through are already in relationships. It's sad."

"It is. Well, I'm going to bed. I'm exhausted." Leigha yawned into the phone. "It's all a bunch of bull, but good luck with Jessie. I know that conversation won't be easy."

"Tell me about it. Hopefully, she doesn't shoot the messenger."

An hour later, I pondered over my introduction once more, as well as Jessie's situation. The clock kept ticking away, with me not only losing much-needed sleep but also my confidence in relationships.

Love, A Many Splendid F#cked up Thing 💖

January 2013

Every relationship starts out perfectly. People wouldn't call it the "honeymoon stage" if relationships didn't. In the beginning, we put on our best behaviors. We do all the "right" things. We say all the "right" things. And we become the best versions of ourselves even when those versions are laced with lies. It's also easier because we haven't put in the time to experience the difficult obstacles or conversations that have defining impact. Everyone is just running through fields of green grass, oblivious to the day they will have to water it. But such is love, right?

    For Jessie, her story was no different. Jordan completely enamored her. She was, as they would say, "head over heels." She was certain, positively certain, that there was a good chance that he was "the one." *How scary is that?* That we could be convinced of someone else's love even when the love was never there in the first place. Jordan was painted as the model boyfriend, not because Jessie controlled the brush, but because he did. He was good at portraying a different side of him, making it seem like he was a great guy. He not only had Jessie fooled but all of us as well. At one point, I was even envious of their relationship. *Again, how scary is that?*

Jessie had always been that friend of mine who believed in love so much. She believed in it so much that she would defend it with every ounce of her being. When it came to her friends, she wasn't afraid of hurting anyone's feelings when she knew it might spare that person further hurt down the road. She has always been one to deliver that reality check or figurative slap in the face when you needed it the most—all in the name of love. She has always been honest, forthcoming, and even through her apparent abrasiveness (or, as she likes to call it, "sass"), she is one of the kindest, most loving people I've ever met, which was why telling her about Jordan wasn't going to be easy.

Blog Post #4

So, I have This Friend...

Most people in their twenties use those years to figure out who they are as individuals. Since most of my twenties were regrettably wrapped up in my ex, I delayed that exploration until recently. But for one of my friends, who had those years of exploration, it almost seemed like it didn't matter.

After going through her fair share of hard lessons in life and thinking that she finally found her reprieve in that of another, it only proved to her once again that everything in life was pretty much short-lived.

During that time of self-exploration, we are handed small pieces of our internal puzzle and try convincing ourselves that we can see the whole picture. That was my mistake. I was so confident at one point that I knew exactly what I wanted when deep down inside, I had no clue. I settled for what I thought I wanted (or needed), only to realize that I hadn't given myself enough time to figure out who I was to even make sense of those needs. The truth is, most of us don't know what we want when we have no idea who we are in the first place. It just doesn't match up. And quite frankly, we haven't lived enough life or have gone through enough lessons to know the things we don't know. It comes from experience. It's not something we can figure out with someone else or in someone else. Period.

When my friend met her most recent boyfriend, she thought the world of him. They had a great relationship on the surface, but no one ever knows what really goes on behind closed doors. Even I thought their relationship was great and had real potential. However, we all know that infamous love story where the girl falls in love with a lie—a story I know for a fact that my friend never wanted to be hers. That was never her idea of her happily ever after.

Cheating is terrible. It's one of those things I will never be able to wrap my head around. If you want something different, then, by all means, go and find it—alone. Don't drag an innocent heart through your duplicitous mud while you try and fix your own. No one deserves that. It's one of the most selfish behaviors one could act upon in a relationship.

But what happens when you decide to forgive a cheater? And what happens when that forgiveness is then blown to pieces when the cheater strikes again? No sooner was an apology uttered to my friend; her boyfriend returned to his selfish ways. But when you are so deep into the weeds of love, it's easy to become blinded. And I don't think my friend ever thought for two seconds that he would be heartless enough to do it again. So, I must ask you: Can you ever really forgive a cheater?

I believe some relationships may come out stronger for it, but you shouldn't have to rise to the level of betrayal and deception to solve your problems. It only ends up creating more or making the existing ones irreparable.

In my friend's defense, she tried to forgive. I can understand how she couldn't let go of all the happy times they shared and how she desperately wanted them back. She may have even felt like it would have been too devastating to allow the fairy tale to shatter—to let all those good times go to waste. But again, I have to ask: Wouldn't it have been easier to let the fairy tale shatter than her heart?

Love, Me.

Telling Jessie wasn't going to be easy. No matter how many times I rehearsed what I would say to her, it all came down to the same inevitable reaction. So, I knew it wasn't going to end well.

"I had a feeling,' she sobbed. "I should have just listened to my gut and not let him back into my life with his bullshit apologies and empty promises."

"We've all been there. You can't blame yourself for wanting to believe him," I said.

"Yes, but you would think I would have learned by now. After all the crappy guys I had dated before him, I should have been able to spot this shit a mile away. But no. Tell me, was I *that* desperate to believe him that I would have believed pretty much anything he said? Or did I honestly believe that this time would have been different?" she asked.

Our conversation ended a short while later. I wish I could have been there so that I could have distracted her from the heartbreak and kept her mind off Jordan, but the distance made that impossible at such short notice. Given the circumstances, I handled the situation as best as possible (at least I thought so when I compared it to the times I rehearsed beforehand). But just as I was about to release a sigh of relief, I heard a knock on my door. It was Noah.

"Hey," I said as he walked right past me and plopped down on my couch. "Well, come right in. Make yourself comfortable," I laughed, shutting the door behind him.

"Hey," he groaned with his face smashed up against a pillow. "I'm kind of bumming right now."

"What's wrong?" I took the seat beside him. "What's going on?"

"I may be overreacting here, but I have a feeling that I'm not." He lifted his face from the couch pillow. "So, I woke up this morning and checked my social media feed and noticed that sometime last night, Katie updated her relationship status to say that she was in a relationship. I immediately thought this was her way of making us official or something—not something I would have done, but it was a nice gesture nonetheless…"

"What am I missing here?" I peered at him.

"I thought it was about us, but now, I'm not too confident that it is," he murmured.

"What makes you say that?" I leaned back into the couch, feeling the sigh of relief I put on hold, leaving me as quickly as it came.

"People started commenting on her status, and I'm assuming they were all referring to her ex-boyfriend because none of them know me, nor did she tag me in her status update." He looked at me, completely unsure of himself.

"Ugh," I sighed—and not out of relief—as my body sank into the cushions under me. "That would have been shitty of her if she got back with her ex and didn't tell you about it or used her status update as a way to tell you. You never know, Noah, maybe it's all a big misunderstanding?" I considered, holding onto the hope that two of my closest friends couldn't possibly be going through heartbreaks at the same time. *What were the odds?* "Have you tried talking to her about it?" I asked.

Sitting there watching Noah look defeated with his body slumped over itself, I was convinced that love was a many, splendid fucked up thing, between Jessie's heartbreak and now possibly his. In a matter of days, the dating world took a massive nosedive into a giant pile of crap. What could this mean for Dan and me—*if* Dan and I were even a thing?

"Of course, I tried to. I called her. I texted her. I did everything short of driving to Michigan to confront her, which was way too crazy for my taste." He shook his head. "She never answered once. Complete radio silence." He pulled his phone out of his pocket to show me the unanswered texts.

My lips pursed, trying hard not to say the wrong thing. Much like my own experience in this department, I could sense that the relationship Noah thought he had, was probably nothing more than a rebound to her. He was merely a pawn in some game she was playing with her ex.

"Are you OK?" I reached for his shoulder, completely bypassing his hands which he had nervously shoved into his pockets. I immediately thought of that day in the diner.

"I'm fine. I'm more pissed off than anything else," Noah huffed. "Why is it so hard for people to be honest? It's as if no one has any regard for anyone's feelings anymore."

"Because some people are selfish. They do whatever they want because they only think of themselves. And if she went back to her ex without giving you the courtesy of letting you know, she never deserved you in the first place. It's her loss," I said, wishing I could have said something along those lines to Jessie early on. "You deserve better."

"I knew she recently broke up with someone, but she never gave me the indication that there was unfinished business there," he said.

"Dating blows. Between you and Jessie, I fear for my heart right now." It was all I could say because it was true.

"People just want their damn cake and eat it, too." He shook his head.

Later that night, I ordered some takeout and relaxed in bed. After watching a few episodes of some syndicated TV show, Dan texted, asking if I wanted to get together again. A part of me was thrilled at the idea of a second date (or non-date), but the other part of me was equally terrified. Between all the heartache I had just witnessed, I was nervous. I didn't need any further complications in my life. And if he planned on being one, I wanted no part of it.

But what did all of this heartache mean? Was there a bigger purpose to all this mess? And why was the dating world willingly allowing itself to play host to the superficial lovers and instant-gratification seekers? And why was so much stock placed on easy attainment and easy detachment (*easy come, easy go?*). The thought plagued me. Unable to make sense of it, I turned my attention over to Dan's text. He seemed sweet and innocent enough. *But don't they all?* It wasn't as if I had picked up on any red flags yet. Or, perhaps, it was way too early to notice any.

I loved our ease of conversation and how he enjoyed sharing his thoughts and ideas with me. He felt comfortable asking for my opinions and valued whatever input I could provide. Not that he had much to contribute on his end with my work because, let's face it, on most days, neither did I. But it wasn't something I felt slighted on in the least. For one, I loved food, so it wasn't much of a stretch for me to savor his passion more than mine. It sure tasted better. Hopefully, not the same as cake.

The Elephant in the Room

February 2013

Blog Post #5

A Trip Down Memory Lane

I hate when I am reminded of all the time I've wasted. I've wasted years of my life in relationships that were, from the very beginning, stamped with expiration dates that I tried my best to ignore or find creative ways of extending their shelf lives. But not all relationships are in it for the long haul. Nor can all relationships be salvaged—no matter the odds. I honestly believed that my ex, **M**, thought we would be together forever. Even I shared those feelings at one point, but at the end of the day, I think we wanted different things out of the relationship. **M** wanted us to work for selfish reasons and what was convenient for him. Listen, I was not perfect by any means, but I gave him some of the best years of my life—some of the best parts of me. I did my best to provide as much as possible even when I was aware of the brutal fact that I wouldn't get much in return. But in the end, who gives to the giver? You can't pour from an empty cup. And he certainly never bothered to replenish mine. So, in the end, I took my cup and ran. I refused to let him deplete me a second longer.

But before **M,** there was **J. J** was my first love. He and I had a huge falling out that somehow landed me in the arms of none other than **M. J,** believing that our fight meant a break more than a *break-up*, wasn't thrilled to discover that I hadn't received that same message. Looking back, I knew I wasn't innocent, nor was I the greatest person when it came to his feelings, but I was young (for lack of a better excuse). I was young and foolish in every regard *because* I had zero regards. I was stubborn, angry, and constantly searching for a reaction rather than a solution from him.

I was angry during our last fight because I felt like he wasn't exactly fighting for me or fighting for us. It wasn't that I was trying to play some game (or, maybe in hindsight, I was), but I wanted him to show me in some way that he cared. I knew that he did, but I just wanted this huge, grand gesture to showcase it (this is another reason I blame movies and books for false expectations). Instead, he looked me in the eyes and told me all the things I needed to hear and none of the things I wanted. But again, when you are young, needs vs. wants are a lost concept. It just doesn't feel as essential or time-crunching to figure out. And it wasn't until I decided to move forward with **M** did I realize that everything **J** had said was, in fact, THE grand gesture. It was only due to my stupidly high expectations that I allowed myself to paint a different picture in my mind on what that grand gesture should have looked like and not appreciate the one he tried painting instead. I was angry with him, yes. But in the end, I was angrier with myself.

Every time something doesn't go your way, you run. You run and try to make me out to be the bad guy, he said to me as he threw his arms up in defeat. He had enough. And it showed.

No, I don't, I said, stopping myself before I started to plead. I was desperate to stand my ground. I didn't want to cave and admit he was right.

He shook his head just before sitting back down upon the edge of his bed. Here was the guy I first said those three little words to—ever. The first guy I believed in my young, foolish heart could be my last. How could I have argued with what he said? He was absolutely right. I was toying with his emotions—whether intentional or not—just because I was confused with my own.

Looking back, did that make me any better than the people who have hurt my friends? Did I have it in me to hurt someone like they have, and in the same manner? A part of me felt stuck and blamed **J** for my inability to grow as a person—as if he was ultimately the one standing in my way of living my life to the fullest. While the other part of me, the rational side, knew he was my solid foundation. However, that side just didn't speak loudly enough.

We fight, and then you go off and meet someone else. And just so that we're clear, this back-and-forth garbage ends today. He looked at me with hopeful eyes. *He's not good for you—and you know it. How many times will we go through these battles until you figure out what you want?* He asked without meeting my gaze as though fearful of my answer.

It was a fair question, which deserved a fair answer. But I didn't have one. If I were to go back in time, I still don't know what I would have said differently at that moment. A part of me was excited at the prospect of discovering what life would be like without him. I was entering into a new territory that made the change alluring. Even with all the uncertainties that wrapped around my decision like a bow, it felt more damning to stay in my comfort zone—the place I knew what to expect—no matter how comfortable it was. Both decisions had their pluses and minuses. So, how fair would it have been if I decided my future with **M** based on **J's** perception of him? Besides, **J** and I were on and off so many times that **M** became the filler during those tumultuous waves—the same waves that **J** wanted to put an end to.

I can't recall how long I stood there wavering on **J's** question. It felt somewhere between fifteen seconds and a year before I watched him pull himself off his bed and walk towards the door.

Just go. Go and make the biggest mistake of your life. Sadly, that ended up being the first and last time I truly listened to what he had said.

A part of me always assumed it was just another fight between us. That I still had the flexibility to choose—that he would be my safety net should my decision fail (and fail it did). Like always, he would tell me to go, and I would leave to somehow find my way back into his arms to pick up where we last left off—and vice versa. Or, maybe, we would somehow reconcile so that the waves would settle, and it would be smooth sailing from there on out. So, I didn't fight him because I thought I had time. I thought there was no way that this was the end. I just grabbed my things and let him show me to the door—a door I never anticipated I'd be banging on years later.

Exhausting, right? Who would want that kind of relationship? My older self is now sickened by how I treated that situation, and most importantly, him. But bang on that door, I did. When he didn't answer, I didn't dare try the doorbell or look through the side window because it was apparent that I wasn't welcome anymore. I knew he didn't deserve to have his life interrupted just because mine was.

But our past is our past. And had I not made those mistakes, I probably wouldn't be the person I am today. I don't think I would value and respect love the way that I do—or relationships—and the people in them. I also don't think we can honestly be proud of every decision life asks us to make, but we can certainly be proud of how we handle the results. The best we can do is hold our heads high and do better. Love better. And whether **M** was my karma in the **J** situation or not, at least I understand both sides now. And I will do better no matter which side of the coin I land on.

Love, Me.

A second date and several weeks later, Dan and I seemed to be hitting it off, or, at least, that's how it seemed. "Seemed" being the operative word. Sure, there were a few things I was still questioning between us, but none of it rose to the level of being red flags just yet. We quickly graduated from sporadic food dates to doing other things such as hanging out at each other's places and staying well past our bedtimes, too.

I learned that Dan was a minimalist. I equated his lack of possessions due to his recent move from North Carolina, but even so, it was pretty sparse considering. Besides the coffee maker, a few dishes, and furniture that came with his rental unit, he could easily pack up everything in several pieces of luggage and leave at a moment's notice. Because of this, I found him hard to nail down. He had nothing for me to use to gauge who he was outside of his food blog. And for someone who loved food as much as he did, he barely had any in his fridge or cupboards.

One morning after staying over at his place, I woke up to find him typing away at his kitchen table. I smiled because I liked working at my table, too, and thought it was something I could check off in our similarity column.

Pouring myself a cup of coffee, I brought the carafe over to the table and topped his mug off. "What are you working on?" I asked. Something about watching him work reminded me of how determined and motivated I should have been about my work (or blog, for that matter). Although proud of my recently published piece about the mayor, I felt like it still lacked any oomph or creativity to have any career-changing potential. I also loved watching how Dan's brow furrowed with intensity when he was into what he was writing, only removing his glasses from time to time when he seemed to be at a loss for words. Lately, they were the words he was looking for me to find.

Without looking up from his laptop, which was adorned with stickers of restaurant logos and random foodie slogans, he cleared his throat to say good morning just before planting a soft kiss on my lips as soon as I finished refilling his mug. He tasted of coffee and the sweet hint of mint. "I'm just messing around with an idea for my blog—nothing important," he responded.

"I'm sure it's not *nothing*." I cocked my head towards him, hoping to inspire him to elaborate more.

With Dan, it seemed (there's that word again) that nothing was ever important, and nothing was ever worth talking about if it didn't have anything to do with his blog, food, or random, impersonal topics. His idea of sharing was letting me know what he ate that day and whether he enjoyed it or not. *So deep, right?*

During those past few weeks, I also noticed how Dan had a great skill at diverting conversations away from anything he deemed too personal. At first, I didn't mind it. I summed it up to nerves or the fear of revealing too much too soon. But it seemed (*Damn that word!*) he was still unable to reveal anything about himself, which only translated into the scary thought of: *What is he hiding?* I was bothered by it as though I was someone unworthy of knowing anything about him. He was tightly guarded—Fort Knox. It wasn't that I expected him to be an open book, but I at least put in enough time to deserve to hear a few pages. When I sat down and thought about that, I realized I didn't know much about him at all. Everything that I did know was barely enough to call it "scratching the surface." I, more or less, hovered over the surface like an aircraft waiting for permission to land. And that's saying a lot when you factored in how much time we had been spending together.

He cleared his throat again before taking a sip of his coffee. I watched as he ran his hand across his mouth to catch a few stray droplets that didn't quite make it between his lips. "I'm just working on a piece for Valentine's Day. You know, to give local date recommendations," he said very casually.

"Nice," I said, not realizing that Valentine's Day was just around the corner, and that was the closest we had ever come to approaching the topic.

"Yeah, I do it every year. I thought it would be a great idea, considering this would be a new area to make recommendations. Plus, I could use our recent culinary adventures as inspiration."

Our? I was hung up on the word *our* like it held more weight than an Amazon delivery truck. Did that mean that there was an *us*? Were we finally establishing what we were? Hold on tight, people.

There was this bubbling excitement within me, begging to spill out and land all over the table. But that excitement, unfortunately, felt a tad bit misplaced. I didn't know it then, but I would come to find out that my excitement was not because of Dan per se or the thought of us becoming an actual couple, but more because I was finally open to the possibility of being with someone again. That was big for me. And it had nothing to do with Dan, but I just didn't realize it at the time.

"It's nothing big. It's just a small blurb. No sense dragging out some lame Valentine's Day piece when I don't have to. I just make them short and sweet—no pun intended." He smirked. "I could care less about this post or the holiday, but it gets a lot of hits each year, so people must want the recommendations," he said without so much as a blink before he dove back into writing his post.

It was apparent that he had no idea what I was thinking or feeling. *Was he insinuating something?* That whatever we were was simply a blurb—a tiny blip in his timeline? Something "short and sweet," as he put it. Like a short story in the literary definition of our "relationship," and this was his way of saying not to expect something more substantial like a novel from him. *Was I digging here?*

"Valentine's Day is nothing more than a dumb, commercialized holiday," he continued with a deep-throated laugh, "that I get to capitalize on a little."

"Yeah. Totally," I half-heartedly agreed. I, too, have always felt like too much pressure was placed on the day. It was perceived as the one day a year, like Halloween, where people rose from the dead—I'm kidding! But it is the one day a year where crushes rise from the shadows to profess their undying love because apparently, no other calendar day of the year would do. Or, if you are already in a relationship, it becomes a competition against other couples regarding who can out-flower or out-chocolate the other more. It's all silly. No amount of flowers, chocolates, or those tacky stuffed bears would ever equate to someone's authentic feelings.

Still, there was always this tiny part of me, like any believer of love, that looked to this day with hope as though something magical could happen. It was never an expectation but more of a dreamlike possibility.

"Any new restaurants you'd like to try next weekend?" I snuck in, wondering if we would see each other at all or if he planned on retreating when the dreaded holiday reared its ugly head, but he didn't so much as look up to me to reply.

It was uncomfortable for a few minutes. The awkwardness hung over the table between us like a dark cloud. I had no choice but to let my question go unanswered as I continued to sip at my coffee, pretending as though Dan's vagueness was once again not an issue. It was hard to tell where things were headed with us or if they were headed anywhere at all because it felt more like a guessing game with zero clues.

I hated that I was allowing myself to be OK with his inability—or refusal—to communicate much of anything with me. Had I asked what his favorite cut of steak was, I wouldn't have been able to shut him up. Was it settling? Was it acceptance? Or was I reverting to old behaviors of making excuses for other people again? If you guessed all the above, you are probably right.

The uncertainty lingered and followed me around like the elephant you never want to share a room with. Maybe one day I'd address that elephant, but I knew that now wasn't the right time. I also considered that I might have been a little hypersensitive given the recent events with Jessie and Noah or, maybe, it was because I knew deep down that something was off between Dan and me. I wanted to get ahead of it before it eventually blew up in my face. Either scenario was plausible. Either scenario wasn't ideal.

But being the type of person I am, I couldn't just sit back and let the silence win.

"Or maybe we could go see a movie? I heard that thriller we've been talking about comes out this week—" I started.

— "I have family coming into town next weekend," he cut in without letting me finish.

"Oh. Maybe we could all go?" I offered. *Ugh, Rachel. What is wrong with you? You don't invite yourself to meet the family—especially the parents! You have to wait for him to ask, dummy! Any chance you could jump in that time machine and remove that last comment from existence?*

"We already have a lot planned," he said very matter of fact. "Maybe another time," he offered, which sounded like more of a statement than a suggestion that lied solely on his terms.

"No worries," I said while hiding my disappointment behind my coffee mug. "You never really talk about your life back in North Carolina." I continued to allow the word vomit to spew from my lips. "What is your family like? Any ex-girlfriends I should know about?" I asked jokingly.

Ugh, you're killing me, Rachel! Shush up! But listen, I get it; I wasn't exactly joking. We all know that half of what people say they are "joking" about is actually serious. I was, in all honesty, slightly embarrassed by my behavior. But could you blame me? I wasn't getting much out of him, and I felt like by me pretending that my interest was all just a rouse, it would somehow disguise how genuinely vulnerable I was.

His body tensed at my question. His posture stiffened as straight as the chair he sat on. I watched as his finger circled the rim of his coffee mug as though searching for an exit that didn't exist. Maybe I didn't read the room correctly? Even the word "ex-girlfriend" didn't roll off my tongue in the same way it sounded in my head.

He didn't say anything for what felt like an awfully long time, and once again, I tried not to appear bothered by it (because who wants to come off as emotionally needy? Or was that some pathetic excuse I gave myself for his lack of communication skills when I didn't want to face the fact that he was purposefully keeping me at arm's length?), but deep down, it was hard not to get offended by how he was acting. Was he hiding something? Or was he just not that interested enough in me to warrant us to get to know each other more? Again, either scenario was plausible. Either scenario wasn't ideal.

I decided to laugh it off and ignore that elephant once more. "Forget I asked," I said. "I was only teasing you."

"No, it's OK." He shrugged. "There's not much to tell. My family was pretty bummed when I said I was moving to New York to take this job. They believed there were more opportunities for me had I stayed in Raleigh. Lucky enough for them, this was only a contract position, so they didn't get on my case too much after that."

"What do you mean? I didn't know this was a contract position?" I'm sure my face said it all—how could it have not? Why would he have even bothered pursuing me—or anyone—if he wasn't planning on staying in the area long? None of what he said made any sense. "How long is your contract for?" I asked, pulling myself together and my emotions into check.

"Six months. I figured it would give me enough time to publish a few pieces for the magazine and my blog before heading back to North Carolina. I plan on making this a thing, though. I'd love to travel across the country and do the same thing I'm doing here but in other states. That is why I love working freelance so much. I'm not tied down."

Double meaning?

What more could I have said? Even if I had found the perfect response, would it have even mattered? Would it have mattered if I called him out on his lack of information while in the same breath telling him it was a dick move on his behalf? Either way, I had no say in what he did with his life. I had no claim on him. I wasn't his girlfriend. I was just some girl he ate and slept with—you know, the basic needs—while being led on by false pretenses. I couldn't bring myself to ask him what we were at that point because I had the gut feeling that I was on contract, too.

It felt like the world was spinning around, yet I remained paralyzed at the table. Coming to, I met the residual discomfort left from our momentary pause as Dan got up from the table and made his way into the kitchen for more coffee.

A small tear that I had no idea was brewing slid down my cheek, which I quickly brushed away. I was grateful that Dan chose to walk away at that moment before he had the chance to witness it. But that elephant certainly didn't miss a beat.

Tiptoeing Around the Hard Stuff

February 2013

I needed a couple of days to myself. After leaving Dan's that morning, I decided it was best to leave things well alone. I wasn't going to poke at something that didn't deserve to be poked. It wasn't that I was completely emotionally invested in the relationship, nor could I have said that I had genuine feelings for Dan, but I knew it wasn't fair, regardless of all that, that Dan was the only one calling the shots. I had a say in all of this, too.

    Until that morning, I had no idea that I had zero voice in the relationship—not even a damn whisper. And the fact that he already laid out our relationship's expiration date (six months to be exact) without ever asking my opinion on the matter pissed me off. Just knowing that he would be returning to North Carolina in three months, I was in no position from there on out to continue forming any type of relationship with him—especially with an end date hanging over my head. *Seriously, who wants to work towards an ending?* Been there, done that.

Dan tried texting me later and well into the days that followed, but I didn't have much to say in response. At least, not until I fully allowed myself the time to soak in everything that had happened. I wasn't trying to be rude or play games, but what the hell did he expect? Did he think I would be happy about all of this? I was so angry that he left that crucial detail out, considering he had plenty of opportunities to tell me about it. And as much as I enjoyed our time together, I wasn't about to go down that dead-end road again.

Blog Post #6

Tiptoeing Around the Hard Stuff

Why does it feel like you're the last single person on earth when you know that isn't the case? Are we not constantly surrounded by couples who inadvertently remind us of all the things we don't have during times of detachment? I have gone so far as to avoid the damn grocery store on certain days to prevent having to share aisles with those happy-looking couples selecting their meals for the week while I'm busy trying to decide which flavor of ice cream to try next.

But all this sounds so "woe is me." Why is that? If I'm being honest here (which writing anonymously makes relatively easy), I *am* seeing someone (if you even want to call it that) who makes me feel as single as ever before. So, you're probably wondering, *What's the point then?* Good question.

What I do know is that our relationship's end had already been established well before the beginning ever was. And the ending, in case you were also wondering, couldn't be any further from that desirable happily ever after we all strive for.

Love is complicated. I know that; you know that. And you certainly don't need this blog to tell you that either. I'm not saying I have, or will, solve the mystery of love or that I will find a way to uncomplicate the complicated. I genuinely believe that there is no magic formula nor a "one size fits all" approach. There is no love potion, song—or shack—to make things as simplistic as we would want them to be or that they *should* be.

So, let me ask YOU a question: Would you ask the hard questions, or would you tiptoe around them?

Love, Me.

Twenty seconds later, I received the following response:

You ask them.

Who was this person? Was it my one and only faithful reader? Or was it someone new? I looked back on prior posts and noticed that my reader count was almost at ten. People appeared interested in what I had to say, and to that, I was extremely grateful. I had my audience. I was building my tribe.

    Since deciding to take those few days off from Dan, I realized how much of my free time was previously absorbed in all things related to him. I would tag along to all the restaurants he invited me to, supporting his passion for expanding his online presence while also being that sounding board whenever he needed to bounce some ideas off. Since I was never actually given the role of supportive girlfriend, it left me feeling more like a groupie than anything else. I held the arm of a food rockstar, ready to swat away any fans who came too close.

At that time, I didn't mind what role he gave me to play, which sounds foolish when I think about that now—especially when I was recovering from all the ones Mike cast me into. But sadly, I wanted to believe that if I worked hard and accepted whatever role he chose me to have, then maybe it would earn me a more significant part later on. I knew I deserved to be more than just the girl with the extra set of eyes to spot his typos and grammatical errors. In the end, it was pretty evident that he and I wanted—and expected—different things from each other, which was the story of my life.

However, I was by no means interested in being so absorbed in his work as he thought I was, but I was at least a good sport about it. I'm not saying I didn't enjoy myself, but I eventually grew tired of being devoted to him every evening. Yes, he valued my opinions and the moral support I provided, but was that *all* he valued? Didn't I deserve to have a little attention with the spotlight on me for once? Or was I just being bitter? Or both?

But I couldn't place all the blame on him. It wasn't like I told him how I felt or pushed any of those difficult topics into our conversations. Nor did I ever stand up for my own needs as well. However, my mind kept circling back to the issue of him never once communicating that he didn't plan on staying in the area for long—and that was utter bullshit.

Later that day, I called Noah to see if he wanted to hang out. We hadn't seen much of each other since the whole Katie catastrophe, so I felt like we were overdue for some friend time. Plus, it would be nice to get his opinion on the Dan situation as well.

"How's everything been?" I asked as soon as he walked into my apartment with coffees in hand.

"I never updated you, did I? Well, it's over. My suspicions were correct." He set the coffees down on the table while he slid off his shoes.

"I'm sorry. Are you OK?" I slumped in the doorway.

Handing me my coffee, he said, "I'm fine," half-smiling. "Better to find out now than later."

After he settled in, I told him about the last morning at Dan's. "I don't know what he wrote; he didn't read it to me," I responded after mentioning the blurb comment. I knew I should have asked Dan to clarify because reading too much into a supposed metaphor was slowly becoming a huge mindfuck. With so much uncertainty surrounding our "relationship," any bit of clarity would have been helpful, and I was desperate to find some.

"How does that make you feel?" He looked at me.

"Not sure," I responded. "I'm just confused. And now that Dan dropped that bomb on me about him being on contract, I'm more confused than ever. Why start a relationship with someone if you don't plan on sustaining it? Unless this was all some casual thing that I have completely romanticized out of proportion." I followed Noah into the living room, where we sat on the couch to drink our coffees.

"Well, he's being very cryptic. We at least know that for sure. Not to mention, it was super shitty on his part to not be upfront about the whole contract thing," he acknowledged. "I wonder why he never said anything?"

I took a long sip and felt the warmth roll down the back of my throat and into the pit of my empty stomach. Like the cream mixing in with the coffee (a metaphor I pondered over more times than I could count), my feelings began to swirl into a ball of confusion until I could no longer separate feeling from fact. Was I feeling comfortable knowing that this could be my out from a relationship I didn't have much invested in? Was I feeling hurt that I was betrayed and misled for whatever reason Dan has yet to justify? Or happiness with knowing that I allowed myself to be open to a new relationship regardless of its lasting potential? The one feeling I did know for sure was that I was worried that Dan and I had gotten too close for comfort, but only he was in control of how close and comfortable we would ever get. It wasn't fair.

"So, what you're telling me is that you think whatever he was writing about also symbolizes your relationship? You know how crazy that sounds, right?" he laughed. "I think by him telling you about the contract was just a nicer way of telling you that it's best not to make any long-term plans together."

"A nicer way? Why would that even be considered as nice, Noah? It's not like he has ever said anything to me directly. Why not be upfront about it and not hide behind supposed 'nice' words?"

"Rachel"—he turned to me— "he is the first guy you've dated since Mike. You can't honestly tell me you saw lasting potential with this guy?"

I shook my head. "Of course not. But I feel like I should have at least some say in this."

"Just let it go. Stop caring about what you two are or what you two are not. Given my track record, I may be a bit cynical here, but nothing in life is ever written in pretty metaphors or perfect symbolism. So, quit digging for hidden meanings when everything you need to know about your situation is staring you right in the face."

"Ouch." I retreated. I knew he was right, but that didn't make his tough love any easier to digest.

"And I'm not saying you need to know or even deserve to know every intimate detail about his past," he continued, "but you are at least entitled to the

CliffsNotes. You need to know where his heart has been. It's the only good way to know where it's going."

"True, but wouldn't that mean that he would deserve the same? Not that he has ever really asked me about my past. He may be judgmental," I sighed.

"Then he's not the one for you," Noah replied.

"I think we already established that," I said.

When the night settled in, so did I. I grabbed a blanket from my bedroom and cozied up on the couch. But just as I was about to select something to watch on TV, I heard a knock on my door. Looking through the peephole, I discovered Dan standing on the other side, about to knock again. Usually, he wasn't one to just show up at my place without calling or texting first. He probably figured I wouldn't have answered if he did. Well played, Dan. Well played.

"Hey," he said as soon as I opened the door. "Are you busy? Can I come in?"

"Sure." I nodded, letting him inside. "What are you doing here?"

"Well, after not hearing from you, I wanted to stop by and see if something was wrong." He looked back at me earnestly, but I looked away. "There *is* something wrong, right?"

"Everything is fine. I'm fine," I lied.

"If that's true, then why haven't I heard from you?" His brow arched inquisitively.

"Not sure." I leaned away from him. "You could have just called or texted."

"So, you could continue to ignore me?" he jested.

Giving in, I cracked a smile. "True."

"I knew something was up after you left my apartment a few days ago, and I knew it even more when I stopped hearing from you. So, I thought about it," he paused, "and I think I know what's wrong." He sat down on the arm of my couch. "It's about my contract."

Dumbfounded, I leaned against the wall for support, remaining silent as my back tried merging with the drywall. It wasn't that I was trying to give him the silent treatment; it was more because I didn't know what to say—again. *And since when do guys search for the deeper meaning?*

"Listen, I get it. It was a shitty move not to be upfront with you about everything. At first, I thought you knew my position was only temporary, and you were cool with everything, but the more we started hanging out, it was obvious that wasn't the case. I should have said something; I get that, but I was a bit nervous about how you'd react," he said.

"So, you just randomly blurt it out without any regard for my feelings?" I stated, holding my place firmly against the drywall, refusing to budge.

"I know. Honestly, I didn't think I would get involved with anyone when I came to New York. And I certainly didn't want to complicate anything, which I did anyway." He scratched his head. "Before I moved here," he continued, "I broke up with my girlfriend because she wasn't exactly pleased with my decision to take this job in the first place."

"Wait," I cut him off as my back lifted away from the wall. "Are you serious?" I asked just then, realizing that out of all the titles I had pondered over in days past, "the rebound" was never one that made the list. Never once did that seem like a possibility. *Again, the story of my life.*

"I know. I'm looking like the world's biggest asshole right now." He slid his body off the armrest onto my couch in one quick, fluid movement.

A part of me was angry, but then this other part of me felt almost sorry for him. I know what you're thinking: *How can you feel sorry for someone who basically led you on for months?* But did he? Or did I *want* to be led on? He was the first guy I opened myself up to since Mike, and even if it didn't go exactly as planned, it still went somewhere. It still opened me up to the realization that I *could* love again—not that I loved Dan. But I knew that I didn't have to settle for anything or anyone anymore. Dan would never be "the one," but that didn't mean I wasn't entitled to feel something here. Had I not, I would have been more worried that my heart had given up, packed its bags, and hightailed it out of my chest. Luckily, that wasn't the case. Feeling *something* was a good sign.

Unsolicited, he began telling me about his breakup with his ex and how she took the move to further prove that he could not commit, especially when he didn't ask her to come along. "What did she expect?" He turned to face me. "This was a contract position, and she had a solid career that she would have essentially been walking away from. I didn't want to be *that guy* who pulled her away from her dreams just so that she could follow me chasing mine. Besides, I planned on coming back—it was temporary." He put his hands up as though trying to emphasize his goodwill in the situation.

"Did she know that?" I asked. "You could have loved it here and wanted to stay. Nothing in life—contract or not—is written in stone," I said, afraid that he would assume there was a double meaning to my words.

"No matter how I spun it, she either wanted me to turn down the opportunity or ask her to come along. And for the sake of full disclosure here, it all came down to trust with her and me. It was always the Achilles heel in our relationship."

"That seems to be everyone's, unfortunately," I said.

"Well, she could be crazy at times," he laughed just as I took the seat beside him on the couch. "But I kind of liked that about her in the beginning. She was unpredictable and always kept me on my toes. But who knew that the one thing that attracted me most to her would be the same thing that would ultimately push me away? Maybe that's why I took the breakup so well? And maybe that's why it was so easy for me to consider moving on as quickly as I have," he tried to justify.

She was, as Dan described her, controlling and untrusting at best. She didn't like that he had a life outside of their relationship, and when his blog built up more momentum, she found it even harder to support something she couldn't quite control. She would throw fits whenever he had to work as though it was an excuse for him to spend time without her.

"The funny part was," he continued, "was that I invited her to come along, but she never wanted to join me." He even told me how she had been cheated on in the past but couldn't let those insecurities go. "I never did anything to hurt her trust," he said. "So, when I got the offer to move to Syracuse, she couldn't handle it. She didn't trust me enough to go here without her."

"You know what makes this whole situation even crazier?" He shook his head at me a few minutes later.

"What?" I asked.

"I never once gave her a reason not to trust me—even though she convinced herself that all men were untrustworthy." He rolled his eyes at the foolishness of it. "Come to find out; she cheated on me after I accepted the job. She confessed it one night after I moved out here. She thought it would make me jealous enough to want her back, but it only made me regret not breaking up with her sooner."

I didn't see that coming. "Does anyone know how to be faithful anymore?" I frowned at the thought.

"I think there are some people out there, which was why I was eager to defend your friend."

"I appreciated that." I smiled.

"So, what about you? What's your story? Now that I've told you mine." He tried locking eyes with me.

Finally, the conversation I desperately wanted to have with him had arrived. But of course, the timing couldn't have been more awful. Because of that, I didn't feel it was necessary to divulge as much as I initially thought I would have. Of course, I appreciated him being so open with me; I felt like I finally received his CliffsNotes—a blurb, if you will (wink, wink).

I did, however, tell Dan how I thought Mike was going through a phase when he transformed into a completely different person when we were still together. I also told him how I lied to myself for years, believing that things would eventually get better—that he would come back to being the person I initially met. I had many theories at that time regarding his transformation. I made up reasons explaining why he lied to me constantly, why he hardly spent any time with me, or how he eventually removed himself so far from the relationship yet demanded that I work harder to make up for his absence.

"It was a year into the relationship when I started noticing subtle behavioral changes. At first, they kind of flew under the radar and weren't cause for any alarm. In hindsight, they were all red flags that I was too naïve to have noticed," I admitted.

Dan leaned back into the couch, rubbing at the back of his neck. He held my gaze for a few moments before responding. "What did you do? How did you handle all of that?"

"I fought for him," I confessed. At that point in the conversation, I knew my admission was disturbing, and I knew Dan was slightly taken aback by it. Trust me; I was aware that my past actions were foolish, but, again, hindsight is always 20/20.

I continued to tell Dan how I fought for Mike even when the evidence was right in front of my face, telling me he wasn't worth the fight. I became untrusting like

Dan's ex in a sense, but for a completely different reason. Where she didn't trust his fidelity, I didn't trust Mike's intentions.

When faced with this type of situation, you find yourself behaving in ways you never imagined you would. You may find yourself rifling through your significant other's belongings as if anything you may uncover might hold the clue to what's going on or to prove your suspicions wrong. No one wants to be that person who goes through someone else's phone, but when you are fearful of your heart, you go through extreme measures to ensure its safety.

For the longest time, I thought I was the crazy one. I thought I was overreacting—making mountains out of damn molehills. But it was just my gut ringing the alarm button to get my attention. *Oh, how I wanted to be the crazy one just so that I could put my suspicions to rest.*

"I guess I believed that the guy I originally fell for would resurface. I wanted to believe in that possibility so much that I allowed myself to sacrifice so much of who I was to keep that dream alive, and it cost me."

"So, he gaslighted you?" Dan looked at me.

"Sure did," I said.

"Damn." He bit his lip

"I knew it was down to me either spending the rest of my life with someone I knew didn't deserve me or leaving and taking the chance of finding someone else who would."

Dan's thumb found the back of my hand as he gently caressed it before locking his eyes with mine. I think that was the first time we really looked at one another and saw *something*. Feeling the familiar intimacy that I had seen played out a million times over in movies and books, I knew what to expect next. It's the romantic, climactic scene where the two lovers overcome an obstacle that rekindles their love so they can finally live happily ever after—the end.

But cut the crap. You and I both know that that's not what's about to happen. Dan and I were not meant for that ending (which would have made this a really short book, huh?). It may have been great at that moment to let everything unfold in that way, but someone had to be smart here. *So, cut! End scene!*

"So, what now?" he asked as his body slowly gravitated towards mine until the space between us became nonexistent.

There it was—the defining moment. The moment where the audience would accept the clichéd kiss and storybook ending. Clue one: His body moved closer. Clue two: He looked into my eyes and then down at my lips. It was going to happen. I knew what he wanted. I knew what I wanted. But remember: Want and need are two different things.

So, I gave us what we both needed. "Friends," I said. "I think you and I should just be friends."

And to my surprise, that seemed like the best title of all.

Perfecting the Art of Loneliness

February 2013

My sword landed upon the ground with a thunderous thud. My armor soon came crashing down along with it as the metal pieces kissed each other with a melodious clank.

I can't do this anymore, I cried.

Throughout the years, I collected battle scars that decorated my skin like tattoos. Up until that point, I had successfully kept them hidden from the world beneath my armor. But at that moment, no matter how hard I tried to keep them covered, they continued revealing themselves despite my effort. One after another, they appeared until there seemed to be no patch of my skin left unscathed.

You can't do this anymore? My enemy snarled as he approached me. He circled me like his prey. The intoxicating scent exuding from him infiltrated the atmosphere around us. It was suffocating. I placed my hand around my throat, begging for air. I watched as he stumbled with each step that he took towards me. I was scared, but I held my ground. I refused to show any sign of weakness.

This! I exclaimed. *I can't take THIS anymore.* I gestured to the space between us with bated breath.

I knew he didn't believe me, yet I couldn't blame him. For so long, when we had approached similar battles, I had threatened similar things. My words were pointless; they held no substance. They were as empty as the space between us.

He laughed a deep belly laugh as his sword shook at his side, which he then placed a hand upon to steady it in place.

The war needed to end. I looked around at the battlefield, at all the destruction that lay in our wake. So many causalities. So much loss.

Off in the distance, a door suddenly appeared. I assumed it was merely a mirage like all the doors I believed to have seen before. He, however, placed himself between the door and me, instantly acknowledging its existence.

You wouldn't dare, he growled. *You are too weak. You need me.*

I took one step forward, and he immediately drew his sword just as quick as my foot hit the ground. It was at that moment I knew that a fight was inevitable. I was either going to fight to stay or fight to leave, and it was up to me to decide which one was worth fighting for. Slowly, I bent down and picked up my sword, dusting a few blades of grass that had decorated its metal surface.

I quickly pushed him aside while holding tightly to my weapon. I picked up speed and ran towards the door with him hot on my tail. I panted hard with each stride, but I continued running, extending my arm to reach the door's handle. I kept extending my arm until I could feel the handle within my shaken grasp.

When the door opened, my body, without hesitation, passed through the threshold just as I quickly slammed the door shut behind me. I never once looked back as the door rattled on its hinges just before I fell into a cloud of cotton…

Wrapped up and tussled in my sheets, I woke with a jolt. Sweat began pouring down my face and onto my chest while my breathing became as equally as heavy as it felt in my dream. Rubbing the sleep out of my eyes, I sat up in bed. That was the first time in a very long time I had experienced such a vivid dream as that. I believed it had a lot to do with my present and past feelings. *Duh, Rachel.*

Realizing that everything was OK, I closed my eyes once more and allowed myself to drift back to sleep.

When I finally decided to wake up for the day, I felt marginally better than how I did earlier. I planned to get up, make some coffee, and start aggressively working on my blog. After last night's events with Dan, I knew I needed to sort things out—and no better place to do it.

Being away, Jessie preferred calling over texting as her way to remain connected to all of us. Calling me that morning, she sounded so much better from the last time we had spoken. I was equally surprised to hear that it was all due to her finding a new perspective on her life. It came from the combination of various self-help books and some podcasts she had been religiously listening to. She said it gave her a whole new lease on her single life.

"I feel like the pressure just fell right off," she explained. "Not only have I stopped caring about Jordan—who, by the way, texts me constantly—but I feel perfectly OK with not being in a relationship right now. It's like I'm finally content with being alone."

"He still texts you?" My lips curled in disgust.

"Yeah, but I don't answer." She brushed me off.

"Well, I'm happy for you. Whatever you're doing, sign me up," I teased before filling her in on what happened with Dan. The relationship dust hadn't settled yet—not that I was heartbroken or anything—but I was more or less dealing with another setback.

"You want to know the real secret to how I'm feeling this way?" she beckoned.

"Yes, please. I think the entire singles population would like to know," I laughed.

"Dating yourself. Seriously, don't laugh"—even though Jessie laughed as she said it—"I never realized how important self-care was until I started setting some quality time aside to devote to it. I've gone out to eat alone; I saw a movie alone; I even went out for a drink alone. It felt so liberating."

"Seriously?" I couldn't imagine doing any of those things alone.

"Don't knock it until you try it." She read my mind. "But I have to run. I will text you some ideas."

So, a week later, I began dating myself.

Jessie was certainly onto something. I had no idea how much I had been neglecting myself and my personal needs until I started putting time aside to take care of them. She recommended that I carve out a two-hour window each week for pampering. And to avoid distractions, she suggested that I silence my phone and completely disconnect from the world to give myself the quality time I deserved.

Think about being on a date with someone who was constantly on their phone, she said. *You would find it rude. So, don't be rude to yourself.*

It felt freeing. I couldn't believe how many times I tried reaching for my phone before I ended up putting it in another room to avoid the temptation. What a damn filler that thing had become. Whenever I didn't want to be alone with my thoughts or needed something to fill the silence or boredom with, there it was. I was never vulnerable with my alone time because I never was truly alone. I needed to learn to master this vulnerability. I needed to deal with my thoughts and actually listen to them, too.

Another thing I started doing again was cooking. Since moving into my apartment, I rarely ever made anything at home. I made myself believe that cooking for one was pointless—that I didn't deserve to make anything more than a sandwich because it was just me. I ended up buying myself a cookbook and dedicated one night a week to trying something new. Just because I lived alone, it didn't mean I didn't deserve to eat well. So, I ate.

And with all that cooking (and eating) I was doing, I decided it was time to focus on my physical health, too.

So, I enrolled in a gym membership. My love for yoga intensified, as did my sudden interest in meditation. Not only was I trying to achieve personal fitness goals, but I knew I needed to try and master the emotional ones, too. I was by no means an expert in the practice of meditation, but it was just another way that helped me sit with my thoughts and reconnect with myself that much more.

My phone was still an issue. I took baby steps each day by silencing it for at least fifteen minutes or more just so that I could fully embrace the time I spent meditating. But I knew in order to organize my thoughts, I needed to organize my surroundings, so I dedicated an entire weekend to unpacking all the remaining boxes and putting my apartment together at last. Doing this helped my mediation. I cleared my head of all the chaos and focused on nothing more than my breathing and positive thinking. I would spend that time thinking about my blog and what I wanted to write next. I also spent time thinking about all the things I wanted to achieve in my life. I pictured myself happy. I imagined myself content. I also imagined what I wanted my future to look like—similar to a visual dream board. But like all good things that come into our lives, everything takes time. And I learned to be gentle with myself about that.

Lastly, I took myself out on one of those solo dates that Jessie recommended. I decided to break into this new activity by bringing my laptop with me. Even though I spent most of that outing writing, the whole experience, as Jessie said, was liberating. I was content going alone with this newly found confidence. It felt as though I could take over the world. I felt like Beyoncé.

Blog Post #7

The Giver, the Taker, and the Cycle-Breaker

Hello, it's me again.
There are some things I have come to terms with lately that I felt the need to share with you. Maybe then someone would hold me accountable to face these things head-on.

Here goes nothing…

I have a big mouth.
I do! And a huge one! But not in the way that you would think. I have a big mouth when it comes to the intimate details about my life—not the lives of others. Sometimes, I find myself being too open with people without first assessing their importance or eventual roles in my life. This assessment helps distinguish between the right kinds of boundaries to assign people. Too often, I

have been burned by placing too much trust in people that were never trustworthy in the first place.

I have no filter.
(Only use them in pictures). I am blunt, honest, and sometimes all-too trusting. I believe in the best of people and can never fathom someone ever being cruel or malicious. As though the odds of someone deliberately hurting someone were out of the question. After all I've been through, you would think that I wouldn't be this way, that I would walk with caution, but sadly, I still believe in people's best.

I am a doormat (sometimes).
So, welcome. I allow people to walk all over me. I exhaust so much of myself into others while barely ever requesting any reciprocation in return. I believe that if I'm needed, then that is all I need to feel fulfilled.

The entire notion is quite silly, to be honest.

But who gives to the giver? Who fills my cup when it's empty? A dear friend asked me this after I had spent some time discussing a past relationship with her. The answer she gave me was just that, "Who gives to the giver?" Not realizing the true impact of her words, they left an everlasting imprint—a permanent acknowledgment that I shouldn't always be so eager to give without getting something in return. She told me how it wasn't selfish of me to expect this. However, I always assumed that "give and take" relationships were things of myths and legends. Giving love without receiving it in return was like serving other people food and claiming that you're fed. It made no sense. And for years, I was complacent with that in my life. I was starving and didn't even care. I was conditioned to believe that giving to someone was far better than anything I could ever receive in return. I lied to myself that I didn't need anything—that I could do without it all. However, I couldn't face the harsh reality that no one gave me anything in return because I had spent years of my life choosing to give to the wrong people. I couldn't bear the thought of not being worthy of anyone's reciprocation; therefore, I never expected or demanded it. But my worthiness was never the reason why I went without receiving anything in return. What I didn't receive was never about me; it was about the giver.

Give and take relationships, like I said, had always felt unrealistic. I had a hard time believing in their existence, to be honest. As a result, it left me open to continual depletion. But how do you break a cycle that you spent years convincing yourself that it was the safest place to be? That it was normal? That to expect anything different was foolish? Well, for starters, you have to tell yourself (and actually believe) that you deserve better and to never (EVER) settle for anything less than that.

But I get it. Demanding things is hard. And having to demand anything taints the whole experience. It ruins the beauty of receiving anything in the first place.

So, if your hand is in, put your hand out.
(And shake it all about.)

Sorry, I had to, lol.

Love, Me.

The Masquerade

March - April 2013

My phone rang just as I stepped out of the shower. Wrapping a towel around myself, I quickly dried myself off as best as possible before answering. It was Noah.

"Hey," I answered, dripping water all over the phone. "What's up?"

"Are you busy?" he asked.

Yes, I was busy, but I didn't tell him that. "No, why? What do you need?" I looked at the face mask I was about to put on and the new shade of nail polish I was desperate to try on my toes.

"I'm at Ella's diner. Want to meet me for brunch? I know you can't resist a good waffle," he laughed, but we both knew it was true.

"You're there now?" I asked, looking at myself in the mirror. "OK." I caved. "Give me a few minutes; I just got out of the shower." After we hung up, I quickly dried my hair, threw on some clothes, and out the door I went—straight to Noah and that waffle.

Heading to the diner, I realized the thought never occurred to me that something could be wrong. It was rather a spontaneous request, considering Noah could have easily met me at my place. However, with both hands gripped around my steering wheel, I contemplated the possibility further until I reached the diner and that answer.

"Hey." I waved as soon as I saw Noah seated, waiting. At first glance, he looked fine. There appeared to be no signs of distress on his face, so the impromptu request still remained a mystery. "What's going on?" I asked as soon as I sat down.

He took a deep breath, shifting his weight from side to side, causing the cushions below him to squeak. But just as he opened his mouth to speak, the waitress interrupted him by bringing our drinks.

"I ordered us coffee. Is that OK?" He looked at me.

"Of course." I smiled.

After the waitress took our orders, I turned my attention to Noah. "Out with it," I said. "I know you didn't drag me here because of the waffles."

He ran his hand down the length of his unshaven face before it reached the base of his neck, where it remained like a makeshift support for his head. His face filled with a pleading expression, and I knew what was to come wasn't going to be good.

"So, tomorrow night is the grand opening of the 315 Eatery," he said as if I didn't know. I had skipped the soft opening on account of not wanting to run into Dan. I didn't want to be forced into having one of those awkward conversations where we both asked each other how we were in the polite attempt at "catching up" while we both wished to be anywhere else.

"Well, I know we planned on going together, but I was hoping we could *really* go together. I think I may need for you to pull out your friend card for me," he said.

I peered across the table at him. "Pulling friend cards now, eh? This must be big. What do you need exactly?"

"I need for you to be my date," he confessed.

"What?" I almost choked on my coffee.

"Well, *pretend* date," he corrected.

I laughed. "What the hell do you want me to do that for?"

"Courtney. She posted on Facebook that she plans on going to the opening, and you know how we promised Leigha we'd be there…" His voice trailed off as though I should have already known where it was headed.

"You still follow her?" I shook my head at that nonsense.

"I know. I know. I'm stupid for it. I get it. Nevertheless, she will be there," he said.

"And why do you care that she will be there? It's been how long since you two broke up?" I tried knocking some sense into him.

"Does it matter? The fact is, she plans on being there with the same guy she cheated on me with. You know they are still together, right?" He looked at me like I should have already known that, too.

"Let me guess; you want me to make her jealous? Noah, you know that plan never works."

"We have to try at least. I'm desperate. Please?" he pleaded. "I have been successful at avoiding her at all costs, but tomorrow night won't be so easy."

My heart started palpitating. I was nervous. The entire idea reeked of failure.

"So?" His eyes widened in anticipation.

"Ugh," I groaned, knowing there was no way out of it. "Doesn't she know who I am? She knows we are just friends."

"Friends become more all the time. How could it *not* work?" He reached across the table, taking my hand into his. Only this time, he left it there and didn't pull back.

A chilly March began as an unseasonably warm April followed in its footsteps. There wasn't much snow left on the ground, but since it was New York, there was no telling whether winter was officially gone for good or if spring was still a distant thought. Syracuse, known for its brutal winters, might have to sneak in one final snowstorm before ending the season. However, something in my bones told me that winter played its last card and that spring was just around the corner. It already smelled like a new beginning.

    Regardless of my new ability to occupy myself with solo activities, I still couldn't escape the negative feelings that camped out in the far corners of my heart which desperately sought companionship. I knew those feelings existed. They were hard to ignore. You see, I love *love* too much to become cynical by all the turmoil it has caused in my life thus far. However, even calling it turmoil felt rather harsh. Yes, love had let me down, but it had also lifted me up. It came and delivered what I needed, but it moved on when it knew it wasn't meant to stay. Maybe that's why it hurts so much sometimes? That when someone we love wrongs us or leaves us without us being ready for their departure, we don't see the positive behind it. We don't see that those wrongdoings and departures were just the universe's way of moving something better in its place. But I get it; when we are right in the eye of a love storm, it's hard to see the rainbow waiting on the other side.

With my twenty-eighth birthday lurking around the corner, it bothered me that my thirtieth wasn't that far behind. Staring down the age barrel at the big 3-0 was unsettling. When would I finally reach that turning point in my life when everything started falling into place? As empowering as any Beyoncé song could be, it still left an empty space that revealed itself when I was at my most vulnerable.

For me, the idea of turning twenty-eight felt bittersweet. I always imagined something different for myself at this age. But with all these constant starts and stops, I felt closer to sputtering off to the side of the road until I found someone worthy enough to restart the ignition.

But life never works out the way we plan. That white picket-fenced dream we have all dreamt of at one point in our lives doesn't always translate into reality, nor is that dream desirable for everyone. *Maybe life had a different plan for me?* I had no desire to accept the grueling fact that I was approaching that pivotal stage in my life where I was supposed to have my shit together. It's the stage where we're supposed to be established and settled (the good kind of settled). Instead, I was about an hour away from pretending like I *had* settled down. However, if I were to have looked at things from a different perspective, would I have really wanted to be engaged or married to any of the guys I had dated thus far? No, I wouldn't. That in and of itself was a blessing—so, Happy Early Birthday to me. But enough of this whining; I had a pretend date to get ready for.

The grand opening started uneventfully. We arrived before our reservation time just to increase our chances of "accidentally" running into Courtney so that Noah could show off his new "girlfriend." So, it became nothing more than an hour of me standing around, nursing several drinks while pretending to be on a date with my fake boyfriend. *Stellar.*

When the hostess finally let us know that our table was ready, Noah took me by the hand and led me through the restaurant as if there was a chance I'd get lost. His behavior was odd until I looked behind me and saw Courtney seated at a nearby table. I couldn't let my eyes linger too long in her direction in fear that she would end up catching me or I'd end up tripping over something, so I turned my attention back to Noah. Thankfully, he slowed his pace when we arrived at our table in the back corner of the room with a direct view of the bar. As Noah pulled out my chair for me, I quickly glanced back in Courtney's direction, who was already getting up to leave. *Seriously?*

Noah's penetrating gaze met mine after I ordered us a bottle of wine because I was desperate to rid myself of the residual awkwardness leftover from our fake date. It wasn't hard to tell that he had a lot on his mind, which would probably take me the rest of the evening to find a middle ground on whatever he was feeling. For one, I knew his plan didn't play out the way he previously envisioned. He imagined some triumph. Some form of regret or jealousy on her part, but there wasn't a reaction of any kind. The only silver lining was that she was gone and that we could get back to just being ourselves.

"Now that we can finally take our fake date masks off," I teased, reaching for my freshly poured glass of wine, "how is my *friend*.' I emphasized the word "friend."

"Fine. Not that anything made a damn bit of difference," Noah huffed as we placed our entrée orders with the waitress.

"What difference were you planning on making?" I asked.

"She acted like she didn't give a care in the world." He slumped in defeat.

"You don't know that, Noah," I said. "For all we know, she might be seething inside, which was why she left as quickly as she did—"

"Or they were already done eating," he cut in as our food arrived.

"Who knows, maybe she will go home and post some cryptic message on social media that no one will understand but is totally meant for you." I smiled. "Just give it time, but honestly, who cares what she thinks or feels? She was the one who hurt you. She doesn't deserve to feel any sort of way, nor should you be feeling any sort of way about her either."

"That may be true, but you said yourself that it was a dumb idea from the start. I just wanted her to see that I was fine—that I'm better off without her," he sighed.

"And you are," I slipped in.

"Our damn masquerade wouldn't have fooled anyone," he chuckled, referring to my previous mask comment. "You were right, though; we are too much of friends to be anything more." He looked at me.

My eyes widened with his sudden bluntness. "You know what? You're exactly right. It *is* a masquerade—and it's best to leave it at that," I said. "She was wrong for what she did, but that doesn't mean it translates into you having anything to prove to her. You were always the better person—then and now. It's time to move on."

"You're right." He nodded. "I should just leave the past in the past where it belongs," he said just as our waitress collected our dinner plates. "Want to split something?" He asked as she handed us the dessert menu.

"Sure. You pick."

While Noah was browsing the menu, I noticed a group of guys congregating near the bar. At first glance, I didn't recognize any of them until one of them turned around. It was Sean Miller, a guy Noah and I went to college with, looking the same as ever as though he had just walked out of an American Eagle photoshoot with his navy-blue sweater and bootcut jeans. Next to him, to my surprise, was another guy we went to college with: Ben Healey. The two of them never struck me as ever running in the same crowds as each other, but then again, a lot can change after college.

Next to Sean, Ben's style was a true throwback to the 90's grunge era, which he modernized with a hipster twist wearing tight-fitted jeans and a plain white t-shirt. The two couldn't have been any more opposite, yet there they were, joined together at the hip in some in-depth conversation where they randomly toasted glasses and laughed amongst the group.

When our dessert arrived, my attention shifted from the guys to the molten lava cake dripping in a raspberry sauce that Noah had selected. As we began devouring it bite by bite, I kept a subtle, ninja-like eye on the group until I accidentally caught Sean's attention which left me with no choice but to awkwardly wave in his direction.

"Is that Sean Miller from college?" Noah turned in the direction I was waving.

"Yep." But before I could say anything more, Sean made his way over to our table.

"Hey! I thought I recognized you both when we walked in," he said while leaning in to get a hug from me before extending his hand to Noah next. Although a nice gesture, the hug felt oddly misplaced, considering he and I never had much of a relationship outside of our occasional run-ins at parties. The most we ever shared between us was maybe a class or a drink. "You look great." He directed his comment towards me. "I hope I didn't interrupt anything here, but I had to stop over." He looked to both Noah and me.

"Not at all." I smiled. "We are here just supporting our friend, Leigha. She's one of the head chefs."

"That's cool," he said. "Well, tell your friend the food was awesome."

After a few more minutes of casually catching up, exchanging our thoughts on the food, and me having to clarify that Noah and I were not on a date, Sean made his way back over to his friends just as Ben glanced over his shoulder to see where Sean ran off to. Sean quickly pointed in my direction as though answering a question that wasn't asked but implied. Ben nodded and waved in return. And for some strange reason, as I waved back, a feeling hit the pit of my stomach, unlike anything I had ever felt before. It was in that moment—as casual and insignificant as it may have seemed on the surface—I knew something within me ignited.

Blog Post #8

What Lies Beneath

When I think back on all of the guys I've dated, I can't help but wonder how many of them I had romanticized beyond their reality? You know, by making them or the relationship out to be far better in my head than what they were in real life.

I once made the drunken effects of infatuation seduce my heart in such a way that sobering up felt painful. I couldn't allow myself the clarity I deserved nor the wisdom that came from achieving it.

I think infatuation stems from falling in love with the idea of someone or something and then convincing ourselves that it is, undeniably, love.

Because in the end, did I really love any of them? Or did I just make myself believe that I did?

Love, Me.

Playground Rules and Other Metaphors

March 2013

I carried on with my self-discovery period and learned how imperative it was to be comfortable in my own skin. I knew the importance of loving myself first before loving someone else. Because you can't begin to love someone the right way if the love you have for your own heart is broken—it's like putting on someone else's air mask on the plane while you are gasping for air. It was also my way to figure out what I wanted—or didn't want—out of relationships in the future. By taking a step back and analyzing where I was in my life, it became easier to separate the needs from the wants. Yes, it was still a learning curve, but I knew that if I didn't nail it down before getting into another relationship, those lines have a tendency of blurring.

I also knew that I was inclined to compromise the needs with the wants when the high of the honeymoon phase clouded my judgment. I didn't want to fall into bad habits by compromising anything before fully comprehending *what* I was compromising. I didn't want or need that to continue in my life.

Coming off my fake date with Noah, it had me thinking: Do we all play games? And is dating perhaps all "fun and games" until someone ends up hurt? It was a constant chase—a cat versus mouse game where we all go into it assuming that we *are* the cat. But as I began my descension into the dating pool, I quickly realized that the rules of dating had evolved in their complexity, making them harder to decipher than ever before.

I was starting to feel lost. Guys slowly became this entirely new species, unexplored or studied beyond the "Men Are from Mars, Woman Are from Venus" garbage. The constant games of playing hard to get by not showing your entire hand—only the right number of cards to keep control and your opponent guessing. It's a game designed to maintain interest by keeping the mystery alive because, apparently, it's considered alluring. It's nuts. And as Leigha has continued to preach from the very beginning of our dating woes: Men love the chase. If she knew anything about "the code" that we have been so desperate to crack, it was that men are natural hunters—and oh, how they loved the challenge.

So, fast forward two weeks after the grand opening:

I was sitting on my couch binge-watching some show when my phone started vibrating beside me. When I looked down, I noticed that I had received a message via social media. It was from Ben. *What could he possibly be messaging me about?* I thought as I rushed to unlock my phone. I knew once I opened the message, he'd know. I needed to chill out. *Relax, Rachel. You don't want to appear too eager.* Pathetic as it was to wait a lousy two minutes to portray some illusion of mystery on my end, I knew I had to. I had to follow the "rules." *Right?*

Hey. How did you like the grand opening?

Bait and catch. I knew it. He knew it. As soon as he cast his line, I took that worm without a second to consider what would happen once he reeled me in. Why I was so anxious with Ben right out the gate will forever remain a mystery to me, but something about him just lit this fire within me. And that said a lot considering we had never actually spoken two words to each other before. Even in college, we were always far removed from one another in some capacity. Yet, I always felt like there was something about him…

To be truly transparent here, our conversation via messaging was, well, boring. There was no substance or flirting—just words sent back and forth like a dull game of tennis. Still, we played—and I enjoyed every second of that match. I loved watching that little bubble appear on my screen, letting me know when he was typing back his reply. And when he asked me out to dinner the following weekend, I just about fell over. Trying not to seem too eager (*Yet, again*), I waited another lousy two minutes before responding. It wasn't that I was anxious to jump back into the dating pool so quickly after Dan; it was more because I wanted to take a swim with Ben. And for the sake of continuing with this cheesy metaphor, I prayed I wouldn't drown.

Let's be real: My date with Ben was nothing spectacular. Dinner was primarily split between me trying to get my nerves under control and him trying to play catch-up with both of our lives since college.

The restaurant he suggested had a casual vibe. Initials, hearts, and the "so and so were here" graffiti were carved into the tables, while the centerpieces were nothing more than the dessert and alcohol specials behaving like small paper teepees over the salt and pepper shakers, camping underneath. Known for its famous barbeque menu, I had no problem ordering my go-to ribs, knowing there was a good chance of me making a damn mess out of myself. But for some reason, I didn't care.

Ben was dressed similarly to when I saw him at the 315 Eatery. He wore a vintage concert t-shirt of some band I had never heard of, while his wallet was tethered to a chain running from his belt loop straight into his pocket. His image suggested that he held on tightly to the age of rock 'n roll, refusing to let it die. And having just learned he was now a lawyer, I laughed, thinking that he was more of a rebel *with* a cause than without.

Catching up with Ben wasn't exactly "catching up" to me. In reality, I was getting to know him because what I did know was only from a peripheral capacity. He told me he was now an attorney specializing in family cases and an aspiring artist by night. He loved to paint.

"I always wanted to pursue art and actually do something with it. But the odds of making it in any creative field is tough," he said, reaching for the menu.

"Tell me about it. When we were kids, I wish they didn't fill our heads with those ideas that we could be whatever we wanted to be. Maybe then we wouldn't grow up feeling so disappointed when we learned that it wasn't true," I replied.

"What did you want to be?" he asked just as our appetizers reached the table.

"A writer. I was convinced that one day I would write the next Great American Novel." I blushed at the absurdity of how it must have sounded. "But I'm stuck writing for a local magazine instead."

"Yeah, but who says you can't write a novel on the side?" He reached for one of the sliders we ordered.

"And who says you can't paint the next masterpiece?" I smirked as I stared into Ben's soulful brown eyes that contrasted against his porcelain-skin complexion. Like Dan's, his hair was longer than most guys I've dated. The only difference was that his hair wasn't messy. It was perfectly styled and tucked behind his ears like a rouge lawyer out to break all the rules.

Smiling became a filler throughout dinner when there was no food or words to fill the quiet spaces suspended between us like a balloon I desperately wanted to pop. One dinner wasn't enough to even begin to scratch the surface of getting to know each other. It appeared we shared many similarities, but it was in those tiny revelations that we learned of the things we didn't have in common, which we quickly cast aside like our finished dinner plates. We paid them no mind. But getting to know Ben was exciting. And I was hooked on every detail he felt compelled to share—hooked, line, and sinker. *Reel me in, Ben. Reel me in.*

If I could have bottled up my emotions from that night, I would have had enough bursts of happiness at my disposal to last close to a lifetime (or, at least, that's how it felt). I just enjoyed being in his presence. I wanted to be near him, which made me hate the table that came between us. What can I say? The heart wants what the heart wants—even when it makes absolutely no sense.

"We all play games," Leigh said later that night when I got home. She, Jessie, and I decided to do a group video chat to catch up. I had just filled them in on my date with Ben and spent the past few minutes obsessing over every tiny detail in hopes that I played my cards right—that I followed all the dating rules. Unlike Dan, who merely showed up in my life and left just as quickly, Ben sort of exploded into it. Because of this, I was hoping that his entrance was no indication of his exit. Either way, my heart and gut both knew that something about him was about to shake up my world.

"Call me old-fashioned," I said, "but I'm not going to wait around for some guy to tap me on the shoulder and say, 'You're it!' for me to chase after him. This isn't a game of playground tag. This is life."

"Isn't it, though?" Jessie chimed in. "It may be life, babe, but it's still a playground. I mean, Leigha isn't wrong. Men love the chase. It feeds right into their biological need to hunt or something."

"For sure." Leigha raised her hands in praise. "It's all about tagging the right partner or worthy opponent. Where's the fun if you're too easy to catch? Game over. Boring. And this goes both ways—in case you were wondering."

"Unless you go back to the theory that you attract exactly what you project. Then you may just be trying to tag the wrong person altogether," I replied.

"That's deep." Jessie reached past her screen and poured herself a glass of wine as Leigha and I followed suit.

"It makes sense." Leigha took a sip of her wine, which I had the sneaking suspicion was the same kind that both Jessie and I were sipping on too. "As we learn more about ourselves, we gravitate towards men who exemplify those discoveries. I remember this one time, I dated a guy who was into craft beer, and before I knew it, he was trying to get me to buy into his microbrewery idea."

"That he was planning on opening in his parent's basement, right?" I laughed.

"Exactly!" she exclaimed. "Just think about it: How many times have we settled for guys when we knew we could do better? We allowed them to 'catch' or 'tag' us when they weren't worthy of playing the game with us in the first place." She set her glass down.

"So true. At my new job, I work with a girl who is gorgeous, funny, and smart. We went out for drinks the other night, and I couldn't believe how many schmucks this girl attracted. It made no sense. Come to find out, the way this girl thought of herself was being personified in the men chasing after her," Jessie said.

"Well, I don't know enough about Ben to size him up just yet. All I can say is that I was instantly intrigued the moment I saw him. I can't explain, so don't ask," I laughed.

"Love at first sight?" Leigha tried hard not to roll her eyes. "You know that's garbage, right?"

I rolled my eyes instead. "I'm not saying that it was love at first sight, but I certainly felt *something*."

"He's either a lesson or a blessing, and only time will tell in the end," Jessie piped up.

"And sometimes they can be both," Leigha added.

Later that night, I couldn't get our conversation out of my head. I thought back on how many games there were on this supposed playground. How many rules? And were they worth following, or better off broken?

Blog Post #9

The Playground Theorem

I have zero qualms in admitting that dating sucks (*Well, sometimes*). It's a cutthroat, brutal sport, and I believe it's more of a battleground than a playground. You have to fight to the death out there. And if you are a bit rusty like I am, you will learn that everything you thought you knew about dating had already expired. Because someone somewhere has already created a faster and more efficient way to either speed up the process or complicate it even more.

I headed into this "battle," believing that I wouldn't have any problems—that it would be easy as it had always been for me. Armed with only weapons acquired from my dating past, I quickly realized that I would soon be waving my little white flag and surrendering. I had no idea how unprepared I was.

Coming down from the high of my latest (and first) date with—well, let's call him **B**—I spent countless hours agonizing over every detail. *Did I say and/or do all the right things? Did I look my best? Did I laugh at all his jokes?* Etc. As if any of those details would indicate our pending relationship's success. I was so caught up in this obsessiveness that I would have gone so far as wishing on a shooting star just for added luck—that's how much I was already feeling for this guy.

It's strange—I get it. It makes no sense—I get that, too. Being that I had just met him, these feelings were rather intense. But sometimes, your heart feels things that your mind simply can't comprehend— like a magnetic pull that even the laws of science can't explain. So, I knew trying to explain this to anyone would be a challenge. All I knew about **B** was that he was different from anyone I had ever been interested in before. I knew that whatever *this* was between us was going to be different, too. And even though I wanted to make sure that I fully understood all the supposed "rules" of dating, I still knew, given how I was feeling, that I was bound to break every last one.

Having been asked out on a date via social media, I couldn't help but reminisce the many ways he would have asked me out in the past. Technological advances have completely altered the way we date and communicate with one another, making social media just another way to reach out to people without ever having to ask for their phone numbers to do it.

Nowadays, it's no longer about waiting for a phone call or text message either. It's waiting for a message from any one of the numerous social media platforms or from some app designed to delete whatever the person had sent you within fifteen seconds of you opening it. There are now hundreds of different communication portals that you have to sift through to check whether or not the object of your affection has contacted you, which just translates into hundreds of more ways you might also be rejected. *Oh, the humanity!*

But I digress...

I had a conversation with my girlfriends the other night when a dating epiphany struck me. It was as though that proverbial light bulb went off in my head, shining a light upon this theory that I knew I had to share with you (whoever YOU are). Whether there is any merit to what I'm saying here is too soon to tell, but still, share it I must.

Like any form of inspiration that has hit me in the past, I played with it; I slept on it; I ate with it and lived with it. I practically formed a relationship with it until it became somewhat of a constant companion. This tiny seedling of an idea bloomed into one of the most basic dating and relationship behavior concepts. Who knew that everything we learned as children out on the playground could be so relatable into adulthood? No wonder dating wasn't fun or even made sense anymore. I had checked out of the playground life years ago and had no idea. Every mistake and every bump in the road could have been easily understood or possibly avoided by what I would now like to call "The Playground Theorem."

And here is the first example.

The first part of this theory that I will be addressing is **The Chase.** The original idea of the chase from days passed has now translated into a whole new meaning in the dating world, altering the way people in relationships behave. The rules feel like nothing more than some makeshift game—a game that, for some of us, we have no desire to play—or, at least, by the rules.

Part One: Tagging the Right Partner

Throughout our lives, we change; we evolve. And it's during those times that the pieces of our internal puzzle start to align, creating a clearer picture of the person we are destined to become. This is called growth. It's part of our self-discovery. But have you ever noticed that during those times of growth and discovery that you may have attracted exactly what you projected? As in, the parts of you still healing were being mirrored back to you in that of another? Let me give you an example:

For most of my early adult years, I was clueless about who I was (still am, sometimes). It took me a while, but I soon realized that much of my life was consumed by titles. I was always someone's friend, daughter, lover, girlfriend, co-worker, acquaintance; someone's *something*—that I never gave myself the time or grace to be my own *whatever*.

After leaving my ex, **M**, it catapulted me into this journey of self-exploration. It was as though I was making up for lost time by locating all those missing pieces of myself that spent years collecting dust in a figurative box somewhere. While he and I were together, I noticed that as I began to grow, it caused us to grow further apart. They always say that growth is continual and that it's important to also grow with your partner to prevent the divide, but with **M**, he didn't care enough about us or the relationship to ensure that the divide wouldn't happen. He didn't support me in any way nor wanted anything to do with the person I was maturing into. It was always about control, and the woman I was becoming, was harder *to* control.

I discovered throughout that growth period that my wants and needs were no longer the same, nor did any of them match up to what he could (or wanted) to provide. So, I had a choice: Settle for what I didn't deserve or reach for something better.

As I discovered more of myself, I gravitated towards men who exemplified each discovery. In hindsight, I see how it was utterly exhausting and unfulfilling. I decided, in some cases, to settle before I had the chance to realize my true worth. I did that with **M**, and I found myself having done that to some degree with **D**, which made me made me worried about **B**. I was never in the right state of mind (or heart) to fully develop into the person I was destined to become when I allowed myself to be limited by the people I let into my life—and that went with friendships as well. I ultimately allowed guys to "catch me" who were not even worthy enough to "tag me" in the first place (I stole that from a friend). So, I couldn't help but ask myself: *Am I doing that now?*

You see, we rise to the challenge of finding a desirable mate when we feel desirable as well. We can't expect to attract what we deserve if we aren't putting it out into the universe that we are worthy of receiving it. Why do you think it's important to set standards for ourselves? Know your worth, and the right guy (or girl) will chase after you. Most importantly. If you find yourself trying to convince your worth to someone, save yourself the heartache and tag someone else. Trust me.
I just never knew I'd end up eating those words.

Love, Me.

The Three Day Rule 📅

April 2013

For the past few days, I began adjusting myself to a routine of coming home, staring at my phone, and then falling asleep to zero messages from Ben. *What gives?*

In my free time, I organized and then re-organized my bookshelves more times than I cared to admit. Not to mention, I did whatever else it took to distract myself—like washing the dishes and tackling my dirty laundry pile—because I couldn't stop thinking about Ben. Since our date, I hadn't heard from him, and I didn't understand why.

Sure, I could have focused on my blog more, but it wasn't like I needed to post something every day, nor would I have the content to support it. So, I chose to investigate instead. I wanted to see what Ben had been up to since I hadn't heard from him by doing what any normal person would do: I searched through his social media for clues. Why wouldn't I? It's the one place where people openly advertise their lives, and I was hoping for some insight. It was the closest thing to an answer, if any. And I was desperate for an answer. DESPERATE.

Don't roll your eyes while reading this. You know you've done it as well. And why not? Most people decorate their social media pages with pictures and status updates about what they are up to, and of course, who they are doing those things with as well. Years ago, you would have never known what someone was doing unless you asked them directly. Or, to further age myself, look at someone's away message on AIM (I'm laughing at this). But because we live in an era that allows sharing to happen instantaneously, some people fall into the trap of oversharing. And aren't we over here just eating it all up? Given all that, how could we ever expect a certain level of privacy from others when we can't even give it to ourselves?

But we buy into it, don't we? We are so heavily involved in each other's lives like it's a modern-day soap opera. We are all voyeurs and proud of it. And there I was, being a voyeur. I was peeking into the window of Ben's life to see if I could figure out why he went MIA.

"I kind of stalked Ben's social media," I confessed to Leigha later that day. "I know how it sounds, but I haven't heard from him since our date, and I didn't know what else to do…"

"Why would you do that?" Leigha asked while munching on something she was cooking.

"Because he hasn't texted or called!" I said as though my reasoning should have been obvious. "Don't guys normally wait a few days before reaching out or something?" I wavered on the possibility. "It just feels like it's taking him longer than it should. Maybe he doesn't want to appear too desperate?"

"Girl, that's stupid," Leigha replied. "Are you referring to the 'three-day rule' garbage? That's just some dumb concept designed by people who needed something to make themselves feel better when the guy—or girl—didn't call them back right away."

"Huh, so…"

"Listen, that rule is nothing more than a window designed by some indecisive guy so that he can bide his time until he figures out what he wants. But seriously, if he needs three days to figure it out, move on," she said.

"Well, that's reassuring," I groaned.

"From experience, if a guy is into you, he's not going to wait three days to lock up that next date. He's going to ask you well before the first date ends."

"Thanks for that. You are making me feel so good right now."

"Let it go. If he's interested, you will know—no games."

I hesitated for a moment before revealing to Leigha that while browsing through Ben's social media, it appeared that he had just recently gotten out of a relationship. And after what happened with Dan, I really wasn't down for a sequel. It made me slightly worried about what that could mean for Ben and me. It was best not to think about it either way. And after talking with Leigha, it was growing more apparent that Ben's explosive entrance gave way to an almost ghost-like departure. *Easy come, easy go.* The fire extinguished as quickly as it was ignited.

After about a week, I just about gave up. I held onto the hope that something happened to prevent him from contacting me, which subsequently extended that three-day rule due to circumstances beyond his control. Like he was helping an elderly woman cross the street and dropped his phone in the process, where it smashed into pieces after an oncoming car ran it over. *That sounds possible, right?*

Who am I kidding? There is no elderly woman—definitely no broken phone. Besides, how many of us have cracked our screens and immediately got them fixed? *Exactly.*

I just didn't understand why everything with Ben felt different. I know I keep saying that everything was *different*, but everything felt that way. I found myself in uncharted waters, and I had no idea if I was heading upstream or down. I was so desperate for some form of communication that I considered reaching out to him myself. Who gives a shit about the three-day rule? Whoever said that our destinies were tied to the actions of another person—and their actions alone? The power shouldn't only be in his hands. Didn't I deserve to have some as well? Therefore, I decided to reach out. What was the worst it would do? Speed up my rejection? Either way, It was time to take action into my own hands.

Blog Post #10

The Playground Theorem
Part Two: Just Let it Slide

Let's talk about social media and our behavior around it. It's easy to pinpoint it as the reason why perception has become one of the most crippling factors in our lives. We all want a perfect life—the perfect house, the perfect job, the perfect look, and of course, the perfect relationship. We create these images of ourselves in our minds and then try projecting them onto the world, showcasing what we so desperately want to believe ourselves. Now,

I'm not saying everyone does this per se, but come on, we all love to advertise a good highlight reel of our lives—do we not?

A friend once told me that no one posts a bad picture. Someone could be downright miserable, but they will still fake a smile for the camera. Why? Because no one wants the world to know that they are unhappy about, well, anything. That little piece of advice has stayed with me for quite some time, and I always refer to it whenever I find myself giving in to that weakness of comparing my life to others. You see, it's down to perception. Perception has altered our realities because we have allowed ourselves to buy into it. When someone posts a picture, we don't stop and consider that it took twenty shots to get it right or fourteen filters to get them looking as flawless as they do. Not to mention, that smiling couple we are envious of may have just had a huge fight before the picture was taken. The point is, you don't know what goes on behind the camera, aka closed doors.

As a disclaimer to this post, I realize that this example doesn't necessarily apply to every single person or situation out there. Still, for most of us—the ones that this example is supposed to reach—it will help make navigating through all the smoke and mirrors a lot easier.

Let's begin...

On one level or another, we strive to be on the same "status update" as everyone else. We have perpetuated the assumption that in order to be happy with our lives, we must mirror the lives of others. This is entirely false. Social media has helped create this unspoken competition between us, making us feel, at times, inadequate with ourselves if we are not reaching the same milestones as everyone else. But here's the thing: We cannot compare. We can't measure the quality of our lives based on the quality we perceive in others. What I may want is not always the same thing that someone else may want (and vice versa)—even if it's perceived that way. **You have to let it slide.** You have to be content with yourself and your life because one thing is for sure: No one has a perfect life (no matter how hard they try selling you on it). You can seemingly have it all but nothing at the same time (*You get what I'm saying?*). And if we constantly compare, we will never be satisfied.

For instance, Michelle just saw on Facebook that Megan recently got engaged. Michelle is upset because she has been with her boyfriend longer than Megan had been with hers. Shouldn't she be the one engaged? Why Megan? Why not her? It seemed so unfair…

But did Michelle ever stop to consider her own relationship? As in, does she even love her boyfriend enough to spend the rest of her life with him? Sure, they have been together for a decent amount of time, but did that mean marriage was in the cards? So, regardless of whether he is "the one" or not, she expects him to act and deliver precisely what "the one" would do. Why? Because she *wants* to be engaged. She *expects* to be engaged. She wants the proposal, the ring, and the fairytale wedding. But did she ever stop and think about *who* she wants those things with? No. She wants to rush up the ladder and slide down the slide into the next milestone, just like everyone else.

A piece of advice (if I haven't given enough of it already) is that getting the same things or accomplishing the same things in life as everyone else does not equate to happiness or fulfillment. Not all slides are created equal (if you catch my drift). And if you think you will receive the same experience or outcome as everyone else, you are sadly mistaken. We need to remember to work at our life's pace, and the universe will deliver precisely what we need, exactly when we need it. So, who cares if you are stuck at the bottom of the ladder for a bit? I promise, one day, you will get your turn. Be patient.

Love, Me.

Action had to be taken. I couldn't expect Ben to make a move if I had no confidence he'd even make one. If Ben didn't respond to me or declined to get together again, at least I would know. Then, I could move on.

Being the first to reach out was completely out of my element, but I had to know something, so I was willing to try something new. I couldn't just wait around in limbo, not knowing what was going on.

After I texted him, I instantly regretted it. I felt like I had cheated on a diet, telling myself, *Ok, just one bite. It won't hurt.* And what did I do? I ate the whole damn pie. I didn't know how to recover from what I felt was a desperate attempt to reach out to him, and I knew whatever lame excuse I would come up with to justify it would make it sound that much worse.

But somehow, ten minutes later, he invited me to a new art exhibit downtown.

I could have cared less about the artwork, as beautiful and compelling as they were, because I was more interested in paying attention to Ben instead. I probably would have agreed to go garbage picking with him if I knew it would have allowed me to spend time with him.

We walked through hallway after hallway, admiring one painting after another, as he gave me his interpretations while asking for mine. We shared similar opinions on a few, but I soon began growing restless after examining what felt like the hundredth painting. Side by side, we made our way further into the gallery as I positioned my hand in every imaginable way in hopes that he would have reached for it—whether in excitement over a painting or for no other reason than him wanting to hold it. But he didn't. Instead, it hung loosely by my side like a dead fish.

When we reached the end of the exhibit, we headed to a nearby bar and grill for a bite to eat. Just like before, we spent the majority of the meal talking about our pasts that neither one of us was a part of, but it was all we had to share. The ease of our conversation gave the illusion that he and I had been dating for a while. And I couldn't help but wonder if he felt it, too. And when he kissed me as he dropped me off at my apartment that night, I was so head-over-freaking-heels-excited. I was ready to scream into my pillow like some lovestruck teenager just before spending the rest of the night scribbling his name all over my notebook. (Just to be clear, I didn't do either of those things.)

I felt like I was on cloud nine—whatever that means. Thanks to the butterflies fluttering around like crazy in my stomach, making it feel as though I could take flight at any moment. That was until my phone went off and as I got ready for bed. It was Ben. And this is what he said:

Thanks for a great night, but I have to be honest with you…

I'm not looking for anything serious right now.

What in the actual fuck? How do I respond to that? What did that even mean? It was like a punch to the gut, causing all those damn butterflies to cease fluttering. I couldn't wrap my head around why he would have said that to me. Yeah, I get that he probably wanted to be upfront (*How thoughtful*), or at least establish a basis on what we were or what we weren't (*I guess I should have been careful with what I wished for. Thanks, Dan*). Still, all I could think about was how or why he would prematurely define us when he never gave the "us" a chance.

So, what's a girl to do? The smart thing would have been to take all the lessons I've learned and apply them. Call it quits on this Ben Healey operation and walk away. But the heart wants what the heart wants. And I knew in that moment mine wanted something it shouldn't.

Three days later, I somehow found myself with him. Again.

What Goes Up, Must Come Down

May 2013

The morning sun peeked through his bedroom blinds, decorating Ben's face like glitter. I rolled over and watched as he slowly opened his eyes due to the penetrating brightness. His soft, cottony sheets smelled deliciously of him. He smelled like a thousand unread books I desperately wanted to read. I inhaled the fibers deeply, never wanting to forget how they smelled or how they felt against my bare skin. There was something about being inside the four walls of his bedroom that made me feel at home. It was as though I was meant to be there—even if I didn't know the reason why.

His eyes closed again as mine scanned his entire room. Ben kept a clean house, but it was far from meticulous. Everything was organized but in a way that only made sense to him. He thrived in chaos that only a creative mind could understand—a mind like mine.

For example, the assortment of books and movies that he had neatly arranged on his living room shelves were in no particular order. I always believed that you could tell a lot about someone by the types of books they read, and he had a mixture of everything from law books to fantasy novels. He, too, was all things to me—a depth that was easily reached since we both allowed ourselves to go there. But he was still a mystery. And I absolutely loved, as I laid there beside him, to have the opportunity to explore that. He was much more than the old movie posters hung upon his bedroom walls or his artwork that he had showcased in each of the rooms. Nor was he the souvenirs he had collected from vacations past or the candles that remained unlit and stationed for aesthetics.

 His fingers entwined with mine as he gently pulled me closer. After the past few days, we found ourselves in a place we hadn't expected. It was the beginning of something that neither one of us knew how to define. Even after he said he wanted nothing serious, his actions began to backpedal as his words began to sing a different tune. *And oh, how I wanted to listen to that song on constant replay.* The connection forming between us was so intense and palpable that I wondered if others felt it, too. Since our first date, my heart ignited with feelings so foreign to me that I had no idea what I was actually feeling. I was in the throes of it all. But it was only at that moment, lying in his bed, that I leaned over and realized what those feelings were. They were *love*.

I get it. Don't roll your eyes at this page. I'm being honest here. I understand love is a strong word to use and possibly not even the correct one. *Passion? Lust? Infatuation?* Maybe. So, again, I get it. I tried to deny the feeling's existence in fear that I would succumb to its effects, or worse, scare the hell out of him. But after spending as much time as we were together, I found myself on this exciting yet terrifying adventure. Knowing perfectly well who was the one steering this magic carpet ride. *Ugh, hadn't I learned from this mistake before?* Why was I already giving up so much control?

Ben and I were still very much in the stage of getting to know one another (*So, how could I love someone I didn't know very well? I hear you loud and clear*); however, even with how strong my feelings were for him, it didn't stop me from pushing toward him and away from him all at the same damn time. I was equal parts open and guarded because I was scared out of my mind. He put the fear of love into me. Something, buried underneath all those butterflies and rainbows, knew that this boy was going to hurt me. He was all kinds of wrong that felt freakishly right. Falling for him was forcing me to worry about how things might end. And as much as I loved the excitement of each day I spent with him, I knew that I would have a difficult time should things go sour. I was in no condition to heal yet another wound when I still had bandages on my heart in need of proper care. So, I knew I was in no position to add any more. Yet, I was fully aware, lying there in his arms, that he was going to add so much more.

But my gut knew what my heart refused to acknowledge. I could tell the two were at odds when Ben told me he wanted nothing serious. My gut knocked upon my heart's door, saying, *Hey, Rachel? Umm…I hate to rain on your little love parade, but I'm here to deliver the first of many red flags.* And boy, did it deliver.

Ben began talking about his ex—openly. He never questioned me about my past, yet, he found it necessary to divulge as much as possible about his (which was a much different experience than what I had with Dan). Ben would squeeze in as much about their relationship in any crevice of our conversations that he could, while Dan preferred the empty craters. Discussing something that big shouldn't have found a place so easily between our words, but he still crammed it in there. Not to mention, I uncovered bits and pieces of their past relationship around his apartment as though they were tokens to remind me that even though she wasn't physically present, the memory of her was.

He had a framed picture of them still on one of his shelves, and various personal items of hers tucked away in a box that he kept in the corner of his bedroom. And in my many attempts to believe that it was all because he hadn't found the time to rid myself of those items or simply because he forgot they were there, I realized that I was slipping further and further into a state of pure denial. And for some strange reason, I didn't care.

Soon, we got up and had breakfast (if you even want to call it that). Breakfast to Ben was a granola bar and a glass of milk, so I always knew after leaving his place that I would have to stop at a coffee shop on the way home to shove a few donuts in my face.

Midway through our morning conversation, I knew that we needed to discuss things, but I was a little gun-shy after the Dan debacle. Regardless, I needed to know how much of his ex was still lingering in his life that went beyond the few talismans she left behind to keep the spirit of their relationship alive. I understand that the ghosts of our exes can haunt us for quite some time (I felt that way with Mike at times), but if he was willingly conjuring her every time I wasn't around, then that was a different story. Because in my case, Mike was fully exorcised.

His lips slightly twitched when he recalled certain snapshots from their sordid past. I had no idea if any emotions were tied to those moments, but I gave him the benefit of the doubt that they held no significant value—just moments with someone he used to know. But we all know that was exactly what my heart *wanted* me to believe.

Damn you, heart!

"We go back and forth all the time," he said as I was instantly struck with déjà vu from Dan. "But this last time was really hard on me." His eyes cast downward.

It was hard not to compare this situation with the one I just had with Dan. Had I not, what would have been the point of learning from previous lessons and not repeating past behaviors? It's about understanding the signs that something doesn't seem right and knowing how to react when those situations present themselves.

But what could I have said back to him at that moment that I haven't already said in others? My response, or lack thereof, was stolen by the sound of his phone going off. He received what sounded like a text message which he quickly silenced. I wanted to believe that he ignored the message because he was invested in our conversation, but there went my gut knocking upon my heart's door again. It knew better. I knew better, But there I was, playing dumb, silencing the knock like Ben did with his phone.

I left his house shortly after my half-eaten granola bar, to which I lied and said that I would finish eating on my way home. As much as I wanted to stay there with him, I knew I had to leave. I always believed that I had to remain present in these moments but staying meant compromising my vulnerability by saying my feelings didn't matter. Not to mention, we were always together, and I began to fear again what it would do to me once inevitability struck. Our conversation provided no reassurance but only seemed to add more insecurities on top of the existing ones I had. The weight of it all came crashing down on me. What is the inevitability, you ask? Come on; you know where this is all going…

What was most confusing to me in all of this mess was that I wanted to be with Ben despite it. I wanted every spare moment to be absorbed by his attention. But in that same breath, I needed space. I was fearful that placing any emotional or physical distance between us wouldn't result in the heart growing fonder but rather the heart *forgetting*. The more he didn't pursue me, the more I pursued him. But like I had once felt with Mike, it started to drain me. I was again putting myself in a position of depleting myself to make up for someone else's inadequacy. Everything in my life was taking a backseat to Ben, who was barely present in the driver's seat.

"Where can I put this?" he asked a week later, waving a red and white toothbrush inside my bathroom.

I stifled a small gasp.

"Oh, and I bought one for you at my place, too," he carried on as he reached for the toothpaste to brush his teeth.

Once he finished, he dropped his toothbrush into the tumbler beside mine—bristles touching and all. What do I make of that? Was this supposed to be one of those symbolic moments in our relationship? But I wasn't prepared if it was. Ben and I were reaching toothbrush status? *Watch out, Facebook.*

"I'm going to hop in the shower—if that's OK?" he semi-asked as he grabbed a fresh towel from my linen closet. The boy knew how to make himself at home.

"Sure." I cracked a half-ass smile. "I'll leave you to it," I said, shutting the bathroom door behind me. Grabbing my phone, I tiptoed into the dining room to make a call. Afraid Ben might overhear, I ducked underneath the table as if it would help.

"Well, look who it is!" Noah answered gleefully.

"Shut-up. I need your help," I whispered into the phone.

"What's the problem? Are you OK?" he asked.

"Ben wants to leave his toothbrush here."

"Please tell me there is more to this," he sighed.

"Noah, this is serious. I'm freaking out. Does this mean we are getting serious? Or is this something all guys do out of convenience?"

"First, calm down. Maybe he is just concerned about his hygiene? You guys sleep over each other's places a lot. Where is he now?" he whispered back into the phone as though Ben could hear him, too.

"He's in the shower," I answered while looking out from my hiding place under the table to make sure the coast was still clear.

"See? Very hygienic of him. And where are you?"

I hesitated. "Underneath the dining room table."

Noah laughed. "Well, why don't you crawl out of your fort and join him. Go be hygienic together."

In the days that passed, I decided to sequester myself from Ben as much as possible. After the whole toothbrush milestone, it opened my eyes to the realization that I was being sucked into the relationship so much that it was starting to become unclear where he ended and I began. Unlike the cream with the coffee, the mix was unhealthy. I was losing so much of myself in the stirring that any form of equality or fairness was no longer present. I needed time to sort out what I wanted and to put some of the focus back onto me. After all the work I put into rediscovering myself, you would have thought that I wouldn't have been so quick to put it all up for sacrifice, but there I was, sacrificing like it was a goat. How sad. However, each time I requested time for myself (as hard as it was to do), I was instantly plagued by the dreaded fear that it would create a strong enough divide to break us. Either we were all in or completely out—there was never an in-between. It made no sense. The balance of our scales were never equal. It became a vicious cycle of me trying to form an alignment between us while that same alignment ate away at me. How was it that we never could get enough of each other, while at the same time, we were getting too much? It was a constant game of tug-o-war, and nothing about it seemed fair. I feared that I would fall flat on my face if he pulled too hard.

As if that wasn't enough, the sound of his phone going off whenever we were together never stopped. No matter what we were doing, his phone would make a noise, and he would immediately silence it. Of course, I wanted to know who it was, but at the same time, I didn't want to expose myself to the truth. But my gut knew. I just didn't want it telling my heart.

During a moment of forced clarity, my gut begged my heart to wake up. I couldn't believe I had allowed myself to be wrapped up comfortably in a blanket of denial, believing it was the safest place to be. *Hadn't I been there before?* I turned to my blog as I should have done from the start. I needed to get everything out of me, and I was surprised at just how much came out. What was even more surprising was how quickly I began to connect the dots to some of my feelings with Ben. It was as though the more cards (especially those that revealed how "committed" he truly was) he showed, the more I continued to fall at warp speed, hoping that it would somehow turn the deck around. I was acting the same way I had once done with Mike by falling into the same behavioral patterns believing the more amazing I was to Ben, the more he would want to be with me in return (but we all know how that story ended).

I was unnaturally consumed by the mere presence of Ben in my life to the point where my friends and family took notice. Everyone was concerned that it would destroy every bit of progress I had made so far (as if it wasn't already). Even I knew it was too much of a sacrifice for anyone to make—for anyone else. So, yes, gut, I know my heart needed to wake up.

"It's like knowing the ground is polluted, yet still wanting to build a house on it," Jessie said to me a week later over the phone. "Sure, the house may look pretty and solid, but you know that there is nothing but shit underneath."

I sat back on my couch. I was at a complete loss for words as I held my phone loosely in my grasp.

"What I'm trying to say is," she continued, "you're an amazing girl with so much to offer, but I need you to see that first before you try getting others to see it. You know that he isn't 'the one' no matter how intense your feelings might be for him. Hands down, he will be the lesson and not the blessing."

"We don't know that for sure," I argued. "You don't see what happens when we are together—"

"Behind closed doors?" she interrupted. "Behind closed doors, Ben could be boyfriend of the year if he wanted to be, but what happens when you two walk through the threshold? Is he the same? Is he the same towards you? Does he acknowledge you as his girlfriend? Rach, you know that he is not committed as he tries to make you believe."

She was right. I was running headfirst into something akin to falling into a bottomless pit. The question was: Would Ben be there to catch me if, and when, I was ready to land?"

I had no choice but to find out.

On a rare occasion one night, Leigha didn't have to work. So, she, Noah, and I decided to meet for drinks at our usual place. I thought for sure that I would have spent the evening with Ben, but he had been strangely distant for most of the day, and I refused to stay home, dwelling about it all night.

"Let's call it 'The Teeter-Totter Syndrome,'" Leigha advised, "for the sake of the playground."

"Teeter-Totter? You mean, seesaw?" I asked while trying to get our waiter, Davis's attention.

"Same damn thing," She rolled her eyes.

"Whatever. Go on," I said.

"Relationships require the work and effort of two people for it to operate efficiently, right?" She looked at both of us. "If they don't work together, the relationship will fall apart. The key here is balance. One side—or person—can't work harder than the other, or worse, stop working altogether. If either scenario happens, the teeter-totter doesn't move, does it?" She looked to both Noah and me again for affirmation. "In the end, you have no choice but to jump your ass off before you go crashing to the ground. The same thing happens with relationships."

"Well, no one wants to be in a one-sided relationship," Noah said before taking a swig of his beer.

"I had one with Mike for years. It sucked," I said while avoiding the fact that I was having another relationship like that with Ben.

"No offense, girl, but aren't you in one now?" Leigha cocked her head towards me, calling me out.

"I don't know," I denied. "It's more like we keep going around and around, never actually landing anywhere. As soon as one of us appears ready, the other spins us around once more. I'm exhausted," I sighed. "We have made zero progress in the progression of our relationship."

"Like the roundabout!" Noah slapped his hand upon the table, interrupting me. "See, I can play this foolish game, too."

Leigha burst out laughing. "Welcome to the playground, Noah. Good job."

"Whoever said I wasn't ever on the playground?" he asked. "Take me, for example; when I was with Courtney, I was certain we were going to spend the rest of our lives together. Unfortunately, I was blinded. I refused to see her fading out of our relationship while I was getting sucked further into it. And I just went around and around unknowingly letting it happen for years."

"I would have jumped ship before I let anyone play me like that," Leigha replied.

"Yeah, but we have all been there—even you, Leigha." He looked over at her accusingly. "Every single one of us has been wrapped up in a relationship where we kept going around in circles without any clear destination. I'm sure you think it's fun at first, like it adds some mysterious element to the relationship, but it's no mystery. You're just left standing there dizzy and confused by the end."

"Or wanting to vomit." Davis snickered as he set our drinks down on the table. "Sorry for butting in, but I had to say something."

"So, you've been in a relationship like that, too?" I asked.

"Girl, more times than I can count," he laughed. "We all know those relationships don't go anywhere, but, oh, how we want them to." He smirked.

"He's not wrong," Leigha acknowledged.

I suddenly felt sick to my stomach.

"After the whole thing with Courtney, I have learned that the people who don't mind being in that type of relationship, or ride, if you will—" he winked— "are the ones who don't care if the relationship has a destination or not. They are not ready to commit, so they don't care—and why should they? Especially when they have someone all-too-willing to participate in their games." He peered over at me as he said it.

"If someone wants to be with you, they will be with you," he continued. "It doesn't take several loops around to figure it out. There are no games. There are no rides." He emphasized his last few words, hoping they would hit home with me.

Blog Post #11

The Playground Theorem
Part Three: The Teeter-Totter (or Seesaw) Conundrum

You know what I'm about to write well before the words have even met your eyes: Balance. This next playground rule landed in my lap like a gift from the universe since it plays perfectly well into my theory, as well as upsets any remaining confidence I have left for my current relationship.

It takes two people to make a relationship work. I knew that when I was with my ex, **M**, and I knew that now with **B**. Yet, how come that knowledge wasn't penetrating through, begging for me to recall the lessons I should have already learned? It's absolutely true that one side cannot work harder than the other, or worse, stop working at the relationship altogether (been there). If either happens, you're not moving anywhere. You may be left dangling your feet in the air with no choice but to jump off (leave) or wait until the idiot you're riding with decides to move their ass (commit).

This theorem example sheds light on the importance of a 50/50 partnership. I have been involved in and have witnessed enough one-sided relationships that always end up the same way. So, why am I sitting here thinking that my relationship (or me) is the exception?

One-sided relationships are depleting. Given how I feel for **B** right now, it wasn't enough to remove the emptiness I felt inside. All I wanted was for some form of reciprocation from his end to solidify that he was present and participating in our relationship.

I'm sure you are, just like me, a giving person. It is in our nature to give our all to those we love. But since when have we allowed ourselves not to demand some level of reciprocation in return? Is it selfish to want those things? NO. I would like to put my hand out and bring something back for once—wouldn't you?

Point blank: Relationships require the work of two people. Both of you have to work at it; otherwise, there will be an imbalance. And if you think that a one-sided relationship has any future, you are the only one invested in that ending.

I'm pretty much talking to myself here...

Love, Me.

Hair a mess, sheets on the floor, and the sounds of dissipating breaths left no opening for me to ask the burning question that was still begging to be answered. It was as though my good friend, the proverbial elephant, tagged along in this relationship, too. There it stood in the corner of the room, shaking its giant head at me. I turned my attention away from it as Ben climbed out of bed and headed towards the kitchen for water.

Lost in the aftermath of passion, I was suddenly knocked back into reality when I heard Ben's phone go off on the nightstand beside me. Ben hadn't returned yet when his phone went off a second time. Deciding to be the one to silence it myself, I reached over to grab it, but my hand slipped, and the phone fell from the nightstand onto the floor. For half a second, I feared I broke it. *What then?* There was no way Ben didn't hear it fall. But luckily, the phone was OK, but sadly, I no longer would be.

When I had picked up his phone, I stared at the screen blankly. Everything I never wanted to be true came to light. My gut was now screaming at my heart to remove myself from the situation, but it was too panicked to listen. My bare feet were frozen to the wooden floorboards below. Even if I had wanted to, my heart refused to acknowledge what my gut was saying. And there, staring me right in the face (something not even rose-colored glasses could distort) was all I needed to know so that I could wash my hands of the entire charade. Instead, I set his phone back down on his nightstand and climbed back into bed. Under that blanket of denial, I went.

There, lying in his bed, I put myself in the worst position possible. I was exposed, vulnerable, and practically two seconds away from bawling. I wanted to close my eyes and pinch myself in hopes that it was all just a nightmare, but it wasn't. I was fully awake—and I needed to start acting like it.

When he walked back into the room and handed me a glass of water, I couldn't grasp what it was about him that made me fall so head over heels when he had barely tripped for me. Sure, he was hot as hell. He was funny, charming, and passionate. But was that enough? What about being trustworthy, honest, or even sincere? He was none of those things, yet I loved him like he was.

My heart constantly ached for him and *because* of him. How could I have allowed myself to give so much of my heart to someone who barely had given me a fraction of theirs in return? How was I OK with that? Haven't I already learned this lesson before? *No, Rachel. You haven't.*

The awkward attempts at determining our status from conversations prior were as pleasant as a root canal. Every time I tried to establish some form of status between us, I was immediately shot down or ignored by his desire to keep things as they were. *Why mess up a good thing?* he'd say. And then I would stand there nodding my head like some stage show puppet.

The situation I had with Ben was different than anything I had ever encountered. At least with Dan, we reached the point of establishment that simply fell short of expectations and timing. Ben, however, wanted to dance around the topic like some ritual to conjure rain. Meanwhile, I sat back, making excuse after excuse, telling myself that he was worth the wait—that he was worth the struggle. That rain or shine, he'd be there with an umbrella. Ben might have been unlike any guy I had ever been with, but that didn't mean he was any better.

But I had to ask the question. So, I did.

"What are we?" I asked while looking more towards the elephant than at him. It raised its trunk as though to applaud my efforts. My words lingered in the air between us like smoke from a blown-out candle. My eyes bore into him pleadingly as though begging him to come to his senses. After a moment or two with no reply, I yanked myself out of bed and started to get dressed. My nervous system felt like a slinky that had just been tossed down a flight of stairs, but instead of landing at the bottom in one pile, it kept descending and descending, never quite landing anywhere.

"I don't know," he finally said as he grabbed the remote to his bedroom TV and turned it on. "We're just hanging out."

I was furious. I was devastated. I wanted to cry. And guess what? I did. I stood there demanding to know what everything between us even meant. I wanted him to dissect every detail with me and tell me that it all meant nothing. I had to hear him say it. I had to hear the words from his lips.

I don't know what came over me, but I was pissed. I was pissed at how much time and energy I had invested (and wasted) into nothing more than someone's idea of "hanging out." But I was in too deep to stop myself from unloading all the pent-up frustration I had been carrying around for weeks. I turned away from him, eyeing the box still residing at the bottom of his closet.

"Listen, I'm not ready for anything serious," he said as though his words were the antidote to solving the problem at hand.

I shook my head in disbelief. "You do realize that we have been doing everything that two people in a relationship do, right? The only thing you're withholding is the title. And you act like it's your decision and your decision alone."

"I know, but I'm not ready to slap a title on this or anything else right now," he said as his phone went off again on his nightstand. "You can understand that, right?" His expression suggested that I was being the unreasonable one.

I knew the sound of another message coming through belonged to *her*. I knew I had been foolish for quite some time, but a part of me hoped that my heart would prove my gut wrong. It was about time I stopped living in denial. I had to leave. I couldn't continue standing there, pretending like I was none-the-wiser, fighting for a relationship that was clearly not worth fighting for. I had already wasted enough years of my life going to battle for love that was nonexistent. So, I dragged myself and my sword out of the room and went home.

When it came down to it, what was so different about Ben? Even as I thought back on our short time together, it was nothing special. It was nothing to write home—or my blog about. But the feelings I had for him were intense, nonetheless. They were unlabeled, undefined, and completely unmanageable, not to mention destructive. He lit this fire within me that was left untamed and to its own devices. It had the power to burn everything down, which, sadly, it did.

I couldn't wrap my head around how every touch, word, and amount of time we spent together meant absolutely nothing to him. How could I have read so much into something that meant so little?

I drove back to my apartment that morning with images of us replaying in my head. I recalled when we once talked about things we wanted to do together in the future, which provided me with nothing more than a false sense of security. But in the end, everything that meant something to me was simply commonplace to him. He was the first person to teach me that two people could look at the exact same thing and see something completely different.

But it was the end. We were over. That whirlwind of a romance arrived like a hurricane, and after the rain and wind had settled, I was left facing all the destruction in its aftermath. In hindsight, the signs were all there. His past was constantly lurking in the shadows, ready to plunge into the depths of our present. Lying there night after night in each other's beds, I knew he wasn't being honest. But to tell you the truth, I wasn't being honest with myself either. And it hurt. He had me believing in one thing while feeling another—like a magician distracting me so he could perform his trick. And the fact that he had me so high on that cloud nine bullshit made me want to swear off love for good. But you know what they say: What goes up, must come down.

And down I went.

The Docking Station

June 2013

Time moves slowly when your heart is in pain. The minutes drag, and all I kept singing in my head was that line from one of Matchbox Twenty's songs, "The clock on the wall has been stuck at three for days and days." Even though I hadn't seen or spoken to Ben in several weeks, it didn't mean that I had successfully escaped from his grasp. He still held a part of me whether I wanted him to or not—and it sucked.

I was hurt. The betrayal still had its teeth sunk into me that not even the jaws of life could loosen or release. Ultimately, I was naïve to have believed that I was immune to any more heartbreak as though I had already paid enough dues in my life when it came to love. And there I was, trying to mend another piece of my heart I allowed someone else to break. And as much as I wanted to spend my days crying this pain out, I realized that it took the same amount of energy to be sad that it did to be happy.

But to be honest, was I sad? Or was I playing the role of the heartbroken girl I was supposed to play? The guy I fell for literally strung me along while I followed him around like a lovestruck fool. If anyone was to blame for how I was feeling, it was most certainly me. I knew better. I just didn't *do* better.

"I don't know, girl." Jessie frowned, reaching for my hand. She had made a trip back home to visit family and friends, and I was her first stop. "I never saw that situation going anywhere positive. And I know you saw that, too," she said. "You need to let him go."

"I feel like I can't. Trust me; if there was some magical button I could press to rid myself of feeling this way, you know for sure I'd press it," I asserted. "I just don't understand how he would want nothing when he treated us like we were *something*."

"But did he though?" She looked at me. "Rachel, come on. You are smarter than this. He did not treat you like you were something. Because if he did, he would have put a lock on it, but he didn't."

"I should have left things well alone. I shouldn't have pushed him…"

"Are you listening to yourself?" She released my hand and pretended to smack some sense into me. "You set the stage for the relationship in the beginning. If you want someone to treat you a certain way, you demand it from the start. He treated you the way you let him treat you."

"I know, but I miss him," I sighed.

"So, miss him," she replied. "But I'm not so sure you really do. I understand my track record isn't exactly perfect, given what I just went through with Jordan, but I did not—and would not—stand for this crap. Yes, it hurt. Yes, I tried to forgive him. But I didn't stay with him because of the few moments of fake love he sprinkled on top of our relationship. Love, like ice cream, is made even better by the sprinkles and the cherry on top. But if the ice cream sucks, then no amount of sprinkles and cherries can make it better."

"So, you're saying he was all sprinkles and no ice cream." I looked at her.

"Precisely." She smiled. "And I'm hungry."

"I just can't believe that I gave Ben so much control over this relationship. And you're right; you would think I would have been smarter about things by now," I laughed even though it was far from being funny.

"Then take back control. I hate to break it to you, sweetie, but all you were was a buffer—a rebound—a damn docking station for him to recharge his battery."

"That's not nice."

"When have I ever sugarcoated things to you? What he did to you has nothing to do with you. He would have done that to anyone. Because it was never about you, it had always been about him."

"So, you're making excuses for him now?" I fumed.

"No, I'm just being real. Broken people can't fix each other. And as much as you would like to think that you are healed, you are not. So, you need to start focusing on your priorities and not on men who don't make you one."

Blog Post #12

The Playground Theorem
Part Four: All About the Roundabout

It was all my fault—that much was clear. I could have been smarter, but I chose to abandon everything I've learned from past heartbreak to nothing more than chance. I tried avoiding the inevitable at every turn, but I knew it would lead me to the same destination no matter what road we ultimately took. So, am I really surprised that **B** and I are over? Kind of. And I will tell you why: Because 1% of me was foolish enough to believe in the possibility that a different destination existed while ignoring the 99% of me that knew the road was a dead-end from the start.

We had THE TALK. Yes, *the* talk. It had to happen. If I didn't initiate it, I would have probably continued living—and loving—a lie. I couldn't keep dancing around this subject with men who were so non-committal. Why were people suddenly so afraid to slap labels on things? As if labels translated into the finality of something.

We have all been in those relationships that go around and around without any clear destination. Sure, it may be thrilling at first, but at the end of the day, you need solid ground. Do you not?

The people who prefer these types of relationships (or playground ride) are the ones who could care less if they land anywhere. They are simply not ready to commit—and why should they? Especially when there are people (myself included) who are all-too-willing to ride that ride and deny the fact that the destination does, in fact, matter. However, here's the kicker: Those willingly riding are only perpetuating the cycle. They are the same people (again, myself included) who believe they have the power to stop the spinning altogether. But what I have learned is that the only aspect I have complete control over is getting the hell off.

It's a hard pill to swallow, knowing that if someone truly wants to be with you, they'd be with you. No games. No guessing. It's simple. It always has been.

So, I guess what I'm trying to say here is that **B** just didn't want what I wanted. There is nothing more to it—and that's OK. I just wished he would have been more vocal about that.

I hope this post offered some valuable insight. If not, maybe this will make sense one day. Maybe…

Love, Me.

I was no stranger to the concept that people in life will always come and go, but that didn't mean I had entirely accepted that truth. I have always been a lover of introductions—new beginnings. I enjoy forming new relationships and always felt compelled to maintain all of them, which is probably why I've hung onto expired things much longer than I should (like that bag of lettuce I swore I'd eat). What an exhausting feat that is. So much of my time and energy had been put into relationships that barely gave me anything in return. A depletion of self-worth came at the cost of needing constant validation. I spent way too long fighting for the undeserving—the ones who wouldn't fight for me.

For the past few weeks, I hibernated inside of my apartment, watching all those movie recommendations Jessie made months prior. I ate junk food and disconnected. I only answered the phone when my parents called so they wouldn't think I was kidnapped and held hostage somewhere. And the only sense of control I had mastered during that time was the ability to turn on and off the TV—and I barely mastered that. Then, there was a knock on my door. It was Agnes, my neighbor. With another houseplant.

"Hi, Agnes," I said, taking the plant from her. I looked down to see that this time she had brought a cactus.

"I doubt you'll kill this one." She smiled. 'I saw the other ones in the trash, so I thought this one might have a fighting chance."

"Well, if I end up killing it, you and I both will know I have a problem," I laughed. "Thank you for thinking of me."

"You're welcome, dear. I also stopped by to see if you'd like to come over for some tea. I just put a pot on." She loosely pointed toward her apartment door as her smile warmed the space between us.

I wanted to decline, but what excuse did I have? That I wanted to veg out in front of the TV for several more hours before I took my one-thousandth nap? The last thing I wanted was to hurt her feelings just because mine were ripped to shreds. I quickly threw my hair up, put on a pair of shoes, and followed her down the hall.

Agnes's apartment had a similar layout as mine; however, she decorated hers with a plethora of floral patterns and knickknacks like she had been imprisoned in the sixties and never quite escaped.

She recently painted a fresh coat of yellow paint in her kitchen that further accentuated the floral patterns she decorated the space with, creating an almost kaleidoscope effect.

"I wanted to create some sunshine in this unpredictable New York weather," she said, noticing me looking at her walls. "That's why I painted the room yellow. It took me six months before the apartment board approved me to do it, but they finally did."

"Well, you definitely did it," I laughed unintentionally. "It's almost banana yellow."

"Whatever, it will fade." She waved me off. "I may repaint the room before I die; who knows?"

"Don't talk like that," I said. Agnes was always joking around about death like it was as casual as discussing the weather. She would always say that there were only two things guaranteed in life: Death and taxes. Agnes once said how her family hated her nonchalance towards the topic, but it was her way of accepting reality. She was a woman pioneering in sarcasm and truth.

"So, what's going on with you, my dear?" she asked while setting a cup of tea before me. "I've noticed that you've barely left your apartment lately." She then grabbed a bowl of sugar cubes and an assortment of honey before setting it down on the table between us.

I sighed as I selected the blueberry-infused honey. "A lot, Agnes. I had a rough few weeks. I broke up with this guy I was seeing…"

A few sugar cubes fell into Agnes's tea. She swirled them around until they fully dissolved before taking my hand into her own. "My dear, you need to stop worrying about chasing after people all the time. Those who deserve a place in your life don't need to be chased after. You would save yourself a lot of heartaches," she said to me.

"Maybe I should reach out to him? See if he regrets how things ended? Maybe he knows he made a mistake but is too afraid to contact me," I said more to my tea than to her.

"Let him live with his mistake, sweetie. It is not your responsibility to show him that he messed up. You can't run around seeking validation from people because you will never truly get it in the end. You have to find validation within yourself because that's something no one could ever take away from you," she said. "Unless, of course, you let them." She pointed her teaspoon at me.

My body slumped into her wooden dining chair as I pulled my tea closer. "I just feel so heartbroken. I thought we had something special. Like, maybe, we were even meant to be."

"You may have been, but that doesn't mean you're meant to be forever."

"I don't understand. How can two people be meant to be if they're not meant to be together forever?" I asked before taking a sip of my tea. A small chip on the rim of the cup scraped against my lip. It hurt, but I ignored it.

"Rachel, it is by no accident who enters and leaves our lives when they do. Every person who crosses our path is there to help guide us to where we need to go next—just as we are there to help them. He may have been meant to be, but only for a short while. You may not know why your time together was so short, but eventually, things will become much clearer."

"Do you believe that?" I was skeptical. My pointer finger circled the rim of my cup, feeling for the small cavity from the crack my lip had found a moment ago.

"Absolutely. Looking back on some of the relationships I've had, whether romantic or platonic, those people came into my life because I needed them, or they needed me—in some way. They were a gift from Fate, or I was a gift to them." She smiled as warm as her tea. "Sometimes, we don't know why we need these people. We may not be able to see within ourselves a must-needed change that only they can help us bring forth. Because it's through each relationship we have—good or bad—that we obtain the knowledge that helps us grow."

I couldn't understand why everything had to be a lesson. Hadn't I been put through enough? What more dues did I need to pay before Cupid finds my heart worthy of good love? It made no sense why the universe felt the need to keep me spinning around the same obstacles as if I was on another roundabout with no end in sight. Then again, perhaps the universe knew that I hadn't learned the lessons I needed to, and I was the only one in denial of that.

"I keep going through the same things," I finally said. "I keep experiencing heartache after heartache…"

"Maybe because you are attracting the same people, you shouldn't be," Agnes interjected as she got up from her seat. "That much is obvious to me, and I have never met these men." She peered over at me.

"I know," I agreed.

Agnes walked over to her China cabinet and stopped just before passing by it. "You know," she began again, "you need to appreciate the people who leave your life as much as the people who stay. You should never expect that everyone has a spot in your life, and you shouldn't try so hard to make them one. If someone wants to be in your life, they will fight for their spot. You will never have to do that for them."

My finger tapped along the edge of my cup in rhythm with the rain pounding against the windows.

"You remind me of my late husband. He was always searching for the meaning behind everything," she chuckled. "But sometimes the meaning doesn't need to be found."

"I understand." I nodded. "I just wished he and I had more time to figure things out. It was as if everything happened so fast. It was a blur without much closure."

"If he is meant to be in your life, then he will find a way back into it."

I nodded again but was hard-pressed in fully understanding Agnes's advice. And just as I was about to take another sip of my tea, Agnes took it away from me. "I just love this cup," she said, scrutinizing it carefully before dropping it onto the hardwood floor. China shattered and mixed in with the tea pooling from all sides. I shot up from the table in shock.

"Agnes!" I shouted. "What did you do that for?"

"Teaching you a lesson," she stated very matter of fact.

"But didn't you just say that you loved that cup?" I looked from her to the mess on the floor.

"You're right; I did. I loved it a lot. There will never be another cup like it," she replied.

"Then why did you break it?" My jaw was seconds away from dropping to the floor next to the shattered pieces of China.

"I have more cups in my cabinet." She shooed me as if I were talking nonsense. "And they don't have any cracks."

"If you knew this one had a crack, then why did you give it to me?" I recalled the feeling of the crack against my lip. I had to remember to avoid it every time I took a sip.

"Because you avoided that crack just like you are avoiding your problems. Instead of asking for something better—something that wouldn't hurt you—you settled for what was given to you. Sure, it may have been a wonderful cup at one point," she continued, "but that doesn't mean it's worth holding onto if it's no longer wonderful. Do you understand?" Her eyes met mine.

"You didn't have to break it, though," I said before directing my gaze back down to the mess.

"I could try and glue it back together, but you and I both know that it will never be the same. So, maybe it's time to let it go and move onto something better."

I smiled. "I get what you are doing here."

"You know, my mother once told me that it's not your job to be the dock whenever someone wants to come to harbor."

"Like a docking station?" I interjected, recalling Jessie's similar metaphor.

Agnes peered over at me as though trying to understand. "Or that. Whatever sends the message home."

Shortly after, I made my way to the door to leave. "Think of this as a gift," she said as I turned back around. "I know it hurts right now, and you don't understand why it's happening, but the universe isn't that complicated. It's just trying to move out what doesn't belong, to move in what does. And sometimes, the transition is downright painful—but it is necessary."

"I've heard that before," I said as I looked behind her at the mess still on the floor. "Are you sure you don't need help cleaning that up?" I offered again.

"I will be fine, dear."

"And you're sure that you're not upset that it's broken?"

"Totally fine," she replied. "But it hasn't been much use to me in quite some time, and I was sick of making excuses why I should hold onto it."

That hit home.

I went back to my apartment to collect my thoughts. I put the remaining junk food away and cleaned up each room that my heartbreak tornado swept through. The sun found its way out from behind the rain clouds and began stretching its arms through my closed blinds. I opened them to feel the embrace. It was time to feel alive again. And it was time to let go of what was no longer wonderful.

When I think about my situation with Ben and all the emotional sacrifices I had made—like they were a toll that I needed to pay to get access to his heart—it made me angry. None of it was worth it in the end because there I was once again, pouring from an empty cup into someone else's who wouldn't have poured anything into mine in return.

As Jessie said, "You set the stage at the beginning of the relationship." Because I didn't establish those boundaries or expectations, he set the stage that he wasn't going to respect them. And it was my fault for letting it go on for as long as it did.

I pulled up a picture of us on my phone. I stared at it for a few seconds before deciding to delete it for good.

It was true. For so long, I was always fighting for people to stay in my life when they were never fighting to stay in it themselves. I did all the pleading. I did all the begging. I did all the convincing. I made all the sacrifices and compromises and received nothing in return. What did they ever do for me? Nothing. And it was about time I put a stop to that.

Beasts, Poisons, and Other Things We Feed Into

July 2013

Mourning the loss of something that meant nothing to someone else was incredibly stupid. Perhaps, it all boiled down to timing. *Wasn't timing everything?* If I had met Ben earlier, who knows what might have happened between us? But again, where was that damn crystal ball when you needed it? What I did know—sans crystal ball and all—was that he was back with *her*. She jumped right out of the shadows and landed back into his present life—an exorcism I know you knew was bound to happen. *But seriously, was she hiding in that damn box in his closet?* WTF.

My heart couldn't take another beating—it just couldn't. It had enough. I get that Ben and I were over and that I should move on, but hearing that bit of news didn't make those other steps in the healing process any easier.

I slowly felt the bitterness take over, making me want nothing more to do with love or relationships. It sucked because I was always a big believer when it came to love. Instead, I was beginning to turn cold at the mere thought of it. Was I no longer a believer? Maybe. If I was such a good person, why was love so damn hard?

"I don't know," Noah said one night when he came over to watch a movie. "Everyone has potential in the beginning, but potential means nothing if they don't live up to it."

"Well, he certainly didn't live up to it, that's for sure," I confirmed. "It makes it so confusing. Like, how do you know when someone is worth it?" I plunged my hand into the bowl of popcorn.

"By their choices and how they treat you. People like to blame others or circumstances as to why they act a certain way when they are entirely in control of their actions. Ben chose how he wanted to treat you. It's that simple."

"I have been beating myself up over this since we broke things off, wondering if my choice to bring up the conversation on what our status was, was the reason why we split?" I looked at Noah.

"Now, that's just dumb. You two were going to end the same way no matter what—you just sped things up a bit." He grabbed the bowl of popcorn away from me.

"I can't believe I thought he had potential," I whined at the mention of it.

"You're just in denial. You refused to acknowledge that Ben was all wrong for you just because he made your palms all sweaty and your heart palpitate." He paused for a moment while he chewed a mouthful of popcorn. "I've learned that it's all about the beasts, poisons, and other things we feed into that end up distorting our perceptions. What you need to do is start feeding into the positive things in your life and not these loser guys you keep letting in."

"Hey now!" I gently shoved him in the shoulder.

"What? Ben was an asshole for what he did to you. He was an asshole back in college, and he's still that same asshole now. He played girls back then—if you remember? So, stop living in la-la land."

"I'm not living in la-la land," I argued.

"I say this as one of your best friends, but he never deserved you. He is not a good guy no matter how hard you try convincing yourself otherwise." His smile flatlined. "It doesn't make him a good guy for toying around with peoples' hearts."

I pushed my hair behind my ears. "I guess I have always tried to see the good in people."

"And where has that gotten you?" Noah interrupted before I could say anything more. "Seeing the good in people doesn't mean that they *are* good. Half the time, we try planting the good in them and then claiming that it was there all along."

I nodded, believing I may have done that with Ben more so than I cared to admit to Noah. I certainly did that a lot with Mike.

"I learned that the hard way with Courtney. When I went and saw a therapist, she told me to stop feeding into poisonous behavior. So, I'm passing this lesson down to you." He smiled.

"Trust me," he continued, "when you stop feeding into it, you'll see that it's OK to acknowledge that the bad parts of people do exist. The bad is far more telling than the good sometimes." He nodded as though he knew it all too well. "I just don't want you to become hardened by those that have hurt you."

"Easier said than done," I said.

"I know. People tend to bring out different beasts within us, which was another thing my therapist said. And as for you, you keep getting involved with the same guys that bring out the same beast within you."

"And what beast is that?" I peered over at him.

"The fighter. Not much of a beast, I get it. But you keep being put back into the same position of fighting for what you know you deserve. And these guys keep presenting you with that same battle because they are not giving it to you. You need to channel that fight for the right guy and not the ones you are so keen on settling for."

I let his words sink into me like an anchor tossed out to sea. Every one of my past relationships presented me with similar struggles and battles. Still, I fought to keep each of them alive regardless of whether they were good for me or not. We never want to believe that someone doesn't want us—and that is what I couldn't come to grips with Ben. One of my biggest issues with relationships centered around me wanting my partner to want me equally in return. Because no matter how much I wanted them, there always seemed to be an imbalance. Secondly, I would always be the one who fought to keep their place in my life when they hardly fought for it themselves. That's messed up. I never stopped to realize that I was fighting for someone else to see my worth when I barely did a thing to defend it. Trying to sell what made me special to someone devalued those same things simultaneously. If Ben didn't realize what he had with me, it wasn't my job to open his eyes to it.

"If he were meant for you, we wouldn't be having this conversation," Noah said as though reading my thoughts.

"Can I ask you something?" I turned the conversation over to him. "What do you want out of a relationship?

What matters the most to you?" It was a question I had been trying to figure out myself. *What did I want?* I knew there were a lot of things I didn't. And it was only thanks to Mike, Joe ("J"), Dan, and now Ben who showed me those very things.

"I want someone I can trust. I want everything I once thought I had with Courtney, but with someone better. I miss having fun with someone," he sighed before taking another mouthful of popcorn. "Ultimately," he said mid-bite, "I want to be in love this time, really in love where there are no strings or games attached. I want off the playground." He winked. "Oh, and I have been reading your blog," he laughed upon admittance.

"You have?" My palm hit my forehead. "What do you think?" I asked, unable to face him.

"I think it's good." He smiled.

Later, consuming more wine than we probably should have, Noah passed out on my couch while I decided to take my unfinished glass over to my laptop and work on my latest post. It probably wasn't the best thing to do semi-intoxicated, but Ernest Hemingway always said to do it.

Blog Post #13

The Playground Theorem
Part Five: When He Doesn't Want to Play with You

If someone ignored you on the playground, it only made you want to play with them more, right? Like, who wants to play alone? When we were kids, we conditioned ourselves to do whatever it took to get other kids to play with us. We would trail behind them, asking permission to join in on their games, or maybe try with all our might to entice them to join in ours.

Now, naturally, as adults, we hate it equally as much when we are ignored. So, what do we do? We revert to our old playground behavior. But this time, the games we play are different as well as our resources. We call. We text. We like their social media posts or send them a DM there. We practically show up at the person's doorstep and wave whatever we have to offer in their face just to get some level of reciprocation.

Let's bare some skin, shall we?

Don't go vanishing between someone's bedsheets just because you think they will somehow see your worth when you do. Good sex does not equate to a good relationship. Sure, it's needed—like a must-needed ingredient to make a great cake—but it's not the whole cake. What I'm saying is, if it's all you have, then it's *all* you have. And if you find yourself compromising in such a way, you may end up losing parts of yourself to someone you may never get back. People choose how much of themselves they want to give to you. So, above all else, pick someone who *chooses* to give you their heart.

I know, tough to hear, right? But if someone doesn't want to "play" with you (meaning "be with you"), don't play with them! Don't overextend yourself just for the possibility of being wanted in return. The only validation you should be striving for is the validation you give yourself. This is the difference between a real relationship and another shitty game on the playground.

I guess what I'm trying to say here is: I'm done playing with you, **B.**

Love, Me.

Noah woke up shortly after I published my post. I probably should have listened to the other half of

Hemingway's advice, but I had no time to sober up to edit before publishing it.

Noah sat up on the couch with his eyes glaring at me as though he was unaware that he had fallen asleep. Looking back at him, I knew how much of a good friend he was. He cared about how I was feeling—even when he didn't agree with any of it. And since the whole Ben ordeal, he catered to my every whim as though I were recovering from major surgery. A surgery involving the removal of another person as though they were a damaged limb in need of immediate amputation. As much as I appreciated Noah's persistence in helping me feel better, I was really OK. I was just wallowing in self-pity and recovering from allowing my heart to be given away so freely.

Yes, Ben was an asshole like Noah said, but I had to take some responsibility here, right? He did say that he wanted nothing serious in the beginning, and I just went along like everything changed when he and I never actually had a discussion that it did. Even though we never brought up the subject again, he acted differently towards me ever since—like an unspoken agreement was made. And I always thought that actions spoke louder than words. *Or am I missing something here?*

I knew that the relationship was headed for disaster well before I even climbed on board. It was as if he told me the boat was bound to sink and threw me a lifejacket to make up for it. But no, I didn't want to be floating around in the cold water, doggy paddling to save my life. Lifejacket or not, someone's arms were bound to get tired eventually. And mine did.

As much self-convincing I had been doing, it was time to put my words into motion and move on. I didn't want to dwell like this anymore. I couldn't allow myself to live in the blind spots because I needed to see things clearly—no matter how hard it was going to be.

Noah reached for his wine glass that still had about a sip or two left before making his way over to the table. After he sat down, he swirled the remaining contents of his glass, inhaling the aroma just before gulping down the rest. I listened as he swished the wine around in his mouth like he just took a mouthful of mouthwash and then swallowed. I was somewhat shocked he didn't gargle.

"Perfect. An excellent year," he joked.

I shook my head and laughed. The year on the bottle was current, and judging from everything I'd been through, I would say it was far from it. But I at least appreciated him trying to make me laugh.

"I always wanted to be one of those people who knew how to taste wine properly. You know an amateur sommelier?" He raised his empty glass. "So, did I pull it off? I probably didn't do it right," he chuckled.

"You pulled off looking ridiculous," I teased.

"Whatever." He waved me off. "Are you doing better now?" He hiccupped. I could tell he had yet to sleep off all the wine he drank.

"Noah, I'm fine," I reassured him. "You didn't need to come over here and take care of me. I know what Ben did was shitty, but there's nothing I can do about it. He made his decision. And I'm quite positive he's not beating himself up with the guilt."

Noah leaned back into his chair, looking me right in the eyes. He held my gaze, similar to when he was still sitting on the couch. "Do you remember the first time we met back in college?" he asked as he brought his chair back down on all four legs. His words sailed over to me in a whisper as though recalling the memory was some sort of shared secret between us. "That's the night I met Courtney for the first time, and I think you had just broken up with Mike for the tenth time. Do you remember?"

I nodded.

"And we sat by that nasty keg talking about our lives before agreeing that you and I were going to be friends forever. Do you remember?"

"I think it was the alcohol talking that night, but yes." I smiled upon recollection.

"Do you think we set ourselves up for failure?" he yawned as his question slipped through. "Like we predetermined our future then?"

My brow furrowed deeply into my skin that I feared it would leave a lasting wrinkle. "What do you mean? What outcome?"

"*Our* outcome. By us saying that we were going to be friends—do you think that stopped us from ever being more?" His eyes fell to the floor.

I didn't know whether to laugh or simply shrug him off as though it was the wine talking and not him. "What are you trying to say here, Noah?"

"I don't know." He yawned again just before getting up from the table and making his way back over to the couch. "Lately, I've been wondering if we had never said that, maybe we could have had the chance at being something more," he continued. "Like we sold ourselves short." He laid his head back down and filled the sudden silence with his snoring.

Confused, I left him asleep on the couch and headed to my bedroom. I looked back at him a few times, wondering if I had imagined the entire conversation. I had a little too much to drink, as well. Anything was possible. But even so, I still heard exactly what he said.

Ugh, what is happening? My mind swirled faster than the wine did in Noah's glass, and I begged for it to slow down. *Did he mean what he said?* It was hard to say. The only thing I knew for sure was that I was too tired to think about it anymore. I needed to get some sleep.

An hour or so later, I woke to the sound of Noah knocking on my bedroom door.

"Hey," he said as soon as I opened it. "I think I pretty much slept all the wine off." He yawned as he looked down at his watch. "I'm going to head home, OK?"

"Right now?" My eyes squinted towards the clock on the wall. "It's really late. You can just stay," I said.

"It's fine. I have a lot going on tomorrow," he yawned again before turning to leave without so much as another word.

I reached for his arm in an attempt to stop him. He may have slept off the wine, but I knew he was still tired. I wanted to get a better look at him—to make sure that he was OK to drive— but he quickly took hold of my arm instead and pulled me in towards him. But before I could even open my mouth to speak, he parted my lips with his own.

Instinctively, I pulled away. I looked back at Noah in disbelief. There was so much I wanted to say, but I couldn't find a single word—let alone a breath—to escape my shock-stricken lips. I quickly wiped the remaining residue of the kiss onto the back of my hand as his body retracted as though it were a complete slap in the face. I didn't mean to hurt his feelings. I was in shock. And as much as I wanted to say something to rid the awkward silence, he left my apartment before I even had the chance to find the words.

I leaned against my bedroom door, trying hard to piece together what had just happened and what led Noah and me to this strange and confusing place. Noah was one of my closest friends who had just crossed a line I never knew I had to guard against him. I steered my mind back to the moment. *Did I kiss him back?* It all happened so fast, so I wasn't entirely sure. No, there was no way that I did—it was Noah, for heaven's sake! And no matter how hard I tried falling back asleep that night, my thoughts tossed and turned as much as I did between my sheets.

Come morning, I thought about everything again (as if I hadn't done that enough already). Noah's lips upon mine felt insanely different—not that I had ever imagined what they would have felt like in the first place. I explored the residual feelings only to come up with the same conclusion each time: It had to have been the wine. *Right?* There was no better explanation—at least, no other explanation I was satisfied with.

After a few cups of coffee, I decided to text Noah. I didn't want there to be anything awkward between us. And for a split second, a part of me did wonder what it would be like to date Noah. But it was all too much. It was all too soon. I was not over Ben (as much as I wanted to be). I was not into Noah (even though he was a great guy). I was merely falling in love with the possibilities and potential—but wasn't that the love story I was trying to avoid? I already knew what falling in love with someone's potential could do. But Noah never responded, which had me thinking it probably wasn't the wine.

Blog Post #14

The Playground Theorem
Part Seven: Don't Be Left Hanging

If used correctly, the monkey bars were designed for someone to grab hold of one bar after another to move from both ends of the playground. It requires a swing-by-swing (step-by-step) approach, which can subsequently describe the same method one could use while dealing with a breakup.

Let's begin.

You break up with a guy you've been dating for a while (me). And you're devasted (also me). Perhaps, even blindsided by the whole ordeal (not exactly me because I had a feeling it was coming). You can't eat; you can't sleep, and you certainly can't fathom how you're ever going to move on without them. But you have to. You must. And the only way you will ever get to a better place is to grab hold of that first bar and hoist yourself up.

Moving between bars (much like the stages of grief and healing) is easy for some. And for those of you who heal this way, bravo. You were blessed with a natural ability to pick yourself back up, dust the emotional dirt off, and carry on with life. But for others (like me), that is not the case. There are those times in our lives when trying to pick ourselves back up is too hard. It feels downright impossible—like we are left hanging without the strength to move on, as though we are destined to fall. And I know exactly what that feels like. Sometimes, I only get so far before I end up losing strength. When that happens, I have no choice but to start the healing process all over again.

Another solid piece of advice a friend once told me was this: "You don't want to look back a year from now and remember how much time you spent grieving over a guy who wouldn't have shed a tear for you. You need to get out of bed, put some lipstick on, and own your life. The only thing worth looking back on is how fabulous you felt despite someone trying to make you feel your worst."

No matter how hard things get or how devastated you may feel, continue grabbing hold of one bar after another until you reach the end. You must endure the stages of grieving so that you can properly heal. And when you do, only then will you finally be able to let go.

So, what bar are *you* on?

Love, Me.

Ten minutes later, I received the following reply:

I'm not even halfway.

So, I replied:

Neither am I. Hang in there. We will get to the end soon enough.

"He what?!" Leigha screamed into the phone. "I'm sorry, but what the hell? Please tell me you're kidding."

"I'm not kidding. And I haven't heard from Noah since, so I'm pretty sure he doesn't know what to do about it all either."

"Yeah, but Noah? Really? I just never saw it coming," she said.

"*You* never saw it coming? What about me? The whole thing is just bizarre. I'm just crossing my fingers that it was all because of the wine, and he is just as embarrassed as I am," I said, still holding onto the wine possibility.

"Girl, he wasn't drunk. He slept off what he drank and then kissed you. That speaks volumes, and besides, most people love to use alcohol as an excuse for their behavior. He hasn't."

"He hasn't *yet*," I added.

"Well, speaking of excuses, I called James last night."

"I'm sorry, but you did what?" I asked, instantly feeling whiplashed between my ordeal and now hers. James was the guy who chased after Leigha for years, but she never seemed interested in him. I always thought he was a nice guy who had a lot to offer, but she rejected him time and time again.

"I know what you're thinking, but things can change. I always thought I wanted something different, but as you know, different never worked out," she mumbled as though what she was admitting was difficult to say.

"How did that even happen?" I asked.

"I ran into him at the restaurant. He came in with a few guys from work, and we ended up talking for a bit. And, well, here we are."

"Wow," I replied.

"Yep. Wow," she repeated. "It's just so weird! If you were to ask me a few years ago if I would ever be ga-ga over James, I would have been more blah-blah over him."

"What do you think changed?" I asked.

"Timing? Who knows?" she speculated. "I wasn't in the right headspace any of the times he tried pursuing me. Now, things just feel natural. Rather than before when it felt forced—like I was forcing myself to like him. It has to be timing."

"Timing..." I thought of Ben. "Timing blows.

Ben. Ben. Ben. Ben. Ben. A flashback of memories crashed into the forefront of my mind, forcing my eyes to close as if it would stop the flood. The fire we once shared extinguished faster than I had the chance to keep it burning. But why was it my sole responsibility to keep it burning? Couldn't he have thrown a log or two to keep it going? Look at me. Still obsessing. Still looking for answers to questions I will never receive.

Knock it off, Rachel. You know the answers. You just failed to accept them because they are not what you wanted to hear. Damn that voice inside of my head. But knowing how much of a forgiving person I was and how many times people trampled all over me in the process, I still allowed it to happen time and time again. I have even let people come back into my life without so much as a decent apology. It was baffling. I was ashamed of the red-carpet treatment I extended those people. And I worried about what that meant for Ben. My forgiving behavior felt hardwired into my DNA, and I knew I needed to rid myself of it—and fast.

Yeah, OK, Rachel. You and I both know you'd open that door wide enough for a cruise ship to sail right through. Damn that voice inside of my head, yet again! It was all just poison. Poisonous thoughts I refused to feed any longer. Enjoy your last meal, boys.

Awkward 😳

August 2013

Why was I so hung up on him? Seriously, if you're reading this, can you explain it to me? And if you don't know, I certainly don't have a prayer in figuring it out either. Or maybe, I didn't explain things well enough? Listen, let me break it down for you: I don't have all day nor an entire book to describe the ins and outs that were Ben and me. Neither one of us has that kind of time. All I can say is that I fell way too fast, too soon. He made me feel things that Mike could only have dreamed of. He was addicting, alluring, and all the things I knew I shouldn't want but still wanted anyway. And if you tried to force me into rehab to get over him, I'd probably say, "No. No. No."

All I knew was that I needed a new lease on life. I needed to kick this toxic behavior to the curb once and for all. And the best thing I could do for myself was put the actual effort into moving on and not just sit around talking about it. I needed to look ahead and not dwell on what was left behind. I wasn't headed in that direction any longer.

Blog Post #15

The Playground Theorem
Part Eight: Life in Full Swing

It's time for this theorem to come to a close. However, I wanted to end things on a high note since most of what I've been talking about seemed rather doom and gloom. I wanted to give you a conclusion that felt uplifting so that maybe both you and I would feel inspired to kick our asses back into gear.

Everyone loves the swing set, do they not? Isn't it the one part of the playground that all kids run to first? I believe it has something to do with the feeling you get from swinging high above the playground as though you are untouchable—like you are flying. However, not everyone can soar as high as they want. Some may pump their legs to the point of exhaustion, only reaching a certain height, while others need a push from time to time. But no matter how you get yourself into the air or to what heights you reach, the point is never to give up. And if someone offers you a little push, take it. There is nothing wrong with accepting help sometimes. It's not a sign of weakness, but rather, strength, to acknowledge when you can't do something on your own.

What I'm trying to say is to live your life in full swing. Enjoy the ride. Take chances. Have fun. And if at any point you feel like you need to regain your footing, jump off. It's perfectly OK if you do.

Above all, always stay true to yourself—no matter what. It's the only survival mechanism to get you off this playground alive.

Love, Me.

"You know, I didn't ask for this," Noah said to me after I finally got him on the phone. I must have called and texted him more in the past few days than I had the entire month. "Listen, that night we first met, I never looked at you as anything more than a friend. Besides, even if I did, both of us were involved with other people. And now look at us." He stopped for a moment before bursting out laughing. "We are the best of friends, and I just messed that all up."

I wondered what caused this sudden turn of events. The memory of the first night we met was suddenly encased in a thick fog, making it difficult to know what really happened anymore—or what we felt back then. *What did that mean for our friendship?*

My heart pounded through the walls of my chest as I recalled the intimacy of Noah's kiss. My palms, sweaty, almost caused my phone to slip right out of my hand. I felt like that cream again slowly stirring into the blackness that was Noah, but what resulted didn't make sense. There was a clear indication of where he ended and I began. We didn't mix. Or, at least, that's what it felt like.

Our friendship had been consumed by our personal heartbreaks, dating woes, and everyday life dilemmas for so long. We watched each other begin and end various relationships on and off throughout the years, and never once did I ever think: *What if?* Noah was always a safe place for me. He was the complete definition of a true friend, and there was no room in the subtexts for the "what ifs."

"Rach, I'm really sorry. I don't know what came over me or why I kissed you. Maybe it was all that wine?" he chuckled. "Either way, I don't want this to ruin our friendship. Can we just forget it ever happened?"

That wasn't what I anticipated him saying when I got him on the phone. However, I was thankful that we could finally move past that night, allowing the awkwardness to dissipate out of our friendship's existence into a mere memory that we would hopefully laugh about in the years to come.

"Yes. Let's just forget about it," I said while thinking I wouldn't be drinking with him for a very long time.

Blog Post #16

Reciprocation Not Included

My mother always told me that you shouldn't view every person who comes into your life as the same. The way you interact, communicate, and even feel towards them should be personalized. Every relationship you have is different. And you simply cannot rely on the hope that just because you are amazing to them, they would be amazing back to you. Reciprocation is never guaranteed.

I have been good to those who have betrayed me and somehow managed to remain good to them despite it. I have opened myself up to people who didn't deserve my honest self and have even kept my heart open longer to those who deserved to have it closed. I have also deeply loved those who had barely loved me a fraction of that in return.

Too often, we are quick to give ourselves away to people without first getting to know their true character. We assume that each person is true to their word, feelings, and sense of self. But the truth of the matter is: You can't always just see the good in people without also recognizing the bad (which is a flaw of mine that I'm desperately trying to work on). This helps establish boundaries. And this has been one hell of a lesson for me to learn.

Just because I give doesn't mean that I will receive. Just because I love doesn't mean that I will be loved in return. And just because I do so much for someone doesn't mean that they will do anything for me in return either. Reciprocation is not guaranteed—like death and taxes (a wonderful new friend would say). So, be careful who you extend yourself to; you have to be willing to accept the gamble that you may lose your entire hand.

Love, Me.

It was 1:00 p.m. as my fingers graced my keyboard while I watched a jumble of letters decorate the blank page on my screen. For some people, blank pages are scary. The idea of finding the perfect opening sentence to set the writing wheels into motion can be quite a challenging endeavor. I can't tell you how often I have changed an opening sentence because I found a better way to phrase something or had a better idea altogether.

Lately, I have been getting a lot of practice in this department. Work has been a bit busier than usual because our internet presence was building a much more robust platform, but with that comes the constant need to produce more. It was starting to become exhausting and unfulfilling.

In other news, Dan was moving back to North Carolina. And according to our company newsletter, Tina had planned a goodbye party for him, which I, unfortunately, had other plans and couldn't attend. Well, I didn't *exactly* have any plans. But no one needed to know that. It wasn't that I was bitter or carried any resentment towards Dan; in fact, it was quite the opposite. I appreciated him in many ways, but I wasn't ready to pretend as though nothing had happened between us. Even after having left things with us just being friends, it still didn't erase the awkwardness that lingered in its wake. *Man, I was just swimming in all kinds of awkwardness lately.*

It's not like we had spoken much since everything ended between us. A few times, he had texted me, asking for my input on something he was working on, but I merely shrugged the exchange off as more of a worktext than anything else. However, there were times that the conversation hung in an awkward place with words exchanged that never really landed anywhere. I didn't want to press him on anything, and I'm almost positive he felt the same with me. It's interesting how things can change with a little bit of time.

Still, time escaped me. I ended up deleting the jumble of words I had written and found my way over to the couch. I fell into the cushions with my phone in my hand, drifting off to sleep just as fast as my head hit the pillow. But I didn't sleep for too long. Several hours later, I realized the day had turned into night, and I was no longer alone.

Missing Persons Alert

August 2013

The rest of the night was a blur like a drug that overtook my senses, making me lose complete control.

As usual, we drowned our sorrows in intoxicating passion and became so drunk off it that neither one of us remembered how we got there or what separated us in the first place. It felt like a hurricane blew through, and I was just waking up to all of the destruction. I looked around, wondering what the hell happened and why everything was destroyed.

With the arrival of morning, so came our inevitable soberness. I awoke to the familiar paintings and posters decorating the walls. The same candle was left unlit upon his dresser collecting dust. We laid awake in bed, staring up at the ceiling as though we had each woken up beside a stranger, unsure of how we got here and why.

I breathed heavy, emitting an unexpected sigh that covered us as long as his sheets. Immediately, I was hit with that familiar ache. It felt as though my gut was throwing a temper tantrum, kicking and screaming as to why I could let this happen *again*. If I were to have stood up at that moment, I would have most likely doubled over. Tell me, why are mornings so revealing and nights so concealing?

"What's wrong?" Ben turned towards me. He laid on his side, drumming his fingers down the length of my bare arm.

"I feel so lost," I said, fighting hard to keep my emotions at bay. *How did we get here again?* The drug that was Ben was finally starting to wear off, and I was reaching a familiar sense of soberness.

"Why?" he asked as if what had happened was normal—as though nothing had transpired between us before. Something in his eyes told me that he was just as lost as I was, but I was the only one brave enough to admit it. And that was our biggest problem: Admitting our honest feelings to one another. We were always great at everything else, but when it came down to communicating on a deeper level, we sucked. I was always the one afraid of getting hurt, and he was always the one afraid of doing the hurting—which is precisely the narrative trap we constantly fell into.

But someone had to say it, and I knew that the responsibility fell on me. It always did. And I would always end up being the one who suffered the consequences no matter how I approached it. After what happened last time, I knew I had to address things sooner. I couldn't allow myself to cower again. I needed something substantial from him going forward. *Didn't I deserve that?* Either he was going to be upfront with his intentions, or I was done. *But wasn't I already done? Didn't I promise myself I would never be in this place again?*

"We keep losing ourselves in each other, and for me, I don't know enough about myself to comprehend exactly what it is that I'm losing," I said while looking deep into his eyes. "I'm afraid," I paused, giving my words a chance to sink their teeth into him. "After everything that happened with us," I continued, hoping the venom of truth was now circulating throughout his body. "I don't trust that you and I are on the same page with things."

He pulled me in close, kissing me on my forehead. I breathed him in deeply. My eyes closed at his touch as my hand instinctively found his. They fit together as though they were made to hold one another. I looked down, marveling at the paint still coating a few of his nails that didn't entirely wash off after working on his latest piece. And without much answer or acknowledgment of what I had just confessed, our bodies once again locked like two perfect pieces of a confusing puzzle, with absolutely nothing keeping us together besides the glue of denial.

"I started getting serious about my painting again—thanks to you," he said, rolling over, unlocking our embrace. He picked at the paint I noticed on his nails only moments ago.

"Really? That's amazing, Ben," I said, catching my breath.

"I'm thinking of trying to get them into a gallery and see what happens. What do you think?"

"I think it's a great idea." I smiled.

"Really? You don't think it's dumb?" He rolled over onto his side and faced me head-on. His eyes penetrated through me as though begging for dissuasion—like he expected me to not believe in him or his abilities. Or maybe it was because he didn't believe enough in himself. I knew he was used to people turning down his creative endeavors, especially when his law career had been so successful. I always tried my best to be supportive. *And look where that has gotten me.*

"It's not dumb, Ben," I said, realizing he completely sidestepped my feelings and switched the conversation over to his. Not even a few hours in, and I was already feeling the sacrifice.

Blog Post #17

Time Traveler

It's incredible what time reveals to us. It shows our strengths, the truth behind well-crafted lies, and, of course, the logic behind feelings once drenched in unabashed emotion. It helps us get over heartbreak, heal wounds, and learn from our mistakes. Most importantly, it helps guide us onto a better path.

We desperately want time to speed up during times of hardship and sadness. Yet, we demand it to slow down during times of complete happiness. But no matter what side of the coin time lands on, we rarely use it wisely. We treat it like we have so much of it at our disposal. We hardly ever live in the moment because we constantly focus on chasing what happens next. Or are we just too immersed in what's going on around us than what is happening directly to us?

How ignorant of me to have once regarded time as the enemy. Time has helped me overcome some hard times in my life and helped me achieve growth and balance. And it has brought me closer to the person I'm destined to become.

Above all, time is a precious gift. Therefore, I promise from here on out that I will treat it as such.

But with all that I've said here, how do I explain my recent behavior? How could I have allowed myself to go back to the one place I knew would never be safe for me, regardless of how much time had passed?

Love, Me.

After I left Ben's and sobered up completely, I checked my phone. Amid all the smoke and mirrors that were Ben and me, Dan had texted. He said that he was packed up and ready to go but wanted the chance to say goodbye.

As much as I wanted to avoid this at all costs, saying goodbye was the right thing to do. The process of watching Dan fade out of my life as quickly as he appeared into it made me wonder if the reason was simply to jumpstart my heart, to let it know it had the strength to feel again. But to be truthful, looking back, Dan would merely be a small hairline crack in my timeline, whereas Ben would eventually leave something more sizeable to the Grand Canyon.

I pulled up to the front of Dan's apartment building as a moving truck kissed the curb in front of me. Dan once told me he scored a month-to-month lease on this historical building which was rehabbed with a modern twist in the heart of the downtown square. For some reason, I have always loved this part of town. Residents had the luxury of living within walking distance to some of the best places to eat or drink. I would have considered living there, too—if it weren't for the increasing crime rates.

A couple of the movers hopped out of the truck as I made my way inside. After punching in the code that was imprinted in my brain, I followed their lead until they veered off in the opposite direction.

"You came!" Dan cheered as he opened the door to find me standing in the hall. He reached in for a hug, pulling me into his apartment. When I didn't reciprocate the embrace, his arms retracted as quickly as they wrapped around me.

"I didn't realize you had that much to pack," I said, noticing all the boxes piled up in the corner. For an apartment I once considered barren, he certainly collected a lot. I wondered if he had hidden things under rugs and behind closed doors like everything else he did in his life. *Whoa, Rachel. Bitter?*

"Why because of my contract?" He looked at me pointedly.

"Well, you weren't planning on staying here long," I sneered as though it still bothered me.

"You never know. They say life happens when you're busy making other plans—or however that saying goes." He smiled, brushing me off.

"What are you talking about?" I shifted my weight where I stood. His joke wasn't lost on me, which made me pissed, considering it was the basis for why we split.

Dan turned towards me, noticing my displeasure. "Bad joke. I'm sorry."

"It's fine," I said, looking towards the door, summoning my exit.

"We can still be friends, right?" He pulled my attention back onto him. "I know we didn't really give it the ol' college try, but maybe we should?" He placed his hand upon my shoulder.

Honestly, what would being friends hurt? He was leaving, and saying that we would remain friends, felt more like an empty promise than a solid commitment—or maybe it was a way for us to have some form of closure between us. I wasn't angry with Dan or upset with what happened between us. It could very well have been my feelings that were misplaced and misdirected onto him. Still, at the bottom of that emotional heap, I did miss his friendship.

When I returned home later that night, I thought about breakups and how each one was different from the next. There is no one-size-fits-all when it comes to healing. My breakup with Mike was a long, drawn-out process, but when I finally reached the finish line, I felt a huge sigh of relief that it was over. My heart never ached after our separation. It only ached after realizing that I had wasted years of my life settling for someone so undeserving and how complacent I had been to stay in an unfulfilling relationship for as long as I did. Before Mike, however, there was Joe. With Joe, I learned the importance of growth and unrealistic expectations. I realized how important it was to put your foot down for what is right, no matter how hard it is to do (which I still needed to work on). And that sometimes the grand gestures in life come in the most unexpected packaging.

On the other hand, Dan showed up as a learning curve, reminding me of the lessons I still had to learn. After Mike, Dan was the trial run I needed to break in my newly found relationship tools. But Ben became the ultimate test, which I continued to fail at miserably. Commitment was a forbidden discussion, yet we were still committing to each other nonetheless. Distance was appreciated but never actualized. And the only time it came to fruition was out of convenience for him. We were entirely too consumed with each other, by each other, and because of each other. And that was never a good thing for anyone.

Listen, I know Ben wasn't right for me. You don't have to shout at the pages because I hear you. Trust me. Ben wasn't right for me in the same way red wine isn't good for pearly white teeth. Sure, it may taste amazing, but smile, and you will look like a hot mess. And I most certainly was a hot mess. It's not exactly the best look to have after spending the better part of the past year trying to better yourself. But like I had mentioned before: You attract what you project. And it was apparent (when I opened my eyes to it) that I was broken. All Ben and I were, were two lonely, broken pieces, trying to make something whole. We believed it was worth trying to round and square our edges to make us fit despite us *not* fitting. However, this time around, I didn't want to alter, remove, or add any elements to myself in order to change my authenticity to match his—when we both knew he wasn't being authentic in the slightest. If things were going to work between us, they would have to do so naturally. I couldn't spend one more day looking in the mirror, asking: *Who am I?*

I wished Ben had responded when I told him I felt lost. Regardless of whether he knew what to say to that or not, he should have at least made me feel like he was listening. This time around, *if* we were going to work, I needed to make sure that I didn't lose sight of myself, even if that meant losing sight of him.

I decided to call Noah. We hadn't spoken much since our last conversation, and I was hoping things were better between us.

"What are you up to?" I asked.

"Just packing a bag. I'm heading home for the weekend," he answered. "My cousin is getting married."

"Want some company while you pack?" I offered.

"It's just one bag," he laughed, "but sure, I'd love some."

Unlike Dan's or even Ben's, Noah's apartment was more grownup in comparison. A frequent shopper of Restoration Hardware and West Elm, he managed to create a den-like atmosphere short of having a bearskin rug and deer heads on the walls.

I told Noah about my time with Dan and how Ben magically resurfaced in my life. A few times, I caught him rolling his eyes at the absurdity of it all while barely saying anything in response.

"What's wrong with you?" I asked.

"Nothing," he stated.

"This is still not about the other night, is it?" I cocked my head at him, but he still said nothing much in reply. "Noah, what the hell? I thought we were past all that. You even blamed the whole thing on the wine—" I stopped myself. I suddenly realized that he probably said that to mask the truth. But why wouldn't he have been honest with me? Friends don't lie to one another. I didn't know whether to feel betrayed or angry, but I knew it was probably best that I left it alone. I wasn't about to have another discussion with him—not like this.

"You know, I didn't ask for this," he shouted towards me as I turned towards the door. "That night, back in college, the thought *did* cross my mind, you know. And I know for a fact it crossed yours, too. So, yes, I have thought about the 'what ifs' from time to time." His eyes narrowed as though trying to read what I was thinking.

"You have always said that you don't believe in the 'what ifs.'" My hand hesitated upon the door handle. I couldn't believe that one of my dearest friends was telling me he had feelings for me, and my only instinct was to run.

"Because then I would be forced to tell you all this." He opened his arms to emphasize his confession.

"Then why did you tell me it didn't mean anything if it did?" My arms crossed over my chest in defiance.

"I felt like it was the right thing to do. Now look at us; I've messed up everything…again." His head bowed.

I leaned onto the door, unsure of what to say. I couldn't go to him. I couldn't smile. I couldn't frown. I couldn't agree, and I couldn't disagree. No matter how I chose to respond, I feared that it would end up getting misinterpreted and hurting his feelings even more. Either scenario wasn't good. I wish I could have just disappeared.

"Our friendship is great, Rachel. You're great. And yes, sometimes I wonder if *we* could be great," he gulped loud enough for me to hear. "I'm not saying we can't be friends. So, please, know that there is no ultimatum here." He bit at his bottom lip.

My heart began knocking much louder than my gut ever did. I could have sworn Noah could hear it from where he was standing. My hand slipped away from the door handle, which I quickly reached for again to steady my balance. I could barely hold it together. Then, Noah made his way towards me, taking my sweaty, nervous hand away from the handle into his.

"I know you want to be with Ben for reasons neither one of us can comprehend, but I will support you all the same."

I nodded, still unsure of what to say.

"I'm going to go missing for a few days in case you try looking for me." He backed away, releasing my hand.

"You'll be back after the wedding?" I asked.

"You could say that."

What You Don't Have, You Can't Lose

September 2013

His soft, cottony sheets most likely served as a resting place for many before me and will undoubtedly continue after. I couldn't allow Ben and I to follow the same path, ignoring the destination. No longer would I allow him to sidestep the conversation every time I was brave enough to bring it up. Everything I had once easily swept under the rug was now causing me to fall face first.

Every second spent with him made it increasingly difficult to ignore his behavior. Knowing how badly he had hurt me the first time, I would have thought he would have been more aware of his actions this time around. The idea of him becoming one of my greatest 'what ifs' in life thus far was slowly fading into feelings of utter repulsion. I was beginning to learn that I had simply become part of the formula he had used on many others before me. I was where he chose to recharge his battery—his preferred docking station. And it was about time to unplug.

What would I have learned (or gained) if I allowed myself to continue repeating past behaviors? Nothing. No matter how good things seemed to be with Ben and me during our second go around the romance sun, I knew things hadn't changed. And why would they? How could I expect things to turn around when I kept enabling the very things that turned us out? I was reaching my breaking point. And I was reaching it fast.

Ben, again, was all-too consuming. It was sickening when I thought about how quickly my feelings evolved with him. If he even felt a fraction of what I had felt for him, maybe we would have stood a chance. But solid relationships are not built on maybes. Maybes are weak. They are sometimes worse than flat-out being told no.

"He's never going to commit to you," Leigh cautioned while on a video call with Jessie and me. "At least, not in the way you want him to. But seriously, what makes you think you're the exception here, girl? It's no secret that he and his ex are not over. They go back and forth like a couple of yo-yos all the damn time. It's what they do. So, why would you even want to be wrapped up in that mess?"

She wasn't wrong. Why would anyone want to be? It made no sense to chase after something so impossible, which was precisely what I kept doing with him. A heart isn't meant to be beaten; it was meant to *beat* for something or someone. Lying beside him night after night only pushed me further down into the denial spiral. Even with my hand intertwined with his, I knew in his mind; he was holding someone else's. And that was a hard feeling to ignore.

Ben had also become somewhat of a permanent fixture in my apartment as I had become one in his. We were like two pieces of furniture or pictures hanging on the walls—so commonplace but admired greatly. I couldn't imagine the day when either one of us would get discarded like pieces of used furniture left outside on the curb. It hurt too much to consider.

"I need you both to listen for a second," Jessie piped up, interrupting my thoughts. "Jordan is dating someone, and apparently," she paused for effect, "he's engaged. He literally just started dating this girl, and he has already asked her to marry him!"

"How did you find that out?" Leigha asked.

"Social media," she replied.

"Didn't you unfriend his ass?" I asked.

"I did, or maybe I thought I did. Either way, you're missing the point here," Jessie objected.

"Just because he can put a ring on it doesn't mean he has what it takes to keep it there. Trust me; what he did with you, he will do to her. You didn't lose a great guy here; you dodged a bullet," Leigha explained.

"That girl must have known he was seeing someone else when she got involved, and if that's the case, karma has a funny way of coming back around," I asserted.

"Ugh, could you have imagined if I had decided to marry him? That would have been awful. He'd be swiping left and right all the way to the alter," she laughed.

"Well, I have some news to share as well," Leigha chimed in.

"Does this have anything to do with James?" I teased.

"Actually, smartass, it does. Things have been great between us—thank you for asking."

"I didn't," I deadpanned.

"Anyway, the other night, I had to work late as usual, and I was complaining to him about how I haven't had time to grocery shop, and do you know what he did?" She paused. "He took my list and restocked my fridge."

"Damn," I said. "That is really sweet."

As Leigha began discussing more details of her blossoming relationship with James, I was, without a doubt, happy for her. But it also made me realize how much I was missing out on being with Ben. Ben would have never done that for me, yet I treated him like he was just as good of a boyfriend as James was to Leigha. Sure, he took me out to dinner. We went to art shows. We went to the movies and spent a lot of time together. But when it came to immersing ourselves into each other's lives, everything halted—like there was a wall that prevented me from passing through.

"You deserve to be happy," Leigha said to me, sensing my silence. "Guys can be stupid sometimes."

"*Love* is stupid," I laughed. "I just hate being with someone that I fear is keeping their ex in their back pocket as a backup. It hurts because I'm not doing that with him," I sighed.

"Then, don't let him. Get over him. I've had produce in my fridge longer than you two have dated," Jessie snorted. "Jokes aside, he was a disaster from the start, and you know it."

"There is always Noah…" Leigha squeezed in.

"There is NOT always Noah," I said, feeling a twinge of pain in my heart.

It was a Saturday night in the middle of September, and Ben had invited me to another art show. Reminiscent of the time before, we walked through the gallery as he admired each piece and provided me with his interpretations.

"When do you plan on putting your work out there?" I asked, not caring too much about the art other than his reaction to it.

He shrugged. "Soon?" he said as though it were a question he hoped I could answer for him. Then, pulling my hand close to him, he led me down another hallway, keeping me by his side. Out of all the moments we had shared, this one immediately became one of my favorites.

As we continued walking, Ben ended up running into someone from work.

"Hey, Trevor," Ben said with a quick wave as Trevor and a girl who I presumed to be his girlfriend made their way over to us.

"Ben," he said with a quick shake of the hand. "I didn't know you were an art guy." He pointed to a few nearby paintings.

"A total art guy. He loves it," I chimed in like an adoring fan. "He may even have his pieces hanging in here one day."

"Really? I didn't know you painted?" Trevor's brow arched with curiosity.

"Kind of," Ben replied with hesitation. "It's just a little hobby—nothing serious," he downplayed.

"Well, I'm sure if you're any good like you were with closing that case today, then you have a bright future ahead of you," Trevor said before being interrupted by his girlfriend's phone ringing, which she quickly walked away to answer.

"Sorry." He shook his head with a grin. "That's Becky, my fiancé. If you think I'm bad with working constantly, you should see her." He winked at Ben which would have been the moment he should have introduced me, but instead, he stood there in silence.

Trevor reached for my hand in an attempt to rid the awkward silence filling the space between us like smoke. "I'm sorry, I didn't catch your name," he said.

"Oh, sorry," Ben spoke up as if the thought had never occurred to him before. "This is my friend, Rachel."

The words stung. They hung loosely in the air as my confident handshake loosened inside Trevor's grasp before slipping through his fingers like sand.

Friend? After Trevor walked away to find his fiancé, I stood there, pulling myself away from Ben more so than I had ever done in the past.

"You're mad at me?" he asked.

"No," I lied. "But I really should be heading home."

"I'm sorry, I panicked. You know I'm not good with the whole title thing." He looked at me as though it should have made up for how I felt. Not even an apology was uttered.

"How many of your friends do you hold hands with?" I asked. "You were holding my hand when you said that. You contradict everything we are all the time."

"Let's just get out of here," he said. "Come back to my place. Please?" He looked at me pleadingly.

And, of course, I buckled.

Come morning, Ben reached over me and grabbed his phone. He responded to a text message right in front of me without much discretion. *Was this transparency? Or have we finally reached the point we no longer cared anymore? Or had I somehow given him the impression that he could do whatever the hell he wanted?* He made everything outside of the world we created meaningless, which inadvertently began to make our world equally so.

"Everything OK?" I asked, hoping he'd clue me into who he was talking to. My body tensed at the thought of it being *her*. It was always her. I didn't want to lose him to her once more. Then again, can you really lose what isn't yours in the first place?

"It's fine. Nothing's wrong." He turned to me, sensing my body language. "I know what you're thinking, but it's just hard sometimes. You wouldn't understand."

My head spun towards him. "What do you mean I wouldn't understand?"

"Look at me." He cupped my face in his hands. "I'm not trying to get back together with my ex, OK?" He brought his lips to my forehead. "You are amazing, and I want to be with you. She and I," he paused, "are over." He kissed me again, leaving an imprint on my heart like footprints in the sand, which I knew in the next breath, would quickly wash away.

"I just think that no matter how you and I feel towards each other, we always come back to this place…" My voice trailed off as it became silenced by another kiss.

"What place?" He pulled his lips away from mine.

"The place where you don't know what you want," I answered.

"Rachel, that's not fair." He removed himself from me, making sure no part of us touched.

"Not fair? Ben, you strung me along last time. And I'm sorry if I'm being a little hypersensitive here, but I can't help but assume that it's her every time your phone goes off." I pulled myself out of bed and reached for my clothes.

Watching him out of the corner of my eye, I tried making out what he was thinking, but he remained rather stoic. *Ugh, I wanted to shake some sense into him!* But who was shaking some sense into me?

"We are together again because I missed you. I missed talking to you, and I missed being with you. I'm sorry about last time; I really am." He picked his face up from the floor. "You won't lose me again." His words floated through the air between us without any place to land.

I had come too far in my life to backpedal like this. Staying with Ben meant that I would have to stay in a place of acceptance. I would have to accept whatever level of commitment he was willing to give me. Maybe I was trying too hard to attach myself to him because of some deep-rooted need that longed-for fulfillment. But no matter what I tried desperately to cling to, nothing with Ben would ever stick.

But I knew something he didn't know—that I could never lose what I never had in the first place.

Blog Post #18

Untitled

With everything I have been through, I'm not entirely sure what love means anymore…

The Exception

September 2013

The relationship between Ben and I accelerated. It went from zero to sixty with no break in-between. As impressive as the progression was, it wasn't all rainbows and puppies. There was still a lingering problem: His phone. It was a tornado in and of itself, leaving a path of destruction that I was the only one paying attention to. And as much as I wanted to make things work, I couldn't be true to myself if I stayed quiet.

All morning, I sat in front of my laptop. I couldn't believe how many readers I had. Even though it was only thirty, it was still a reason to celebrate. But just as I was about to take that first jump of joy. I received a text. It was Dan.

> I could be wrong here, but... Are you the Author of The Salt City Diaries Blog?

I about fell to the floor. Forget jumping. *How the hell did he find my blog? And how the hell did he figure out it was me?*

I texted back:

> What makes you say that?

Dan:

> You have edited enough of my work for me to know your writing style. Not to mention, a few posts felt rather personal.

What do I do? Do I admit that the blog is mine and completely blow my cover? Or do I try to deny it like any normal person would when caught red-handed? But before I could even respond to him, he called.

I took a deep breath. Dan had discovered my identity. My absolute biggest fear concerning my blog had been actualized. How was that even possible?

"As your friend," he laughed, knowing that our newly formed friendship felt more like an inside joke than anything else. "You have a serious problem we need to fix."

"And what's that? Horrible grammar? Did I misspell a few words?" I rolled my eyes.

"Not that I have any right to say this, but this *B* guy has got to go. After reading your posts, it's obvious he's no good for you," he said.

"You're right; you don't have any right to say that to me. Where do you get off?" I bit my cheek, afraid I'd say more.

"Don't you want your readers to share their perspective—or am I missing the entire purpose behind this blog of yours?" he mused.

"Oh, I'm sorry," I jeered. "Just because I'm not 'Dan the Food Man' with over a million followers doesn't mean you can talk down to my blog no matter how little it is."

"I'm not talking down your blog," he objected. "I accidentally stumbled upon it by accident when I was googling something else." He paused for a few seconds. "I'm, believe it or not, a faithful reader."

I wanted to hang up, but I didn't. "Are you just saying that?" I questioned.

"Listen, you are a very talented writer—" he hesitated— "and a rare breed. You deserve so much more than what you've been willing to settle for, and I feel like a complete jackass for how I handled things with you," he apologized. "When you see it in black and white, the grey area of interpretation no longer exists."

Thinking of Ben, I knew I gave him no standards to adhere to, yet I silently slapped on expectations that I knew he'd never meet. A tear rolled down my cheek, which I quickly brushed away. "In my defense..." I began.

"No excuses," he cut in.

"Dan, this whole conversation has caught me off guard. You and I have never spoken so candidly to each other like this before," I countered.

"I get it. I'm sorry. But if you would let me say one more thing?"

"What is it?" I asked.

"Stop treating these guys like they are the exception. Rachel, *you* are the exception. And I know you're going to do what you want to do, but honestly, this *B* character doesn't deserve you."

The words slapped me across the face more viciously than if it were a hand. I sat there, fumbling with my couch pillow, unsure of what to say. I didn't want to believe that Ben wasn't the guy. It hurt too much to question it more than what I already had.

"Anyway, I wanted to call you and tell you that I enjoy what you're doing," he changed the subject. "And I would love to help you in any way that I can—if you'd like?"

"Dan, I'm trying to remain anonymous here. I doubt there is any marketing you can do to a nameless author," I said.

"Sure, there is. We can brainstorm. Just because I'm no longer in the area doesn't mean we can't help each other. You've helped me so much that's only fair that I return the favor," he asserted.

"That's very nice of you to offer," I said. "Can I think about it?"

"Sure. I'm here whenever you need me," he replied.

"You write about food," I piped up unexpectedly. "What insight could you possibly give me on my blog? Besides, it's not like you have any experience writing about love and heartbreak," I pointed out.

"True," he wavered.

"So, how are you going to help when I get lost?" I asked.

"Well, getting lost is an important part of the process. Sometimes, getting lost is the only way to find where you're destined to go."

"I appreciate that sentiment," I said with a smile he couldn't see.

"But this is your journey, Dorothy. I'm just offering to be Toto." And with that, he hung up.

Dan would be a good resource, but the question of whether or not I could trust him was too soon to answer. Now that he knew the blog belonged to me (however the hell he figured that out), I now had no choice but to trust that he would keep that information private. Thankfully, he wasn't upset about anything I wrote about him. And at least there was nothing left unsaid between us. Perhaps becoming friends wouldn't be as hard as I had initially expected.

Blog Post #19

A Call to Action

When I meet someone new now, my first thought is to assess their impact on my life or what kind of impact I might have on theirs. Have you ever wondered that? With all the people I have crossed paths with, have I ever made a lasting impression on any of them? Am I ever thought of? I've been thinking a lot about that lately. I have surmised the possibilities, but I know no matter how long I try dissecting the details of any relationship I've ever been in, I will never be promised the answer.

At this stage in my life, I have learned that most of the impact I have received thus far was solely based on departures. Some departures in my life have been easily identified and understood, while others, not so much. Some departures had been very hard to accept, whereas others, I wanted. Either way, I don't see how you can ever escape a goodbye without it leaving some kind of mark behind.

But goodbyes are not always easily recognized. They don't come to us delivered as a wave, a hug, or even with spoken words sometimes. They can sneak up on you when you least expect it—regardless of who ends up initiating it. Then, there are those goodbyes that happen as a person slowly fades into the background of your life—sometimes vanishing for good.

However, there are a few exceptions where those departed individuals resurface. And they seem to resurface at specific points in our lives to either test us, teach us, or maybe to pick up where their story left off. But it isn't always easy to figure out Fate's intentions in these scenarios. That is why it's important never to force anything in life. Anything forced cannot stay because it will eventually leave as it was always meant to do.

But is that always the case? Is Fate always in control? I have battled with this for quite some time, and now, I feel I've reached that proverbial fork in the road. I'm being called into action. But is Fate the one doing the calling? Is it telling me to stop forcing this situation to work when it was never supposed to work in the first place?

When something doesn't belong, every possible obstacle, reason, and circumstance is presented to reveal why that is. And it's our responsibility to take notice so that we can act appropriately. **B** and I were full of obstacles, reasons, and circumstances from our inability to commit to our failure to be honest with each other properly. We would never be that couple (you know, that teensy, weensy 1% exception) who comes out stronger in the end. Because of that, I had to act. And I had to act now.

Love, Me.

My feet slid across the pavement as though it were comprised of ice. No matter how many times I tried pulling myself back to the starting line, I had to keep sliding forward. I couldn't allow myself to backtrack as I had done so many times before. Nor could I fully trust my feet's intentions. All they wanted was to lead me in the opposite direction, but thankfully, an invisible force kept pulling me towards the door.

I wanted to run. I wanted to abort this mission and pretend as though I never embarked on it in the first place. But I couldn't do that. My fear wouldn't let me. It anchored me to the ground forbidding me to jump ship. And no matter how hard I tried inching my way to the edge to peer into the waters below, I knew what was best for me.

There were no more choices or decisions. What had to be done was done. And somehow, after contemplating the mission at hand to the point of obsession, I knew it was finally time to accept and face the inevitable. So, I removed my blinders and allowed myself to see things for what they were. And no matter how painful it was to do that, I could no longer live in my blind spot.

And just as the door opened, I heard my gut whisper to my heart: *Do better for yourself because better was never here.*

When You Are the Cake

September-October 2013

It was there in the center of Ben's kitchen where I placed myself in the middle of that proverbial fork in the road. It was that "now or never moment"—the climax of the story—where I had to choose which direction I would be heading. But before the words even came out, something between Ben and I shifted. And I knew he felt it, too.

He looked at me, concerned that I would tell him something he wasn't prepared to address. But what was new? He never wanted to address anything when it came to us. He tried sidestepping all the important topics like our relationship was a game of hopscotch.

Coming to this decision, my gut knew what I would be walking into. How it knew as strongly as it did will forever remain a mystery, but I think that's why I decided to forge a strong bond with it going forward. I registered Ben's immediate trepidation as though it was intended for me, but I quickly realized it was reserved only for him. The insecurities that wreaked havoc on my heart had worn me down for so long that I had accepted all the obstacles, reasons, and circumstances as indicators of strength, perseverance, and the eventual happy ending. I never once considered them as reasons to break us than *make* us.

Earlier that day, before I had decided to head over, I tinkered around my apartment, desperate to find anything to drown out my thoughts so that I could crawl back into that familiar place of denial. It felt temporarily safe so that I didn't have to face the hurt I knew was bubbling under the surface, ready to erupt into a full-blown meltdown when I least expected it. But no matter how hard I tried, nothing could be ignored. The rug was mounded too high to allow anything more to be swept underneath it. The only thing I could do was try and prove my gut wrong, but as usual, it was ready to call my bluff instead. And boy, it certainly did.

I grabbed my phone and texted Ben. I sat down, watching and waiting for that notification that he had read my message. But as the minutes rolled on by, I hovered more and more over my phone like an anxious fisherman, waiting impatiently for a bite. And when I finally saw that my message was received and read without any response. My gut shook its head, telling me: *I told you so.*

I knew something was wrong, but I couldn't quite put my pathetic finger on it. I was familiar with this feeling all-too-much for me to simply shrug it off. But I battled the notion that things had been so good between us that there would be no reason to think otherwise. He told me how he felt the last time we were together, which dissipated some of the lingering doubt that haunted our relationship—like the ghost of breakups past. Unfortunately, nothing he could ever say—or do—would ever keep those doubts at bay.

Again, the knife began twisting into my back, reopening the wound that, to be honest, never closed in the first place. All the pain ignited like a stick of dynamite, blowing my heart into shreds. I had no idea where to go from there. My heart had enough. Something so broken that I desperately wanted to work on was beyond my ability to repair. There was no use trying to salvage what was left of Ben and me. We were done. All I would have been doing was piling on more bandages, denying the wound left underneath.

Love is a strong word. I get it. It's not like I pass that word around like candy. And perhaps I never gave the word the justice it deserved or explained its existence better in the first place, but it was there. At least, that's what my heart believed. But did it check all the boxes?

No. It may have provided the fireworks and butterflies, but falling deeply for someone doesn't mean that what you fell into was *love*. Instead, I found myself in love with the idea and potential of someone rather than their reality. Had I allowed myself to love the truth of the situation, I doubt love would have existed at all.

Ben and I had this intoxicating and addictive quality about us, and when I stopped to consider that, intoxication and addiction weren't exactly synonymous with healthy love.

The trouble with living in the past is that you prevent yourself from seeing clearly into the future. You remain stuck. And it's not because you are comfortable with where you are per se; you may just be too afraid to take the next step in fear of the unknown. So, you stay put, regardless of whether the place is good or bad, because you know what to expect. In a way, maybe it is comfort. But we all know that nothing good ever grows from a comfort zone. And standing there in his kitchen, I had to explain all this to him without any hope of finding the words.

I was tired of battling his relationship with his ex. The sad part was how he was so adamant about holding onto that toxic relationship, while in the same breath, I was doing the same with him. I was a hypocrite. No longer would I give in to flights of delusion, dreaming of the possibility that we had a chance to make it when every flag had been thrown on the field. In the end, I allowed myself to be whatever he wanted me to be at the sacrifice of *me*—and that is a price no one should ever be willing to pay. It was time I stood up for myself because someone had to.

As confusing of a mess, I knew I was in, there was still a chance for me to escape it—to remove myself from under that blanket of denial. With Ben, I should have known this day was bound to come. Our relationship was too cyclical: One minute, he was pulling me in extremely close, and in the next, he was pushing me away. The entire time I was with him, I was left with this nameless longing because I was always searching for the answers—answers that were always there that I had chosen to ignore.

But there in his kitchen, I couldn't place ultimatums or even beg for things to change. I always came with one condition that I barely defended. I never set the stage from the beginning as I should have. Had I done that, he would have never gotten away with everything he had. He said I would never lose him again, and that may have been true—but what about me? What about me losing myself in him again?

Shamefully, I still stand by that I loved him—or, at least, the idea of him. I couldn't have ever seen myself being that way for someone had I not loved them to some degree. Or to be so forgiving and understanding.

But I just couldn't be those things anymore. They weren't helping either one of us. *Rachel, you have to face the music.*

Staring at Ben, I realized I didn't like him anymore. I may have loved him on some deeper level, but I just didn't like him. *And how could I?* That was the point my gut began prepping my heart for battle, to finally be strong enough to tell him that I was done and actually mean the words this time.

"Just tell me." I looked at him. "Be honest. I deserve to know."

He stood there, shoving his hands nervously into his pockets. His eyes fell to the floor as though the answer to my question lied buried beneath the floorboards. "You know how I feel about you," he started to say while holding out on the "but" we both knew was coming.

As I continued looking at him, I wondered what would have happened to us had we been completely honest with ourselves and each other from the start? Could we have handled it? We say we want honesty and even demand it from others; yet, for some reason, we can't even be honest with ourselves. We both needed to be. There was no way around it this time, no matter how painful the truth was. *No excuses, Rachel.*

"*But,*" I said, "I'm not doing this anymore. I can't do this anymore. It's not fair."

"I'm trying." His eyes shifted. "It's just hard, but I want this to work."

"But it can't." My jaw hardened. "You can't have your cake and eat it, too, Ben."

"How can you say that? You think that's what's happening here?" His body materialized by my side as the space between us began to diminish.

"Yes, Ben. That's exactly what is happening here," I said as confidently as I could while trying to keep my heart from racing out of my chest. Before, I would have let him pull me in and cloud my senses beyond control.

"It's over, isn't it?" His chin trembled at the words as he pulled me closer, causing the remaining space between us to vanish. But I had to be strong. I couldn't revert to bad habits.

Answering his question was pointless. Instead, I savored the goodbye by inhaling that scent of a thousand books I once desperately wanted to read, wondering just how many of them I was actually given the chance to. Because, on most days, it felt like I was stuck rereading the same one.

I slowly pulled away from his embrace. I needed this to end before the intoxication set in, and I was back at square one. It was time to close the book on Ben for good. I needed to do what was best for me; otherwise, everything I had fought so hard for when I left Mike would have been for nothing. I didn't fight for a better life or for the chance to find a better love, just to be put back into a loveless, noncommittal, and toxic relationship. So, without another word, I walked out the door. It was the first time in my life that I realized how tightly you could hold onto something but still having no choice but to let go of it in the end.

It was all a game. And while I was all-too-familiar with the playground, it was getting dark, and I needed to get home. I was done playing. I was done chasing. I now had to grab hold of that first monkey bar and begin the stages of healing. Ashamedly, when Ben came back into my life this time around, I convinced myself that he came back because it *was* love. But he wasn't fighting to be with me. He wanted the best of both worlds. I let him back into my life without so much as an apology or for him to mean the things he'd say. All he wanted was his cake and to eat it, too. And for so long, I willingly handed him the knife that cut slice after slice until there was barely anything left. And I refused to be the cake anymore.

Blog Post #20

Beneath the Sheets

The only way I can describe what transpired between **B** and me was that the stars aligned perfectly, yet, at the most inconvenient times. It was "love" so passionate and, unfortunately, almost secretive that even whispering it amongst each other felt like betrayal at times.

I held this man on a pedestal of my own making. I praised him daily as though he had become a religious custom of mine, and I loved every fiber that collectively made up his entire being. I took all that he had—both the good and the bad—and still wanted all of him. Even when I wasn't sure of what we were, I was still confident with how I felt. When he was at his lowest and turned to me in need of reassurance that he was worthy of love, I wanted him. I wanted all of him. But I never *had* all of him.

I wasn't prepared to have the relationship I had with him. It wasn't like he nor I premediated our demise or knew how wrong it was for two broken people to try and make something whole. After so many years apart, we reconnected at a time in our lives when connecting with anyone else seemed impossible. They say you don't always have control over your heart's wants—or why it even wants what it does—and I believe that to be true. Looking back, it sickens me that I ever allowed myself to want what I did.

But how can you share your heart with someone? It's not a timeshare. And somehow, **B** rented his out like he was making bank. His relationship with his ex was as tumultuous as what I had once shared with **M.** *Who would want that?* He was never going to leave her—not entirely. He was never going to be that brave. And how dare he force me into being his rebound by wrapping up my place in his life in a pretty bow of lies and deception. You can't treat someone like a girlfriend and then deny them of the title. **B** was always afraid to grasp onto anything unknown to him. If it didn't live and breathe in his comfort zone, it was too much of a risk to him. And he didn't know what to expect because I was too far outside the boundaries. I was the unknown.

Every time I tried to draw that line in the sand to define the boundaries of our relationship, one of us always made an excuse to cross it and draw yet another line. And for months, we cultivated this confusing relationship and bonded over all the superficial things one would ignorantly mistake for intimacy. He has left the most prominent scar of all the men I've dated so far.

The wound began to reopen each time we went to blows with one another about the level of commitment we did or didn't have. We'd fight about how unfair it was to expect anything from each other when we didn't know what we *were* to each other. When I finally stood up for what I wanted—and needed—neither he nor I could face that truth. There was too much at stake to try and fight to keep something alive when we both knew we'd end up crippling in the aftermath. And that in the end, we would resent one another for our inabilities to accept anything we could or couldn't give to the relationship. Anything we tried building couldn't sustain—or weather—any storms we knew would eventually come. I loved myself too much to round and square my edges to fit his another day more. The road we were on simply ran out of pavement. The recovery would be difficult since I allowed my heart to be as open as it was to something it should have been closed off to. But I am no stranger to heartbreak. This too, I shall mend.

Without a doubt, he was my soulmate—and not the kind of soulmate you're supposed to be with for the rest of your life. He wasn't a perfect fit for the healed version of me—no matter how much I wanted that to be true. Instead, he was the kind of soulmate that forced me to face some of my most significant flaws when it came to love. He forced me to pay attention to the details instead of cowering in their presence. With him, I learned the importance of setting the stage for what I deserved early on and not to feel bad for demanding it. Being with him changed my life. For the first time in a very long time, I opened myself back up to love. I became as vulnerable as I possibly could just so that I wouldn't settle for anything less than what I deserved, again. I could never have been with him forever. It would have been too toxic. Too taxing. He successfully broke my heart in such a way that it made me feel alive again. By him being everything that was wrong for me, it helped me realize how much I deserved to have everything right.

M forced me to have the courage to walk away from something no matter how much time and energy I invested into it. He ignited the fire within me to go after a better life. **J** was the teacher of reasonable expectations and did not allow stubbornness to dictate his actions. **D** helped me get back onto the right path in finding good love. Whereas **B** forced me to acknowledge all the reasons I was preventing myself from finding it. He was the test.

B also awakened this part of my heart that had stopped beating for years to this unfamiliar yearning to be treated better. To want someone to love me the way I deserved to be loved. He unknowingly taught me so much in such a short period of time, yet to love and lose him was the only way to gain myself. He put the weapons in my hands to finally fight for a better life—even when he was too afraid to use them himself. Either way, I don't think I could ever thank him enough.

But I would like to think that I gave him something in return as well. I saw this passion within him, a desire to do more with his life, and I hope the person he ends up with nurtures that, too. He was the first person I thought of when I closed my eyes at night and again when they opened come morning. Just the sound of his voice or laugh set my body on fire, making me crave him in such a way no words could ever suffice in this blog.

As I lay that relationship to rest, I would like to believe we shared something meaningful—no matter how short-lived it ended up being. He and I would have never known what a future together would have looked like because we were too broken to travel that far. He was always grounded in his past, and I was still recovering from mine. He may never have intended to hurt me in the ways that he had or by making it so difficult to love him—because had that not happened, I may not have learned to love myself more.

Still, we were what we both needed at the exact moment we needed each other. I agree, he didn't do right by me—but I didn't do right by me either. He wasn't perfect or even a stand-up guy when it boiled down to it. But I would be a liar if I discounted all the good he did bring to our relationship in those fleeting moments when he freed himself from the chains of his past and opened himself up to love. He listened to the things I had to say. He nurtured my writing passion as I did his art. We connected and understood each other—even when we didn't like what the other person had to say. There was a friendship there, but it would have never been able to come out of this alive. There was no saving it. It, too, went down with the ship.

But our story is done. Our parts have been played. I can't, for the sake of myself, sacrifice anything more to him—or for him. He made his bed, and now he must lie in it. However, I'm sure a part of me is still haunting him beneath those sheets.

Love, Me.

Stupid Love

November 2013

Getting dumped sucks. Well, even though I was the one who ended things with Ben, it still felt like the roles were reversed as though he put me up to it—but dumped? *Ugh, I hate that word.* What does it even mean to get dumped anyway? It wasn't like Ben dropped me off in the middle of nowhere before driving away from me and the relationship.

Was I still upset? Yes. Was I still hurt? Double yes. Did it also feel like a huge sigh of relief? Triple freaking, YES. A huge weight had been lifted off my shoulders because I no longer had to live in that limbo of hurt anymore. But breaking up with people is tough. I hate it. I remembered how it once took me years to break up with my hairstylist. She would continuously mess up my hair, yet I would still tip her and tell her thanks. I didn't want to hurt her feelings. I just wanted to spare us that awkward conversation where I would have to say to her that it wasn't *her*—that it was me—or my hair, for that matter. And how she did beautiful work, but my hair was so damn unappreciative of her talents—that she would be far better off working on hair that wasn't as selfish as my mane.

Unfortunately, my breakup with Ben was a little more earth-shattering than a loss of a hairstylist. Nevertheless, I was rocked to my core, and I had nothing left to do but put myself back together, put those big girl pants back on, and move the hell on. As much as I would have loved this to have been a Hallmark movie ending, I would have had more of a chance getting struck by lightning.

I wanted to rid myself of him completely. To do this, nothing was off the table, which meant even my apartment. I rearranged my furniture, the books on my shelves, threw out his toothbrush, and bought new bedding. I was determined to create a space entirely void of his existence. Nothing felt worse than falling asleep in a bed you once shared with someone—even worse when their scent still lingered like a fading memory, transporting you back in time. I needed a refresh. I needed a clean slate. I didn't need another houseplant (*Thanks, Agnes*). The ghost of Ben's presence wasn't allowed to lay rest at my place. Oh, no. He didn't deserve to exist even as a shadow. Harsh? Maybe. But when it comes to matters of a broken heart, nothing is off-limits when it comes to healing. So, I burned some sage and pressed on.

Let's circle back to the beginning, shall we?

Present Day: November 2013

"I just don't understand why he repeatedly runs back to her when it's such a toxic relationship. He once told me how she treated him like crap, yet there he goes, right back to her," I said, pulling up the social media evidence I found on my phone. I took a sip of my wine, wondering if my tears were responsible for the glass constantly refilling.

"Kind of the pot calling the kettle black, don't you think?" Leigha peered over at me. "Weren't you doing the same exact thing?"

"Touché." I winced.

"I don't know why you wanted to be with him so badly," she pointed out as only a true friend would. And she was right to say that, because really, why did I? Why did I fight so hard to make something work when it never was going to in the first place? Why did I overcompensate for his lack of fighting as a reason for me to keep fighting more?

"Because I thought things with us were different," I admitted. "I wanted to believe that we were the exception and that things would have worked out if we tried hard enough." My words sounded as weak as they felt inside.

"But it wasn't healthy—and what were you actually working on? From this side of the room, it was like you were trying to force something to happen. That's not 'work,' that's stupidity," Leigha asserted.

"Trust me; I get that now. I was always blaming myself for why he didn't reciprocate anything on any level or why he didn't realize how great I was? Blah, blah, blah. I gave that boy way too much power over me." I downed the rest of my glass.

"You should have never given him or anyone else that kind of power. If he can't see how wonderful you are, that's on him. It's not your job to convince people of your worth. If they can't see it, that's their loss—not yours," she advised.

"I know," I sighed. "But enough about me. How are you and James?"

She looked down as she fidgeted with a string on her sleeve. "I don't know. Things were going great, but they were just moving way too fast. It was suffocating," she paused for a second as she ran her fingers through her hair. "I kind of freaked out."

"You're scared. It's all new," I consoled.

"You think?" she considered. "Well, he seems to think it's because I'm not into him or that I don't want to be together…"

"He's probably scared, too," I said. "But it will be OK. He's a great guy—just be open to everything," I said, wishing I had her dilemma over mine. "Reach out to him and explain how you are feeling. Slow things down if you need to."

"And say what?" she interjected. "That I'm an idiot who has commitment issues? And how for years I've complained about that very thing with every guy only to end up acting the same damn way? I'm a freakin' hypocrite."

"We all are," I laughed. "Just tell him how you feel. I'm sure that he'd understand. And if you need him to pump the brakes a little, I'm sure he would," I said.

"Or he'll stop the car altogether and tell me to get out," she laughed. "I tell you; love is so—"

"Stupid?" I cut in.

"Soo stupid."

"I can drink to that," I cheered.

Later that night, I climbed into my new bedding. I knew no matter how hard our choices are in life, they must be made. The harder the decision, the better the outcome. Maybe the idea of "breaking up" is really just another way of saying that in order to move on up to something better, you have to break away from something that's holding you down.

Blog Post #21

To Be Continued...

At the end of the day, everyone wants the same thing: to be happy. People dedicate their lives to the pursuit of it. We search, chase, and sacrifice so much at the chance of finding it. The only difference is that happiness can mean many things to different people. What makes you happy might not be the same for someone else—and that's where people tend to get hurt.

Staying with someone because you "love" them doesn't mean you will be happy. Love is not the only number in the question. You need trust. You need respect. You need honesty. And if you don't have those things, despite all the love you believe the other person is providing, there is no way that it can equate to happiness.

Regardless of how some of my relationships have ended, I'm just proud I once tried for something—and that I will continue trying no matter what. I'm also proud that I didn't settle even when it could have been so easy for me to do just that. What I can say is that love is, well, stupid sometimes. It can make us do and feel some of the craziest things. And no one is immune to its effects—no matter how hard we try convincing ourselves otherwise.

But I know the journey is going to be long. It's going to be hard. It's going to be rough. And there will be times (and guys) that will make me feel like giving up. However, I've always believed that nothing good in life ever comes easy. So, I will fight and always stay true to myself and my heart. And who knows, maybe one day I'll find someone who will make the fight easy by them fighting for one for once. Until then, I need some rest. I'm exhausted, and so is my heart.

So, goodnight. Farewell. And we will continue this journey another day.

Love, Me.

Acknowledgments

It's funny how much time changes things. Had I published this book seven years ago, this acknowledgment section would have looked entirely different. All I can say is that the people still in my life fought for their spot, and I couldn't be more blessed to have them here.

A huge THANK YOU to my fantastic team at Cupid's, who saw my vision and helped me execute it. I couldn't be more pleased with how *Book One* has kicked off this series.

To my sister, Ashley, who always reads my books first. And my husband, Josh, who continuously supports and believes in everything I do.

Lastly, to my daughter, Aven: I love you with all my heart and soul. I began writing the final draft up until the day you came into this world. And between you grabbing my laptop and helping me type, I know you are bound to write your own book one day. Josh, I think we may have a future author on our hands.

About the Author

Danielle Dexter, who also writes under the pen name, Danie Jaye, is an Award-Winning author of three novels, including the Literary Titan Gold Medal Winner, *The Taming of Lions*. She lives in New York with her husband, daughter, and three dogs. She holds a Political Science degree from the University of Arizona with a minor in English.

For updates, blog information, and appearances, you can contact press management at www.daniejaye.com or follow Danielle on:

◉ @authordaniejaye
   @thesaltcitiesdiaries
❶ Danie Jaye, Author

…..And let's talk Book Two:

Slated for the end of 2022, Cupid's Arrow Publishing hopes to publish Danielle Dexter's second installment of *The Salt City Diaries*. The following is a sneak peek into Book Two.

Arrested Development

April 2014

It had been six months since Dan moved back to North Carolina. Six months since Ben and I called it quits. Six months from when Jordan got engaged and then called off his engagement. Word on the social media streets was that his ex-fiance accused him of giving her an unexpected pre-wedding gift: an STD. *Burn!* (Pun intended). It had also been six months during which Jessie started dating again, Leigha and James went on a break, and my friendship with Noah finally started to get back on track—even my blog started to gain traction (thanks to Dan on that one). And lastly, it had been almost six months since I found myself in a rather strange predicament. But I'm getting ahead of myself here.

Let's back up a bit, shall we?

February 2014

During those six months, a lot happened. Obviously. And it was during that time I had reached a point of acceptance that was unfortunately sprinkled in with unpredictable bouts of depression. I was hot, then cold, then cold, then hot. I was all over the map with my emotions, and if I couldn't figure out what was going on with how I was feeling, certainly no one else could.

You are probably wondering if I was finally over Ben. And for the most part, I was. There were, however, parts of me that still wondered about him and other parts that couldn't care less. I half-related to Bella from *Twilight* when she was sitting by her bedroom window, watching the seasons change. Not going to lie; I dislike those movies to my core. And I always thought that scene was way too dramatic. But now, I found myself saying: *OK, I get it, girl—a little. But whereas you were nursing a broken heart over a million-year-old vampire, I was nursing a broken heart over a guy who, instead of blood, sucked the love right of me.*

And there is nothing worse than nursing a broken heart that just won't heal as quickly as you would like it to. And all I could do in the meantime was sound like a broken record about it. I repeated the same damn stories a million times over. Round and round, I would go over the same questions, asking, *How could he not miss me? Why did he do what he did?* Until I pissed both my heart and gut off along with everyone else. Even my readers begged me to get a grip—to move on from it already. *What a pillar of strength I was.* It was downright laughable. My behavior was exhausting and pathetic. But at that time, I wasn't too concerned with the perception or opinions of others. I just wanted to do what was best for me, all in the name of healing.

Dan's departure was almost like a re-entrance into my life. *Weird, huh?* Suddenly, we were spending countless nights on the phone, bouncing ideas off one another until we both became so heavily involved in each other's blogs that it became increasingly difficult to switch between food and heartbreak. But it was great. Our past didn't define us, nor did it hinder our ability to move forward with our newly-formed friendship. And for that, I was grateful that we decided to give it the ol' college try. It made me realize that not every attraction has to turn into something more. Sometimes, friendship *is* the destination, but we overcloud the roadmap to get there with unrealistic expectations.

Not to mention, thirty was peeking over the horizon, waving at me like, *Girl, I'm coming for you! So, you better start getting your act together.* But I knew I wouldn't—or couldn't. Who's to say? There wasn't enough time for me to sort through all the bullshit I still happily surrounded my life with like bubble wrap. And if I chose to rush things, I would most likely feel like I missed out on something. Like I had chosen the scenic route but closed my eyes the entire time. Or that I planned on this exquisite destination only to settle for a Motel 6 because I refused to travel a second longer. No, thank you.

And that's where the story gets interesting. Meet DC (we will touch on the other highlights from the recap later).

Dave Collins is his name, and confusion is his game. If I were to label this time in my dating life, I would probably go with: "What in the Damn Fuck." So, I think that should sum it up for you.

"DC" had been Dave's nickname since high school when he went to school with another guy named Dave Collins. So, in the interest of keeping them both separate and distinctive, one of them chose a nickname instead. However, besides sharing the same name, the two couldn't have been more opposite. The DC in this story is the optime of a laidback, casual guy. Creating the nickname "DC" was an example of just how far his creativity went.

Anyway, DC was of average height and build with very prominent features—eyes, nose, and lips that could be easily picked out of a lineup. Back in the day, he always had a thin mop of hair, which through time, disappeared along with his youth. In its place was a bald head concealed underneath a baseball cap, which he wore religiously like an old guy would a toupee. It may sound like I'm painting a not-so-attractive picture of this guy when in all actuality, he *was* attractive. His casual vibe and baldness suited him—much like Vin Diesel or The Rock, but without all the muscles.

I should have picked up early on that his casual demeanor was nothing more than an indicator that there wasn't much variety or spontaneity with him than just his desire to wear nothing but leisurewear wherever we went. Sometimes, he would throw on a pair of jeans for good measure. But the boy was very basic—like a girl with a Starbucks coffee in her hand at Target.

However, DC was the first guy who ever taught me that it was OK not to be perfect. He announced his imperfections to me as though they were characteristics that would attract rather than deter. And I found myself constantly getting angry at him for his lack of self-esteem. I wanted (ashamedly) the perfection of others when I knew damn well that I could never deliver that in return. The wall surrounding my heart was built upon unrealistic standards and expectations, which I knew was all due to the side effects from the heartaches I endured during the past few years. It wasn't like I was perfect by any means. Hell, I had enough imperfections to land a season spot on *The Maury Show*, yet, I still carried myself around like I wasn't the mess I knew deep down inside I was.

I met DC or, rather, reunited with him while shopping at one of the local bookstores in Syracuse. I was browsing titles of books I knew I wouldn't get the chance to read for months when I saw him. I didn't immediately recognize him from a cursory glance since he was always someone I never had a direct relationship with. It was always a six-degree-separation-from-Kevin-Bacon-type-of-relationship.

He didn't notice me at first, but he wasn't the least bit shy with approaching me as soon as he did. "Rachel? Rachel Parker?" he asked.

"That's me," I said as though I was some D-list celebrity who was excited to be recognized out in public.

"It's me—DC," he said as though I had no idea who he was. So, I played along.

"DC? Oh, my God! I didn't even recognize you!" I lied. "How are you?"

Smooth, Rachel.

"I almost didn't recognize you either." He smiled. "Looking for anything in particular?" he asked as I suddenly realized that we both somehow ventured into the self-help aisle.

I wanted to say, *Yes, actually. I probably need every one of these books.* But I contained my sarcasm in case my joke didn't land as I hoped.

He began telling me that he was a cop now—a city cop—before showing me his shiny, little badge to prove it. And after several minutes of catching up while I stole peripheral glances at some of the "Get Over Heartbreak" titles that were staring down at me from the shelves, I was ready to disband the reunion.

"It was really nice running into you," he said just before reaching in for a hug. He smelled of coffee and something else I couldn't quite put my finger on. It could have been either his body wash or cologne, but whatever it was, it wasn't the least bit intoxicating.

"It was nice running into you, too," I said before pulling away.

"Yeah, it's been forever," he continued. "Why don't I get your number, and we can get together sometime?" He asked as he pulled out his phone.

Honestly, I had no idea what to say. In my defense, I was taking the "Let me get your number" thing farther than I should have. *What's new, right?* You would have thought he asked for my hand in marriage the way I backed away from him. I felt like Kevin McCallister in *Home Alone* when that scary neighbor entered the store while he was trying to buy a freakin' toothbrush. *Ugh, the toothbrush…Damn it, how these things have to haunt me.*

More to come… Obviously.

COMING SOON!

The Salt City Diaries Blog

Get behind the book content
Bonus content
And stupid shit that didn't make the book
& More!

Find the blog at www.daniejaye.com

CPSIA information can be obtained
at www.ICGtesting.com
Printed in the USA
LVHW110721120822
725756LV00004B/23